A
Tales from Post-Colonial Africa

Verulamium Press

18 Icknield Close
St Albans
Hertfordshire
England AL3 4NQ

First published by Verulamium Press 2014

verpress.com

Copyright © Robert Gurney 2014

Robert Gurney asserts the moral rights to be the author of this work.

A catalogue record for this book is available from the British Library.

ISBN 978-0-9547166-4-6

Printed and bound in Great Britain by JamJar Print

www.jamjarprint.co.uk

Limited Edition of 100 copies

All rights are reserved. No part of this publication may be reproduced, stored in a retrieval system or transmitted in any form or by any means, electronic, mechanical, photocopying, recording or otherwise, without prior permission of VP.

This book is sold subject to the condition that it shall not, by way of trade or otherwise, be lent, resold, hired out, or otherwise circulated without the publisher's prior consent in any form of binding or cover other than that in which it is published and without a similar condition including this condition being imposed on the subsequent publisher.

Acknowledgements

Gratitude is expressed particularly to Clive Mann for all the help he has given me with this book, not only with proof-reading but also with a host of clear memories and anecdotes. His photographic memory has proved to be second to none. I am grateful to him for his patience and constant encouragement between 2012 and 2014.

Thanks are also extended to the following for weathering a storm of e-mails in 2012 and 2014 and for their replies: Brian Van Arkadie, David Simmonds (DS), Clive Lovelock, Niall Herriott, Trevor Wilson, Colin Townsend, Andrew Carothers, Charles Barton, David Smith (DAS), Charles Good, Mike Tribe, John Warren, Lilian Hayball and Mike Clarke. Gratitude is expressed also to Steve Lord, Don Knies, Alex Fleming, Brooks Goddard, Mike Rainy, Dave Marshall, David Greenstein, Bill Jones, Paul Cant, Ed Schmidt, Henry Hamburger, and Derek Pomeroy for their contributions. They have been a willing and necessary audience and, in most instances, have made substantial contributions to the book. Where an email was the catalyst or trigger for a certain piece, special mention is made at the end of the text in question, e.g. (CM). This book is very much a group effort.

I would like to thank Brian Van Arkadie for suggesting the subtitle of the book.

The cover photograph of the sausage tree (*Kigelia africana*) is reproduced with the kind permission of the biologist, Dr Clive Mann.

By the same author:

La poesía de Juan Larrea (1985)
Poemas a la Patagonia (2004, second edition 2009)
Luton Poems (2005)
Nueve monedas para el barquero, antología (2005)
El cuarto oscuro y otros poemas (2008)
La libélula y otros poemas/The Dragonfly and Other Poems (2012)
La casa de empeño y otros poemas/The Pawn Shop and Other Poems (2014)

Translation:
The River and Other Poems, Andrés Bohoslavsky *(2004)*

Contents

Night in Buganda - **6** The Beggar - **6** Rimbaud's House - **6** Rimbaud Square - **6** The Hills of Buganda - **6** Rimbaud's Ostrich - **7** The Invisible Ones - **7** The Cage - **8** The Eyes - **8** A Garden in Africa - **8** Gisenyi - **8** Goma 1965 - **9** Goma 2012 - **9** The Zoo - **9** The Elbow - **10** Heat - **10** Guilt - **10** Overlapping Films - **11** World War Three - **12** Sitting on a Fortune - **12** Imagine - **13** The Snake - **13** The Cobra - **14** Spitting Cobras - **14** The Black Mamba - **15** The Polish - **15** Magic - **15** The Witch - **16** The Nile Virgins - **17** The Spirit of The Falls - **18** Where Are They Now? - **18** The Earthquake - **18** The Two Ladies - **19** The Sausage Tree - **19** The Silhouette - **20** Mwizi - **20** The Sun Glasses - **20** The Hippotami - **21** Wandegeya - **21** The Killing - **21** Diplomacy - **22** The Chemist - **22** Butterflies - **23** Impact - **23** The Lepers - **23** Lawrence - **24** The Mercenary - **25** The Occupation - **25** Chastity - **26** The Antidote - **26** The Stories - **27** The Bishop - **27** Silences - **27** Change - **27** The Wheel of Fortune - **29** Mukasa - **29** Ice Cold in Kampala - **30** The Message - **33** A Bird's Eye View - **34** The Spirit of Africa - **34** The Calf - **35** UFOs over Kampala - **35** Harambee - **35** Magnets - **36** The Void - **36** The Pioneer - **37** The Jembe - **38** Bark Cloth - **40** The Egg Sandwich - **40** Moira's Curse - **41** The Kingu of Sebei - **41** Breathless - **43** Tremors - **44** Things Fall Apart - **44** Hornbills - **45** The Frogman - **45** The Spy - **46** Bodies - **49** The Future Dictator - **50** The Rock - **50** The Club - **51** The Prisoner - **51** Rebels versus Assassins - **51** The Night Watchmen - **52** The Kick - **52** Mountains - **53** The Crooked Path - **53** The Termite Eaters - **53** Johnny - **54** The Sixty Second Friend - **54** Burn's Night - **55** The Saviour - **55** The Bullet in the Neck - **55** Rule by Helicopter - **56** A Perfect Storm - **57** Guardian Angels - **57** Amin's Eyes - **58** Light and Shade - **58** Newton's Cradle - **59** The Nighty Ritual - **59** The Diaspora - **59** Obote and Nyerere - **60** Respect - **60** The Other - **61** La Révolution - **61** Frogs in Bujumbura - **62** The Fuse - **62** The Sea Venom Pilot - **62** The Car-Wrestling Snake - **64** The Scramble for Africa - **65** The Philosophers - **67** The English Pope - **69** Reality and Desire - **70** The Explosion - **71** Heat 2 - **72** The Marabou - **74** Magpies and Marabous - **76** Dying Vultures - **76** The Post-Mortem - **77** The Secretary Bird - **78** Secretary Birds - **79** Insects - **79** Lucinda and Clive - **80** Jiggers - **81** The Howl - **81** Wings - **82** Seeds - **82** Small Beer - **82** The Fox and the Python - **82** Cashpoint - **83** The Dreamliner - **83** The Kampala Club - **85** The Swap - **86** The Cockroaches - **86** Hissing Cockroaches - **87** The Sack of Mangoes - **87** The Development Economist - **89** The Gash - **90** The Clutch - **91** The Flight of the Phoenix - **91** Porous Borders - **91** A Bad Day - **92** The Conundrum - **93** The Anthropologist's Dilemma - **95** The Billiard Table - **96** Explosions - **97** Realities - **97** The Pitcher Man - **98** The Real - **99** Fort St George - **99** Brief Encounter - **100** The Last Straw - **102** The Heart of Africa - **104** The Gallery - **105** The Dead Man - **105** The Complainer - **106** The Stone Thrower 1 - **107** The Stone Thrower 2 - **108** Guy Fawkes and the Kikuyu - **109** The Lock - **110** The Bullet Car - **111** Seigneur Hugh de Gournai - **113** Henry - **117** The Lazy Man - **117** Charlie - **120** Kay - **120** The Spider Man - **121** The Greedy Academic - **121** The Praying Mantis - **124** The Green-Eyed Monster - **127** Kabs - **134** What do you write about Africa? - **136** Warmth - **136** Baring the Load - **137** Dalí and Josefu - **138** Ostriches - **138** Brief Encounter 2 - **139** John Kakonge - **144** A Night in Buganda - **146** Notes - **148** Contributors - **150**

Night in Buganda

I stand by my window in Namilyango, twelve miles from Kampala. I look out across the tops of the trees. Orange beams from fires I cannot see reach up here and there into the darkness. Bursts of drum beats: village talking to village. I drum my fingertips on the fridge door. I ask the brothers on the campus what it is all about. Nobody seems to know.

The Beggar

I haven't been there long. He comes towards me on a low wooden trolley. It looks like a skateboard. He has no legs. I give him something. Then I see the lorry that goes round early each morning throwing him and other beggars off at street corners. I begin to turn away and he stops asking.

Rimbaud's House

I haven't been there, to the Bet Rimbaud, Rimbaud's house, in Harar. It's not for want of trying. They say that the lady who lives there shows you a trunk that was made by him. She urges you to open it and feel the old clothes and newspapers inside. Some say the house was built after his death.

Rimbaud Square

Rimbaud once wrote in a Cairo newspaper in eighteen eighty-seven that the French should build Djibouti so that Harar could have a port. There was nothing there then, he said, but desert. Now French soldiers amble in and out of bars and nightclubs, flirting with girls from all over Ethiopia: The Sainte Amour, the Flèche Rouge, James's Bar and Mick Mack, the Joyeux Noël and Intimité, Semiramis and the Bar Pile ou Face. Dates come from Saudi Arabia, oranges from Kenya, refrigerators from the Gulf, meat and wine from France and *khat* from Harar. 'Place Rimbaud' has been renamed Place Mahmoud Harbi, after a hero of Djiboutian independence.

The Hills of Buganda

We met, by chance, on the veranda of the City Bar. He said that he had just measured two hundred slopes in Buganda. "Whenever I return," I said, "from Ankole, or Karamoja, I find that there is something reassuring about the elongated hills of Buganda and their flattened summits that surround this shore of Lake

Victoria. They feel as familiar to me now as the Chiltern Hills where I was born. They remind me of Mayan pyramids in Guatemala. You feel that there could be something mysterious inside them: sacred tombs, perhaps, hieroglyphs, statues, brass lions." "They are," he responded dryly, "the product of erosion. In the past, the surface was unbroken." It was as if he had poured cold water on what I had said. "I don't care," I said. "I always feel at home when these flat-topped hills heave into view." "Some of them are rounded," he added. "Not many," I said. I didn't ask him his name. It was often like that in Kampala. It seemed that the city and the whole of Africa was full of people measuring things. At times, the poet in me was losing the will to live.

Rimbaud's Ostrich

I am standing outside a three-storey house that faces the sea, in Aden. It was here that Rimbaud once worked as a coffee trader in the eighteen-eighties: the Maison Bardey. It was here that he buried deep inside him the poet he had been. It was to here that Alfred Bardey brought the ostrich given to him by Abou Bekr, Sultan of Tadjourah on the Somali Coast. It was here, on its first night, that the ostrich died, kicking down the door of the shed where it had been stabled.

The Invisible Ones

I never felt really at ease in Kenya. The next game of rugby was in Eldoret. The others went by car. I travelled on a Vespa. I wanted to feel the air in my hair. I loved swooping through clouds of yellow butterflies. I crossed the border at Tororo where the tarmac ran out. The heavens opened. The road turned to mud. I saw a track and struggled down it in search of shelter from the downpour. At the end of a path, I could see a thatched roof. The family beckoned me in. Their Swahili was different from mine. They made me tea. They made me feel at home. The sun came out and the mud dried out. I set off, arriving late in Eldoret, at half time, to be precise. In the clubhouse afterwards, I told them the story of the kind people who had taken me in during the storm. A man, dressed as Long John Silver, with a parrot on his shoulder, shouted out in disbelief: "But there aren't any people on that stretch of the road!" No, I never felt completely at ease in Kenya.

The Cage

There was a feeling of freedom in the air, in Africa, in the 1960s. The space seemed almost too great to explore. And yet, there was another feeling: that of being caged in. I remember the tiger I used to watch inside Whipsnade Zoo. It spent its time pacing up and down. The view it had of the Vale of Aylesbury was magnificent but it was still trapped. That's how it was, as I stared into near-infinity on the rim of the Rift Valley. There was no way out. Return flights home were simply too expensive. It wasn't just that. I remember standing, facing a wall in Burundi, arms outstretched. Guards with guns were taking the car apart. On my way out of that country I tried another route. I drove down a steep track towards the river that forms the border with Rwanda, the Kagera. I could see the bridge that would take me to freedom. There were no guards. Scaffold bars had been welded across it. On an island near Cape Town a good man entered a cell that had one foot in the sea.

The Eyes

I was sitting in an office in Nairobi trying to get a visa for Ethiopia. It was nineteen sixty-four. I was the only *mzungu*, the only European. The other men, Somalis, were very pleasant. There was something strange about them. Their dress was very different but it wasn't that. Then it suddenly hit me. They all had blue eyes.

A Garden in Africa

There was a garden In Africa that filled with scent after sunset. Flowers used it to attract fruit bats and moths. Bats drank the nectar and ate the petals. Night Jasmine was as sweet as desserts in Valencia. You felt that you were walking through a symphony of scents. Honeysuckle was in there. The most cloying was Gardenia. Each bush resembled a young woman reaching out for your arm from the darkness, beckoning you to draw near and enjoy her fragrance.

Gisenyi

I loved driving down to Rwanda. To me, Mick Nolan's game lodge, in the north of the country, was the nearest thing to heaven on earth, better, even, than the mountain tops of Kigezi in the south of Uganda. There was something about the altitude, the air and the light. They were pure. One day I had to go Goma to pick up some medicine. They didn't have it in Kisenyi, as Gisenyi was called then. Gisenyi and Goma are, in effect, two halves of one town that straddles the border between two separate countries, Rwanda and what is called now the DRC. There were soldiers then, crouching in the ditches that line the road linking the two countries. Hundreds of rifles pointed at my car as I drove by.

Goma 1965

I had an email today from a friend about the Congo in the mid nineteen-sixties. It said that he, too, had decided to drive into Goma, just to look around. The border guards, on the Congo side of the barrier, were drunk and difficult but they let him through. He asked them to stamp his passport to show that he had taken his car in but they refused. He saw mortar holes in the roads of Goma. Shops were boarded up or just burnt out. The odd soldier was firing his rifle into the air. He decided not to stay, turned his car round and drove straight back towards the customs post. The guard had changed. A new set of soldiers, also drunk, stopped his car. They wouldn't let him back into Rwanda because his passport had not been stamped an hour or so earlier. He had no official proof that he had taken his car in. Body language was threatening. Cash changed hands. After that, he never went back to the Congo. (CM)

Goma 2012

Today, in the year two thousand and twelve, I caught a glimpse on the TV of the same Belgian-style curb on the side of the road down which I passed, head down, nearly fifty years before. I experienced a sharp shock of recognition. Goma still looks the same but is now ten times larger. There are still soldiers on the streets. Today they are not firing guns. Some say the growing chaos in the Congo was the reason why the British left Uganda early.

The Zoo

You must get out more, I was told. You must get out of your Kampala cage. You must see the crocodiles slide towards your boat from the banks of the Nile at Murchison Falls. You must experience getting close to giraffes in Nairobi National Park. Make sure, though, that they don't jab their legs through the roof of your car. You must get close to a gorilla on a volcano in the Virungas. You must stare into its eyes. You must come face to face with an elephant but be careful, back off if it throws a branch down in front of your Land Rover. You must experience the thrill of looking into a lion's eyes, while you pass water in the middle of nowhere. You must experience the buzz of dodging stampeding hippopotami by Lake Victoria in Kisumu. There is nothing like ducking the venom of an angry roadside snake spitting on your windscreen, when you try to turn round on a narrow dirt road. There is nothing to beat being in a storm of invading locusts and then picking some up to roast under the grill. And you can't beat the excitement of dashing for your vehicle when a line of angry buffaloes, emerging from the jungle, comes charging towards you. Often I was quite happy, to be honest, observing see-through geckos moving up the living-room wall and watching chameleons change colour on the trunks of trees in the garden. Yes, living in Africa in the nineteen-sixties was like living in an open zoo. Apart from packs of abandoned dogs and the bats that seemed to be staring at you from the shower room floor, more dangerous than a rat, Kampala felt safe. The crocodiles, the lions, the hippopotami stayed outside the city limits. Even the leopards that would cross the road as we drove back from the girls' school in Gayasa stayed away from the city centre. It was only in the nineteen-seventies, they say, under Idi Amin, that pythons took up residence at the municipal dump and Kampala began to feel dangerous.

The Elbow

We were in 'The Harp', a pub off Trafalgar Square, said by some to be the smallest in London. You have to be careful when weaving your way back to your seat from the bar. You can easily get an elbow in your eye. My French friend had, he said, been to Uganda "pour voir les animaux". I asked him if he had slept with a gorilla. "Vous avez couché avec un gorille? Did you stare into its eyes?" I know, I know, it was cruel of me. "My one experience of getting close to a gorilla was when one charged us on a hillside in The Forêt Impénétrable, in Kigezi," he said, wide-eyed. "The idiot in front of me panicked, swung round and stuck his elbow in my eye. I was briefly knocked out." (CM)

Heat

I don't remember a heat as intense as that which filled the valley I had to cross each day in Kampala. I had to pause in the shade of every tree. It was like entering an oven. Later, at dusk, the sky would darken with bats and the air would become cold.

Guilt

It was a Sunday morning. We were in Fort Portal, in the Kingdom of Toro, in the West of Uganda. The sun felt good on my bare arms. I had filled my trolley up to the gunwales. I steered it this way and that between other heavily laden trolleys pushed by European ladies. Suddenly short men appear, ducking and diving between the cars. For a split second I think that they are extras in a film, like cowboys and Indians. One stands beside me, scantily dressed, an arrow in his bow. The bowstring is held taut between his fingers. He fires and misses. I cannot see at whom or at what he is firing. His arrow bounces off the windscreen of a camper van. I don't know why but I have often felt guilty, just recalling that scene. Today, a Sunday, I decided to explore the concept of two overlapping worlds and I felt a little better. I tell myself that I have often felt guilty on a Sunday morning. (2010)

Overlapping Films

I set out this morning to write about the Omukama, the King, of Toro. I struggled and struggled with the theme, about how he was reduced to asking a friend of mine in London for a loan and how his successor was discovered in a nursery in Lewisham. I was struggling and struggling until, suddenly, this text shot out: I was shopping in a supermarket in Fort Portal in the west of Uganda. It was more modern than any I had seen in Kampala or Nairobi. It was spacious, airy and well stocked. It seemed to be ahead of those that were shooting up around towns in the south of England. It had everything you could desire: kippers, bacon, Typhoo Tea, Turkish Delight, the lot. It had gleaming new trolleys and a perfectly laid-out car park with arrows for the traffic and proper white-lined bays. I was loading up the car when an arrow shot past my head, then another and another. A spear went flying through the air just above my car. Then some men appeared, most of them quite small, crouching, popping up and down behind the cars like meerkats. They didn't have much on and what they did have was minimalist, traditional. I think I remember red paint, in stripes, on their temples but I may be imagining that. They weren't aiming at me but I ducked down all the same. They moved quickly on, darting this way and that amongst the weekend women shoppers, most of whom appeared to hail from the Home Counties around London. The scene reminded me of when, as children, we played cowboys and Indians in the local park on the way back home from watching westerns during Saturday morning pictures. No one said a word. It was all over very quickly. The ladies carried on robotically loading. To this day, I don't, for the life of me, know what it was all about. It felt tribal. There was nothing about it in the papers. It may have been an everyday occurrence. It was as if two films were being shown on the same screen and at the same time, one superimposed on top of the other, one from the past, the other from the future. I know that the Soviets were in the area at the time but no one paid them much attention. It didn't really feel like anything to do with 'The Cold War'. It felt more like a Saturday afternoon scrap between Luton Town and Millwall football fans, except that these chaps were quite well armed. I was asked the other day if they were Bamba or Bakonjo, Batooro or Bakiga, Banyoro or Banyankole. I was ashamed to reply that I just didn't know. I have a friend who comes from Luton and who is a leading figure in London's liberal elite. He totally shocked me recently when he said: "What do you expect, when you drop someone from another planet into the middle of a Stone Age culture?" It didn't feel correct. I nearly said, "You can't say that!" I didn't. I was lost for words. I have to admit that this is the first time that I have told the full story for years and years. It's just not the sort of tale you are supposed to tell. Even now, a part of me wishes that I hadn't done it. Perhaps I should have told it in a different way but how? The combatants, it must be said, in mitigation, seemed to have more life about them than the Stepford Wives who appeared to be oblivious to what was going on as they went about their business. That's a better ending, perhaps. Does it get me off the hook? The wives, you say, perhaps they weren't really 'Stepford'. It was more, let's say, like British sang-froid, stiff upper lip, unflappability. (2012)

World War Three

An image has been haunting me for some time now. I used to go to the house of a friend I met in the City Bar in Kampala. It was on top of a mountain in Kigezi, in the south of the country. Most days his house was above the clouds. We used to sit on his veranda and look out across the clouds. They were like a roll of cotton wool that had been opened. The earth had disappeared. It felt, in a way, like being in heaven. We were, it turned out, sitting on a wolfram mine. Wolfram is the mineral that is used to make tungsten. Tungsten is used to make armour- and rock-piercing missiles. One day I asked him what more could he want. "A World Wide War," he replied. I was shocked. A friend of mine, who lives in Chiswick, says that we all say things like that from time to time. I am not so sure.

Sitting on a Fortune

There was another wolfram miner. He, too, lived on top of a hill, at a place called Rwanza, on that corner between Rwanda and the Congo and Uganda. His house was a mansion. To get to it from Kisoro, you had to pass through two international borders. The wolframite was pouring out of the mine but there was no demand in the days before Vietnam. He spent a fortune on storing it. His palace began to fall down. There was no money left over for repairs. You would go though a door, from one room, which was in a reasonable state, into another, only to be confronted by a huge pile of rubble that had collapsed onto a snooker table. He still had servants but the cages where he had once kept animals were now empty. His wife went back to Europe. She could not stand it. His one pride and joy, a pink Cadillac, in which he had driven her to Entebbe airport for their final farewell, ran over a nail in his garage when he got back and never emerged again. Eventually the roof fell in on it. The car is probably still there under a pile of tiles and rotting beams. His life was lonely. His newspapers would be taken up the mountain by Walter Baumgartel, owner of 'The Traveller's Rest' in Kisoro. My friend in Chiswick would go with him. It was all very expensive. An immigration officer had to go with them to get them through the borders. I didn't know that wolfram miner. I don't even know his name. They say it was Greek and that he came from Cyprus. He didn't frequent the City Bar. He could not afford it. He didn't even come up to Kampala. He didn't have two pennies to rub together, even though he was sitting on a fortune. (CM)

Imagine

"What did it feel like in Africa?" my sons and their friends used to ask me, as we sat making sandcastles on the beach in Port Eynon. "Imagine," I said, "coming face to face with a red-necked wallaby. It wouldn't be too bad. Imagine finding yourself standing next to a ring-tailed lemur, a Chinese muntjac or a bar-headed goose. You can, at Whipsnade Zoo. It feels fine. But imagine you are on a road in the north of Uganda and an elephant takes umbrage at having to share a space with you. Imagine a row of African buffaloes suddenly emerging from the forest in Rwanda just as you have stepped out of the car to do some exploring. Imagine a black mamba snake, lying curled up in your porch just before the ten o'clock curfew. Imagine there are soldiers in the road cocking their rifles just outside your flat. It's not quite the same when there are no bars, no glass, no wire, no walls between you and them. The feeling is different. It doesn't feel too good." "So it didn't feel too good then?" they asked. "No, sometimes it didn't," I replied.

The Snake

I got back late. There was a curfew in Kampala. There were soldiers on the road outside my flat on top of Nakasero Hill. They had said on television that anyone out after ten would be shot. It was five to ten. The streetlights were out. There was just a crescent moon. Then I saw it, curled up, on the top step, by the door: the snake. I heard a rifle being cocked. What was it to be, the soldiers or the snake? Would they shoot? They won't kill me. They will kill me. Were they from the north? Should I call out, tell them who I am? Would they speak Swahili, Luganda, English, or something else, like Lugbara? My knowledge of snakes was sketchy. A bite could be fatal. Key in hand I jumped over the snake and was inside in a flash, locking the door behind me. Through the mosquito screen that covered the kitchen window I saw the soldiers ambling back towards their barracks inside Lugard's Fort.

The Cobra

It was in the days before TV. My birthday parties included watching black and white films. My dad brought them home from a chap in the town. The films were highly popular with the kids in the street. There was one we waited for with bated breath: *The Wild Women of Borneo*. We were totally intrigued by these out-of-control Amazons running round and round a campfire completely naked. As if to calm us down, the next short film was of a man wrestling with a giant snake. It filled us with terror. It would be no exaggeration to say that I dislike snakes. I find it difficult even to write about them. I am sure they have their good points but I cannot, for the life of me, see what they are. I had a student at Hendon who kept them in his flat. He would pass photographs of them around the class. They were huge. He genuinely loved them. I know it was to do with association but he was my least favourite student. A friend of mine had just come back from Africa. We got onto snakes. We had agreed to meet in 'The Spaniards' on the edge of Hampstead Heath. He said he had occasionally come across snakes. Usually they had beaten a hasty retreat. Once he had left a pile of mist-nets (used for catching birds for ringing) tangled up on the floor of his house in Soroti and had gone away for a few weeks. When he returned, there was, he said, a ghastly stench permeating every room. A cobra had got into the nets, become terribly tangled up and had died. Yes, even writing about snakes makes me feel ill but I know that I have to do it. It's like a compulsion. I often wonder if it is to do with that snake film we used to watch, birthday after birthday, as children in Luton. I sometimes wonder, too, if that's why I went to Africa, to get snakes out of my system. (CM)

Spitting Cobras

I didn't venture out far from Kampala, not as much as I should have done, perhaps. I had read somewhere that some Spitting Cobras can spit more than six feet, and that their venom can blind you. Stories like that made me want to stay in Babu's City Bar. A friend of mine did venture out, though, far more than

I did. He told me the other day that he was turning his Land Rover round on a murram road in Kenya. His bonnet pressed into the embankment. A cobra rose up and spat at the windscreen straight at his eyes. If the glass hadn't been there, he would have gone blind. Since then he has always carried a carton of milk, when driving in Kenya. He says it's an antidote. He says that if washed out quickly with milk, the venom has no lasting effect. (CM)

The Black Mamba

We all have had our favourite places. As a child, mine lay among the ornately painted disused carts and carriages which had been left to moulder inside a large corrugated iron shed in an abandoned orchard down our street. Robins nested in the abandoned vehicles. I used to lie and contemplate the redness of their breasts. You felt you could warm your hands on them.

A friend of mine had such a place in Gedi, a mysterious town abandoned centuries ago on the Kenya coast. He went there to watch a bird called the African Pitta. He loved its colours: black and yellow, brown and red, olive green and dark azure, pink, buff and grey. He liked to sit and observe it from a bank of coral.

One day he shared his secret with an American who asked him if he knew of a hole in the coral near the point where he sat. He said that he did. He was told it was the lair of a black mamba and that he was lucky to still be alive. (CM)

The Polish

As you drive into towns in South Wales, you will often see housewives busily polishing their steps. A friend of mine in Kampala swore by the same polish. His balcony was always polished with the distinctive red product. Snakes were unable to move on the slippery surface and couldn't get into his house. I often think of that balcony in Uganda, as I drive towards St Elli's Shopping Centre in Llanelli. (JW)

Magic

I was sitting in a bar in Mukono, on the Kampala to Jinja Road, not that far from the turn-off to Namilyango. I was reading the local paper when I came across an article about a talking chicken. I leant over to my friend Clive who was busy texting a friend and asked him, straight out, without a hint of a smile, if he had ever come across a talking chicken. He said that he hadn't but that one of his Kenyan servants had poisoned a pair of owls that he had been raising because, it was claimed, they brought bad luck and were responsible for the school lorry overturning and the death of two schoolboys. He didn't look up. He just carried on texting a friend in Brunei. Then he added, a bit later, that one of the African teachers, at the school in Kenya, a young Kikuyu, had committed suicide in a rather unpleasant manner, and that was also blamed on the grass owls.

"What's a grass owl when it's at home?" the barman asked, rather insensitively, I felt, in Luganda. I could tell Clive was upset.

"They are," he explained, "like English barn owls but larger and darker".

"It says here," I went on, "that Idi Amin freaked in nineteen seventy-eight when someone informed him that a talking tortoise had predicted his downfall. It says the story terrified him so much that he constantly changed bodyguards as well as the cars in which he travelled and that he changed his schedules and sleeping places to avoid the tortoise's prophecy."

"Didn't do him much good," Clive mumbled, without looking up. "Didn't he get his comeuppance the following year at the hands of Julius Nyerere? I once had some bird nets stolen," he continued, still texting. "I used them to catch birds that I wanted to ring. I wanted to study them. I put the word round that anyone using those nets other than me would become leprous."

"Did it work?" I asked.

"A day or two later I found them outside the rest house in Kakamega Forest from where they had been stolen."

"Mm, so it did, then," I said, sipping my Bell.

'Mm," he replied. (CM)

The Witch

Sometimes it leaves a lingering doubt in your mind, when you write about Africa today. You feel that you shouldn't really do it. You have no hesitation describing witchcraft in Clophill in Bedfordshire or witches' covens in Bricket Wood in Hertfordshire but when it comes to superstitions in Tanzania, I don't

16

know, it feels, somehow, not quite right. Why is that? I don't know. Well, I do but you wouldn't like the answer. It's complex and it's not what you think. Be that as it may, a friend of a friend, an African American, came to work in Africa. He was from the wrong side of the tracks in Detroit. We had agreed to meet in Jackie's Bar in Haile Selassie Avenue in downtown Dar. He told me that some Tanzanians didn't know what to make of him. Was he a missionary? Was he a teacher? Was he an aid worker? He told me he just wanted to 'hang out' for a bit in Africa, 'the land of his fathers'. He said he liked keeping chickens that he kept healthy by giving them injections. They all survived the Newcastle Disease outbreak that decimated his neighbours' flocks. Villagers couldn't understand it. Rumours began to spread. One day they stopped his Land Rover. Some one shouted: "He's carrying *mumias!*" *Mumias* are local vampires. The angry crowd pulled him out and set fire to his vehicle. A passing policeman stopped him being strung up on the spot. "But, he's a witch!" someone cried. At this, he was arrested but was later released by the local police inspector who decided that a man from Detroit would, on balance, probably not be into black magic. Why is it I feel bad telling you this? It puts some people in Africa in a bad light, some will say. So what do you write? Should I have described that settler with a parrot on his shoulder or should I just have ignored him? Do you just tell the good, edifying stories? Should I wear rose-tinted spectacles? I don't know. I just ask the questions. It's up to you, dear reader, to provide the answers. (BVA)

The Nile Virgins

I can't understand why my mind keeps going back to the Nile virgins, after all these years. An academic I know, who lectures in ornithology at Makerere, sat up when I asked this very question. You could see his ears pricking up. I had this obsession to find the 'true' source of the Nile. I was never quite sure where to look for it. Was it in Rwanda? Was it in Uganda? Was it somewhere else, in Ethiopia or Tanzania, perhaps? Eventually I settled on a point near Lake Victoria. It made sense and I didn't have to go too far. 'This is where it starts', the locals said. I stood and stared at the magical place. It wasn't much. It was more like a rivulet that trickled into the river. A Mugandan whispered in my ear that virgins used to throw offerings into the water at that spot to make sure that they were fertile. It comes back to me again and again, even now, and I still don't really know why. The other day I asked a friend of mine who has worked for years as a missionary-type lecturer in a Catholic seminary in Jinja, if he had heard of the Nile virgins. He replied, rather abruptly I thought, that he hadn't.

The Spirit of The Falls

I often wonder what happened to the man with the pipe and the dreadlocks? They say he could walk on water. He used to bury the bodies that collected among the rocks at the source of the Nile near Jinja. They say that they had floated all the way from the Kagera River, that they were Tutsis who had been murdered in Rwanda in 1994. (It seems that many bodies were given shallow graves all along the shore of Lake Victoria, on the Ssese Islands and at Entebbe.) His name was Jaja Bujabald. He was a herbal doctor. He said that many would die and others would go mad, if they built the Bujagali dam. He was, they say, the thirty-ninth incarnation of the 'Spirit of Bujabald', the Spirit of the Falls. He must be a hundred now, if reports are to be believed.

Where Are They Now?
         To David Bowie

I dreamt that there was a current that ran north from the Kagera river. I imagined that it ran past the Ssese Islands. I saw it leaving the lake at Bujagali. I dreamt that it was filled with swimmers. It was just the movement of the water that made their bodies look alive.

The Earthquake

I was fast asleep when it happened. I always was a sound sleeper. They say it began with an eerie silence and that even the dogs in the town and the cicadas fell silent. There was, they say, a tearing sound and then a roar like a heavy fruit train approaching in Patagonia. Whatever it was, it passed by under the houses like a prehistoric monster. People fell to the floor. Shelves came crashing down. Houses moved from side to side, cracks appeared in walls and in lintels above doors. Outside, the earth moved this way and that. People tried to stand up but were hurled back down to the ground. The car alarms in Fort Portal all went off at the same time. Mothers became hysterical. The Mountains of the Moon, weighing billions of tons, were on the move along a fault-line. The noise was deafening, worse than the presses in H Block at Vauxhall in Luton. At first, I didn't wake up but with large clumps of clay coming away from the walls and cascading on to my bed, I came round for a moment, only to have the thought that my host kept an untidy hut. It went on for two hours but, apart from those few seconds, I slept through it all. Even now I am sorry that I missed it.

The Two Ladies

I don't know why I cannot get certain images out of my mind. I had an email today from a lady who worked in Kampala but now lives in Cyprus. She told me that she, too, had found herself in the middle of the Bundibugyo earthquake. She said that as she drove out of the area affected, she passed a naked lady walking along the road, carrying her clothes bundled up under her arm. She told me that the lady in question was remarkable, not only for her nakedness, but for her prodigious size. I then had another e-mail from a friend who, on that very same day, and at the very same time, was three hundred kilometers away, in Kampala, on the first floor of University Hall. The building began to shake. He managed to get his dressing gown and his flip flops on and fled outside into the quadrangle. He particularly remembers a 'lady' wandering around, who couldn't remember whose room she had come from. I don't know, it's funny how certain things stick in the mind. (LH, MT)

The Sausage Tree

I can see him now, clearly. I was looking for the place from which I had been told Baker looked back at the Sudan. The plain was deserted. I found the tree. Its fruit looked like giant sausages. Suddenly he was standing there next to me. I was drinking a Coke. He jabbed at it with his finger. His body language was unsettling. We had no common language. His hair had been shaped with mud. I couldn't read its language. Where he was from? Which clan did he belong to? Was he married? What position in society did he have? I just didn't know. He was wearing beads, and multi-coloured clothes and was carrying a spear that was as tall as he was. His gestures became frantic. The can was almost empty. I thought he wanted a drink. I don't like sharing a can with anybody. I don't know why. It's just how I am. "To hell with this!" I said to myself and gave him the can. I waited for the explosion: there was nothing left. It was empty. I felt a heel. Why had I done it? It's just that I felt that he was being rude. His behaviour felt bullying. Call it a clash of cultures, if you like. To my surprise, he uttered a great whoop of joy and went running off down the road, throwing the tin can into the air. When I got back to the bar in Moroto Club I told them all about my strange story. "You bloody fool!" an old-timer shouted. "Don't you know that we have been trying for years to stop them killing each other by removing the metal tips from their spears?"

The Silhouette

To Alex Fleming

I drove into Nairobi and pulled up outside a nightclub. Above me there was a window. Three feet wide by five feet high, it had an old-fashioned shape. It was filled with a yellowy-white light. A dark figure appeared, sideways on. The timing was immaculate. Hitchcock couldn't have done it better. A silhouette is a person, an object or scene represented as a solid shape of a single color, usually black, its edges matching the outline of the subject. The interior of a silhouette is basically featureless. This was the best example of a silhouette I had ever seen. In his back dinner suit and black bow tie, he looked like a taller version of Humphrey Bogarde in 'Rick's Bar' in Casablanca. At dawn we retired to his garage that he had converted into a bar for passing tourists, while giraffes strolled rhythmically by the bottom of his garden.

Mwizi

You have to be careful when walking along Tom Mboya Street in Nairobi. A chap I heard of almost got into serious trouble. "Mwizi, mwizi!" ("Stop thief") he heard. A woman came towards him. "No, no, he didn't come this way," he says. She pushes him. On the ground he sees a handbag with just one strap. The other is in her hand. Three men arrive and go through his pockets. The woman starts to mutter that she will shout 'mwizi'. An irate crowd can beat a man to death, if they think he is a thief. He calls her bluff and pushes her away. Passers by don't seem to be interested. She picks up her bag and vanishes. It happened, I heard, right in front of the Odeon Cinema.

The Sun Glasses

I don't know why this image keeps coming back to me. Is it because I have never visited Dar-es-Salaam even though I have always wanted to do so? Is it because the name means Haven of Peace or Port Safety? I have often tried to imagine what it is like. I know it is hot. I know the light can be blinding. A few years ago a friend of mine was driving past Kariakor market. He was wearing the latest, top-of-the-range sun glasses: Ray Ban Aviators. A young man leant in through the car window and deftly removed them. It was all over in a second. Decisions had to be made. Should my friend give chase? Should he shout "Stop Thief," "Mwizi"? Would this lead to the man being lynched? Would it lead to his being beaten or stoned to death, or 'necklaced' with a burning tyre? Was a pair of sun glasses worth a man's life? He kept quiet, did nothing and told his chauffeur to drive on. (BVA)

The Hippopotami

An image often comes back to my mind. It is accompanied by a feeling of being closed in, unable to get out. It is dark. I am in a club in Kisumu, in Kenya, on the edge of Lake Victoria. I suggest we all go for a walk to see the stars. "Not at this time of the night," comes the reply. "One of our members tried to do that a few years back. We found him the next day face down in the mud as flat as a pancake. He had panicked the hippos that were grazing on the shore. They all rushed into the water when they heard him coming".

Wandegeya

There was a roundabout called Wandegeya. It was just by Makerere University Campus. It is still there. Its name derives from the weaverbirds - Endegeya in Luganda - that used to nest there before the nineteen nineties. You could hear their calls: "chit-chit" changing to a chesty "cheee-eee-ee" above the noise of the cars. It wasn't the only sound heard there one day in the nineteen sixties. The air was filled with "Mwivi, mwivi". The shouting got nearer, "Mwivi, mwivi!" ("Stop thief!"). A man appeared from up one of the roads and stopped, trapped against a wall. A hail of stones drove him to his knees, his hands cupping his bloody head. "Watakufa yeye. They are going to kill him," someone shouted. "Nzuri ... yeye ni mwivu tu! That's fine. He's only a thief." Today, you might not hear either sound above the roar of the traffic.

The Killing

Teaching in Uganda was rarely dull. At lunchtime on a Friday at Kibuli the students would go with Sheikh Mukasa and the local mullah for prayers in the mosque on top of the hill. They would then come back down the hill and go back into classes: Chemistry, Biology, Physics, etc. The school was an oasis of peace. But then, one afternoon, cries could be heard, getting closer and closer. One the boys stood up and ran for the door. Through the Science Block windows a man could be seen running followed by a growing crowd, shouting "mwivi, mwivi". The teachers followed, trying to keep up with the boys. They asked what was happening. A man had been seen stealing shoes from outside the mosque during the second service for the general public. The man was running fast and seemed to be getting away but when he ran into the village, his fate was sealed. The villagers surrounded him. The beating began with fists, sticks and feet. The maluka chief appeared and tried to calm the anger, stepping between the man and the irate crowd. The teachers tried to intervene to save the poor man's life. It was no good. He was beaten to death while the boys looked on. He died before their very eyes. The students returned quietly to their classes, saying that there was no place in their community for a thief. They expected classes to go on as usual, which they did, but, for the staff, it was with difficulty. They had never seen a man die before. (TW)

Diplomacy

Come on, we have all been there. I was taken to a local market in San Vicente de Abando in Bilbao. "You must try this. It's typical of the region," my Basque host urged. We went into a covered hall. There were tall pot plants dotted around. Portions of ham were lovingly placed on a plate. I put the ham on my tongue. The effect was immediate. A feeling of nausea and disgust overwhelmed me. It tasted extremely greasy. "Just look at those hams hanging up there!" I exclaimed. My friends looked up. I took the ham from my mouth and slipped it behind one of the plants. "Rico? Tasty?" the local priest asked me. "Riquísimo, delicious," I replied, lying through my teeth. It happens when you travel. Ken and I decided to climb Kilimanjaro. We approached the bottom and started to climb. The heat was overpowering. Ken stripped off and plunged into a pool. I collapsed onto a rock. Some locals arrived and invited us to a bar. It was a humble construction: a hut with wooden sides through which you see the vegetation outside. There was a bench round the sides. Beer was poured into wooden cups from a white gourd. "Maisha marefu! Afya! Cheers," we lifted our beers. "Down the hatch! Bottoms Up." I was feeling nervous. The liquid was dreadful. It reminded me of the vinegar I had once tried in my mother's pantry. It had the consistency of runny, lumpy porridge. When our hosts were not looking I poured it onto the bare earth beneath my seat. "Very nice," I gasped, smiling. "Mzuri sana!" I later heard that it had probably been made from peanuts although someone else said it might have been *mbege,* which is made from bananas.

The Chemist

I had a friend in Africa whose curiosity knew no bounds. One day he set out to investigate the local beer, *pombe,* brewed in Kibuli village in a fifty-gallon oil drum. Millet was allowed to germinate and placed in the drum filled with water and heated over a wood fire. A couple of shovels of soil were added to allow the yeasts in the soil to start the fermentation. By Thursday the *pombe* was ready to drink! *Waragi* was fermented from bananas in an equally unhygienic fashion. Tests that my friend carried out revealed a fair proportion of brain killing ketones. (JW and TW)

Butterflies

> The butterfly counts not months but moments
> and has time enough.
>
> RabindranathTagore

They want to cut more of the forest down in Uganda. I once rode my Vespa through a great cloud of butterflies in Mabira Forest. They were all yellow. A friend told me recently that he, too, had passed that way, a long time ago. He had driven through the same spot on his motorbike. He had sunscreen on his face. A huge number of butterflies stuck to his face. They made him look like a brave in war paint. I asked him the other day, fifty years later, if he could remember the colours. They were, he said, all different: black, yellow, red, green and white. They say that the butterflies are in danger of disappearing on that road to Kenya. On a good day, a lepidopterist could once catch up to fifty in his bait traps. Now he would be lucky if he caught more than five. They want to cut the forest down in Uganda. They want to grow sugar cane in its place. Like the fruit bats on Kampala Road the butterflies are living on borrowed time. (CM)

Impact

I was reading a book called *The Africans*. In it Uganda's President was saying that Britain had left no mark on Uganda, that our presence was fleeting, that we had not really made much of an impact. Today I received an email from a friend I last saw fifty years ago in Kampala. In it he said that one of the most memorable things for him about Kampala Rugby Club was the cycle path that ran diagonally across the pitch. He said he had a vivid recollection of a chap pushing a bike across it loaded with bananas. They went flying in all directions, as the pack surged over him. I don't think that that poor soul would have agreed with Yoweri Museveni. (JW)

The Lepers

I don't know where it happened or even, for that matter, if it did. It was somewhere in East Africa. I thought it took place in Marsabit but my friends think that it didn't. I had a friend called Lawrence who loved a bit of adventure. He asked me to go with him but I had made a previous arrangement. When he got back, I asked him how the trip had gone. He didn't say much but later, in the Staff Bar at Makerere, I was told that he had been seen beating back begging lepers by hitting them on their stumps with a stick. The story made me feel sick.

Many years later, however, I heard another story of a wealthy shoe-maker from the Midlands who spent time each year measuring lepers' feet in a colony called Kumi not too far from Soroti. He would then go back to England where he had the special shoes made and shipped out to the lepers. They had the smartest feet in Teso. The story of the millionaire cobbler made me feel better.

It reminded me of the life-changing experience Che Guevara had had in Peru, in the Clínica de San Pablo, and the thoughts he had had about social justice on the banks of the River Cenepa, as he watched the lepers crossing in a boat that was inferior to that used by those who were well. (CM)

Lawrence

I can't remember a great deal about Lawrence on that five-week cruise from London Docks to Mombasa on The Rhodesia Castle. It was quite a long time ago, almost fifty years, in fact. I had forgotten that he had put a sign up on his door that said: "Dr Lawrence Jones, Professor of English, Makerere University". He was neither a Dr nor a Professor. He did it, he said, so that he did not have to share a cabin. I had forgotten that our 'minder', Moira, from The Ministry of Overseas Development insisted that the captain make him take it down. He claimed to be fluent in thirty-four languages. I had forgotten that. In Gibraltar he pretended to engage one of the locals in conversation. Through binoculars from the ship we could read his lips and see that all he was saying was "Sí, sí, sí". He said that he was fluent in KiSwahili. In the first lesson on the boat it was clear that he didn't know the first word. When the teacher challenged him, Lawrence replied that he only knew Zanzibari. "That's what I am trying to teach you," came the reply. He claimed that his brain was so active that he had to read three books at the same time. He would walk about the ship with at least three open. Later, in Kampala he did the same thing, especially in lectures. It got up lecturers' noses and was one factor that explained his fall from grace. At receptions he would grab six drinks at a time and hold the glass stems between his fingers whilst, at the same time, he juggled several plates of food. At lunch in the restaurant he would bellow "Waiter! More Melton Mowbray Pie!" which he would shovel into a brief case for a stowaway whom, he claimed, he had hidden in his cabin, while the ship was docked in Genoa. He insisted on having Lobster Thermidor for dinner every night. I know, because I joined him. We had never had that in Luton. I had joined him, too, on top of the Rock of Gibraltar, when the ship docked there. I remember him approach one particularly nasty-looking specimen with evil-looking fangs, a Barbary Ape or Barbary Macaque, as some call it. He gave us a lecture about its Latin name, *Macaca sylvanus*, and where it had come from, in Algeria and Morocco. Holding out his hand to one that was sitting on a fence, he told us that the apes were an endangered species. Just as he did so, one leapt onto his arm and sank its teeth into his hand. A swift taxi ride back to the ship's doctor was the only thing that would console him. It was the first chink that I saw in his armour. When all is said and done, it can never be claimed that life with Lawrence was dull. (CM)

The Mercenary

"Spitfire pilot. In the Congo." He spat dust on the floor. "That's what we had wanted to be! You were our hero," I stuttered. He said that he had flown in the Battle of Britain and that he had shot down Messerschmidts and Junkers. I looked at him with admiration. He was middle aged. His face was bloated. He was covered in dust. He said that he was bombing the rebels. Later I heard that Che Guevara might have been among them. Che, too, was one of the heroes at that time. One hero pitted against another. It seemed as if the world had gone mad.

The Occupation

I don't know if I would have been there, at the Foreign Office in Downing Street in 1972, had I been invited. People were beginning to say that Lord Douglas-Home, Secretary of State at the Foreign and Commonwealth Office, may have been about to sell out to Ian Smith in rebel Rhodesia. It must have been one of the most distinguished gatherings of Africanists ever seen in London. Brian Van Arkadie, who ran our 'tutorials' in the City Bar in Kampala in the sixties, was there at the front. There was David Caute whose *The Decline of The West* was compulsory reading among the Makerere crowd and Basil Davidson whose book *Black Mother* is still the first one friends' hands go to when they look at my bookshelf. Ruth First, who was later killed by a parcel bomb in Lorenço Marques, now Maputo, was there too. Ronald Segal, founder of the Penguin Africa Library, whose book *Race War* had sent shivers down our spines in Kampala, was doing the organising. Richard Gott of *The Guardian,* whose articles on Latin America were firing my generation's indignation, was there to advise on how to navigate the corridors of power. Guy Clutton-Brock, now a Zimbabwean national hero, whose African enabling centre, Cold Comfort Farm, in the then Southern Rhodesia was causing more than a stir, was the spokesman. (He had been at Rugby and Magdalene with the senior official on duty.) Having made their way in, by asking to see the library, they announced to the bewildered doorman that they were occupying the building and proceeded to sit down on the stairs. They refused to negotiate with the senior civil servant. Only the minister, Lord Alec Douglas-Home, would do. (It was only four years after the 1968 student occupations at Hornsey, later Middlesex University, and the LSE.) George Melly began to sing Fats Waller's *Ain't Misbehavin'* while Queen Victoria and Lord Curzon looked down disapprovingly. Having realized who the guests were, some burly policemen showed them the door. I am not sure I would have gone there, if I had been invited. As Brian said in Dar the other day Berkeley-style radicalism never really worked on the British mainland. The authorities would just refuse to play the game. They refused to be oppressive and the sit-in knew it. (BVA)

Chastity

She came slowly up the steps of the City Bar. She was tall, blonde, young and healthy, most young men's dream. She said that she had nowhere to stay. I offered her my bed. I said I would sleep on the floor. As it turned out, she was the perfect lady. She insisted on sleeping on a mattress on the floor. We exchanged tales until we fell asleep. I was too weak, after my operation in Mulago for peritonitis, even to make her a cup of tea. She left to marry a famous writer. That's how it was in Kampala. Best not to mention it, though, in case he puts a curse on me in his next book.

The Antidote

Brian was often there, in the City Bar, bouncing ideas off people and letting others bounce theirs off him. It was one reason why I had come to Africa: to find some new ideas. New philosophies seemed possible - different from those we had chewed over to extinction in our armchairs in St Andrews. There was Nyerere's *Ujamaa*, based on an idea that the individual became a person through working with other people. It sounded good. It felt like a perfect model, based on ethical and cooperative economics. Development economists from all over the globe joined in the ongoing conversation. Reference was made to Kenyatta's *Harambee* in Kenya. African nationalist refugees from South Africa and Rhodesia joined in the discussion with theories like *Ubuntu*. It was just what I needed. Ideas flew this way and that. *Encounter*, the magazine, had, it was felt, let us down. Its editor, the poet Stephen Spender, had just resigned. The penny dropped when it became clear that we had been manipulated by what some in the group called 'dark forces', to counteract our alleged intellectual neutrality, which, in the UK, we had got used to calling academic objectivity, dangerous, it was deemed by some, during the Cold War. The City Bar arguments were the perfect antidote.

The Stories

Were they true? Were they false? They did your head in those stories. Someone whispered that on a Sunday an earlier king of Buganda would throw people to the crocodiles that he kept in his private lake, just for his pleasure. Another told me that a Muganda king thought that 'fat was beautiful' and kept a hut full of women whom he force-fed on a diet of milk and who became so huge that they could not get up off their backs. There was another story that one kabaka used his courtiers for target practice. Whatever the truth, it is clear now that someone was feeding a certain narrative that made us favour a new status quo.

The Bishop

The myths we heard were strange. I had always been told that Bishop Hannington was roasted alive in a pot then eaten. Now they say that he was speared to death, naked, on a rock in Busoga.

Silences

I have always been interested in silences, the gaps, the parts, the people that have been airbrushed out of history. I once got into trouble at an undergraduate conference in Scotland for listing and examining the voids, 'the missing parts', in Miguel de Cervantes's *Exemplary Novels*. How could I know what was missing, I was asked? How could I possibly know what may or may not have been left out? How could I assert that Jane Austen's world was based on slavery? I asked. It didn't go down very well. In my lectures in London I loved to ask and analyse why certain writers, often women, were glossed over or ignored and absent from the canon. We were surrounded with areas of reality in Uganda, where most of us just did not go. Those who did, like my neighbour at Namilyango, John Weatherby, who dared to enter the Sebei caves, seemed to disappear off the radar.

Change

An atmosphere of paranoia was beginning to descend upon the city. That's what people were beginning to say. Before the storming of the Kabaka's Palace in 1966 and the arrest of cabinet ministers, life had been good. You could say anything you liked, within reason. It was a free country, a free press, free unions, a free parliament, a free business community, a free judiciary. There was freedom of thought in the university, freedom of assembly, freedom to form a political party, a free opposition. All of the freedoms we had taken for granted were in place. Even freedom from hunger and disease was moving into place. They were like the air we breathed and the clean, drinkable water that came out of the tap in Kampala. Everything seemed perfect. There was respect for the individual and even for property. Then things began to curdle. The milk started to go off in the fridge. You could feel the change in the atmosphere. The very air we breathed was changing. You began to look over your shoulder, whenever you were talking politics, or, indeed, eventually, when discussing anything in the local bars. It was a strange feeling because Obote had been popular in some of the circles in which I moved. No, strange is not the correct word, 'bad', a bad feeling, is more exact. It began to feel bad. One minute we were in a fully functioning parliamentary democracy, the next minute we weren't, well, not quite. One minute you felt completely free, the next, you didn't, well, less so, anyway. People began to say, "Oh, well, the country has to modernise and democracy, well, you know, it's a bit of an English fad". A friend of mine, Obote's niece, said "Oh, you English and your freedom. You are always banging on about freedom. Why do you go on so much about that?" "We have other priorities," they began to say. Sadly, people began to turn a blind eye to what was happening. I felt uneasy when she said that about freedom because at the back of my mind there was a voice that kept saying, "And what about freedoms before independence?" There were some 'freedoms from' but not so many 'freedoms to'. Anyway, that is how I saw it but others in my group of friends were not too bothered. A rumour started about the creation of a secret police. Soon it was said that it was more than a rumour. People were saying that the Prime Minister no longer felt safe and that he had to be sure of what was going on. There was talk, by some, of his growing paranoia, that he felt that the Baganda, or at least some Baganda, were out to get him. This appeared to be nonsense but we didn't know what was happening behind the scenes. After all, his wife Miriam was a Muganda. We did not have all the facts. They may have been in the Catholic paper *Munno* but we couldn't read Luganda. The rumours made you feel uneasy but the sun carried on shining and life was not that bad, far from it, really, particularly in the centre of the city. Everything was running smoothly. Mulago hospital was the best in Africa between Cairo and Johannesburg. The University was going from strength to strength. Cultural life was stimulating. The latest films and songs seemed to arrive in Uganda even before the public was aware of them in England. The jukebox in The Gardenia seemed to be ahead of those in London. Surely it was all a minor hiccup, a teething problem that would soon go away?

The Wheel of Fortune

I don't know if I am proud or ashamed of this story. I was told that what was about to happen was very important and that it would change my life. My finances were in a disastrous state. I can see myself, even now, walking up those steep stairs in that warehouse in Kampala. It seemed to be one the highest flights of stairs I had ever climbed. Was I walking up to Hell? They say that before you die, your whole life flashes before you. I had that thought but I didn't see my life flashing. There he was, sitting behind a desk, facing sideways. Was he the man who employed the beggars who worked the streets of Kampala? He was very fat. The idea was that he would put thousands of pounds into my account. When I got to London I would transfer them into his account and would keep some for myself. What on earth was I doing there? What was I thinking? Perhaps it would make a good chapter in the book about Buganda I might never write. Is that why I had allowed myself to be there? I recalled *The Life of Lazarillo de Tormes and of his Fortunes and Adversities,* the first picaresque novel. I remembered the peak of his good fortune, 'la cumbre de buena fortuna'. I thought of the giant wheel of fortune turning in that book. Was I at the top? What happens when it turns and you reach the bottom? I felt sick. I declined his offer, and beat a hasty retreat. Some time later I heard that guards on the Congolese border had shot a large man in a white Mercedes whose tyres were stuffed with dollars and diamonds. His wheel of fortune had turned. Did 'Little Lazarus' from the banks of the River Tormes in Salamanca save me? He probably did.

Mukasa

I was driving south from Kampala towards the town of Masaka, determined to find the brass lions that had once stood guard at the entrance to a forgotten king's palace that I had seen in a dream. Was it in a dream or had I read about it in an old book or did someone tell me about it? I am not sure now. I searched and searched slashing the undergrowth with a panga but just couldn't find them. I was soaked in perspiration. It was then that I saw the sign, 'Canoes, Lake Victoria'. An arrow pointed east. The canoes turned out to be dugouts, trunks of trees that had been hollowed out with axes. I paid my money and set off across the water. The boat was solid. It felt safe. It felt 'tight'. "Be careful of the crocodiles," the owner shouted out, as I drifted out of earshot. My paddling became bolder. I couldn't see any crocodiles. Suddenly the canoe turned turtle. I found myself upside down in the murky water. The mud in the water made it impossible to see more than two yards. I put my hands up to the sides of the boat above me, to ease myself out of its grip. I couldn't move. I was stuck. It could only be seconds before the crocodiles arrived to get me, I thought. Was I being punished for looking for the lions? What would I have done with them if I had found them? I pushed harder and harder, twisting this way and that. With a jerk I was free and bobbed up to catch air. I swam as quickly as I could back to the shore, using my usual sidestroke, pulling the canoe along behind me. "Mukasa was guarding you', the boatman said. I didn't know what he meant. "My guardian angel," I replied. He nodded. It wasn't until years later that I learned that Mukasa was the God of the Lake. Oh, and for all I know, the lions, if they exist, are still there somewhere under the ground.

Ice Cold in Kampala

What can I say about it now? It was my own stupid fault. I should have stayed away but that's how I was then. I was too curious. I am not now. Now I keep my head down. I am not proud of the story. I wish it hadn't happened but it did.

There was an almighty bang. We all ran out into the access road below our front windows. Up there, on Nakasero Hill, it was like a balcony overlooking the city. On the hill opposite ours a pall of smoke was rising. The crackle of gunfire could be heard. Then there was another crash and another. The whole town shook.

My neighbour and I stood shoulder to shoulder on the top of the hill, up by Lugard's Fort. It's strange how a catastrophe can bring people close together. We call it 'the Blitz Spirit' in England, from the time when Nazi bombs and missiles were raining down on us.

"What on Earth's going on?" he asked. He was from the south of Uganda. He was high up in the Ugandan CID but even he didn't know what was happening. I knew him well. We liked each other. He was always asking me, in the nicest possible way, who the numerous English friends were who used my flat when they were in Kampala. I would ask him in. Looking back, it must have seemed that a clandestine English army was forming. They were, in fact, mainly teachers.

"They are going for the King!" he gasped.

"Let's go and have a look," I said to Horace, who had just dropped by. He is Afro-American but he looks Mugandan. He taught history at the university in Kampala.

"Just look, Horace!" I said. "It's history in the making!"

"Ok, let's go!" he said.

We dived into my car, a light green Ford Zephyr 4, and shot up the steep road that led up to the Palace. We saw men with long rifles crouching behind bushes. The undergrowth had been cleared. The thought crossed my mind that it had been burnt.

We were at the top of the hill, when it happened. Three soldiers stepped out, holding rifles. Their faces and their bodies were thin. They were from the north.

"Kwenda chini," one shouted pointing his gun.

What did he mean? All three were shaking with fear.

"Horace," I whispered, "Does he mean 'Get out of the car', 'Get on to the ground' or 'Go back down the hill?'"

A shot rang out. A bullet broke the glass of the small, triangular ventilation window by my right hand and embedded itself in the door at my side, just a few inches away.

Horace was already out, lying on the ground. I stepped out.

"Lie down," Horace hissed.

"Get up!" I hissed back. "You are presenting yourself as a victim."

I heard an Englishwoman screaming frantically for help in the bushes. I think she was English but she could have been Ugandan. She had a cultured voice. There was nothing we could do.

"Get up off the ground, Horace," I shouted. It was then that the kicking started. Horace started laughing.

"Why are you laughing?" I gasped between my teeth.

"I get the xxxx kicked out of me in America and I get it kicked out of me here, in the land of my fathers," he gasped. He carried on laughing as the boots thudded into his ribs. I turned to the soldier who had fired the shot.

"We are teachers. I am at Kitante School. He's American. Makerere." They looked blank.

"Sisi walimu. Mimi Kitante," I repeated. "Yeye muamerica. Makerere". I wasn't sure if my upcountry Swahili was correct.

It was then, at that moment, that I knew what I had to do. I have always had a strong survival instinct. It was simple. I felt sad. He looked a nice chap. I had to take his gun. I might have to kill him. I had no choice. It was him or me. That's how it is, when the chips are down. There were no ifs or buts, just the decision, as clear as crystal. It was made in a second. I simply didn't want to die.

I became pure consciousness, totally alert, unaware of my body, unaware that I might be about to be riddled with bullets. I was as cold as ice. I remember being surprised at my focus. The gun, give me the gun. I needed to hypnotise him. I didn't want to kill him but if I had to, I would.

I got ready to spring. His gun was raised, pointing right at me. Could I reach him before he squeezed the trigger again? Would the others react? I felt sure I could see, out of the corner of my eye, water seeping through his trousers but I couldn't look down to check. I couldn't lower my gaze. We were staring each other in the eye. They looked young, younger than me and I was young.

The next sequence of events began to play out, in slow motion, in my imagination. Anguished cries for help were still coming from the side of the road, from behind the coffee bushes and the banana trees, now louder, more urgent. She was hysterical. Was she being attacked? I could help the woman, if only I could get the gun.

A line from a lecture I had attended at Makerere about the Pax Britannica and Colonialism ran through my head: 'The role of hegemon didn't extend far inland'.

I hesitated. The stand-off lasted just seconds.

It was at that moment that a black Mercedes Benz came speeding up the hill. The soldiers' eyes shifted towards it. Four men in dark, smart suits jumped out, their hands in the air. I thought they were Baganda but I couldn't be sure. They looked tall. The soldiers strolled casually towards them, dragging their rifles.

I told Horace to get into the car. He crawled up to the door and slowly got in. I started the engine, turned the car round and drove back down the hill, holding my breath as I did so, gradually increasing the pressure on the accelerator.

The bullets didn't come.

I went straight to the City Bar and ordered a cold lager and another and another, pure *Ice Cold in Alex*.

Horace wouldn't come in. He wanted to get back. I don't know why he didn't come in but then, he never would. It always puzzled me. I felt that he might feel ill at ease in there. I was totally unaware, then, of what society was really like then, in America.

It's funny. I didn't start shaking until three hours later, after I had gone over the tale again and again with Babu, the bar owner. A stranger at the bar said that that was why he liked the English. Unlike the French, he said, who started shaking at the slightest provocation, the English stay calm and do their shaking later. I didn't feel calm and I didn't like overmuch the sound of what he was saying.

I know it sounds ridiculous but the thought has occurred to me, at times, that perhaps that diversion, those few seconds, gave King Freddy his chance to get over the wall and escape to Rwanda and thence to London but, then, I have to admit, it wasn't raining when we were shot at. The storm broke later, at three, at the normal time and that, they say, is when he left.

The Message

In the gardens of the Lubiri (Mengo or the Kabaka's Palace) there are some cells where prisoners were once shot dead. The walls are pockmarked with holes from machine gun bullets. All over the city we could hear those guns chattering on that fateful day in May 1966, when things changed forever. Handprints of those about to die can still be seen on the walls of the cells. There is writing on the wall that translates as "Obote, you have killed me, but what about my children?" It's not really part of the guided tour. You have to ask the guide, if you want to see it. It mentions the name of the man overseeing the killing: Idi Amin. I often wonder if those four men who accidentally saved my life that day on Mengo Hill were among his victims.

A Bird's Eye View

We bumped into each other on the Northern Line. I had got on at Hendon Central, he at Belsize Park. We talked about the Battle of Mengo in 1966. He said that he remembered helping me to remove the bullet from my car door, the one that had almost killed me during the battle. He then told me something I had never heard: the things he had seen on that day when, for the first time in the country's history, the Ugandan army turned on its own citizens. He said that he and the Biology teacher could see Kabaka Anjagala, the main avenue that leads up to the Kabaka's Palace in Kampala, from the top of the minaret of Kibuli mosque. They could see the troops at the top end away from the palace and the gunfire as they attacked. He mentioned how, at lunchtime, it started to rain cats and dogs and how the army took a break. He said that it is rumoured that is when King Freddie, the Kabaka, escaped over the back wall. Lubiri School, he added, lay inside the Mengo grounds but much of it was destroyed during the fighting so the children came to use the old buildings at his school at Kibuli. He remembered going with the Lubiri Chemistry teacher to retrieve equipment from inside the palace grounds. They saved a lot but quite a bit had been looted. "What are you doing with all these super stories?" he asked, as he got off the train at Mornington Crescent. "Mind the doors!" a recorded voice called out. "Absorbing it, transforming it, writing it down," I said, as the doors closed and the train moved off towards The Elephant and Castle. "Did you see me down there at the palace?" I shouted. He gestured that he couldn't hear me.

The Spirit of Africa

I often felt ill at ease outside the cities in Africa. 'Hypervigilant' is perhaps the correct word. Elephants would block the road. Buffalos would threaten to charge. Crocodiles would take to the water, bats to the air. That night it was different. I was driving down a murram road somewhere in the middle of Buganda. I could see nothing ahead except the patch of earth lit up by my dipped headlights. Something stirred, almost imperceptibly, like a spirit inside the circle of light. A guinea fowl appeared, white dots on black feathers, just visible, just sitting there, enjoying the warmth of the dust that had still not cooled. It seemed to have no fear, as I drew near. It didn't seem to want to get out of the way. As my car approached, it moved slowly off into the undergrowth, trying to ignore me. For an instant, I felt at one with Africa. For a moment, I felt I loved the place. I remember it now, however, as a black and white image, rectangular, projected onto a screen.

The Calf

I hitched a lift on the dirt road that ran between Kenya and Uganda. A calf, startled, ran out in front of us trying to join its mother on the other side. There was a bang. The car felt as if it was about to take off into the air. The inside of the car filled with dust. I turned round. The calf lay on its back with its feet in the air. It looked dead. He drove straight on without stopping. "Never stop when that happens," was his reply to my puzzled stare. "You never know what will happen."

UFOs over Kampala

> Est-ce ma faute, si je trouve partout des bornes,
> si ce qui est fini n'a pour moi aucune valeur?
>
> René de Chateaubriand (1768-1848)

Let me explain. I used to lie in the sun in my garden on top of a hill in Kampala and close my eyes. As you know, black dots can appear. They are scars from damage done by the sun. Most people have them. They are like bits of dead nerve. I used to try to follow them but they always seemed to slip away to the side or up, or down, in the luminous void inside my head. I tried to imagine they were hot air balloons or space ships. I began to form a plan to write a whole saga based on my travels on earth and in space in one of these craft. Just imagine if you could get inside one and just sit there and enjoy the trip, as in some sort of *Hitch Hiker's Guide to the Galaxy*. But I could never catch one. They would never sit still long enough for me to get on board. It was as if even they were slipping away from me. "I Can't Get No Satisfaction" by the Rolling Stones was being played in bars and parties all over the city. The old Empire was melting like a snowman before our very eyes. We were in that gap between being Top Dog and becoming America's Poodle. There was no escape. There was nowhere to go to, except home.

Harambee

I can't remember exactly what we were doing. Studying volcanoes in the Rift Valley, I think. Through the classroom window we could see a group of men who were raising a pole by pulling rhythmically on a rope. We could hear the words they were singing. A solitary voice would start by telling what sounded like a story. Then, as one, the workmen would chant and pull. "Harambee!" ("All together now!") Little by little the post went up. Even now that sound from Tororo, on the Uganda-Kenya border, is echoing in my head.

Magnets

I used to stand and stare at the Catholic Cathedral in Kampala. Sometimes I felt like going in. Then I would look at the Anglican Cathedral and then at the Mosque. They were all on hills, at three points of a triangle. I remembered an experiment that we did at school in England. A sheet of paper was placed over three magnets and iron filings were sprinkled on top. Curving lines formed, each pointing to an underlying magnet. On one occasion a line formed away from all three. The Baha'i Temple in Buganda was outside the city. You could see right through it. You could walk in one side and out the other, in a straight line, without even opening or shutting a door. It was always empty, whenever I was there. It felt unfinished.

The Void

Uganda was full of religions, Christian, Judaic, Muslim, Hindu, Sikh and Baha'i but I can't remember, behind the noise and the evangelical din of the churches around Makerere, and the call of the muezzins in the suburbs in the night, any mention of Kiganda religion. I was never really aware of Katonda the remote Creator of the Baganda, the one who brought into being the heavens, the earth and all that they contain. Nor was I aware of the balubaale, the semi-gods beneath him. Some say there are thirty, others say up to seventy. Semi-god is not quite the right word. They were, or are, perhaps, more like saints or a cross between saints and guardian angels. They were the spirits of real men and women and were known for something outstanding. They were above the king in people's minds but we were never told that. It's what I wanted at Makerere but we didn't get it. Perhaps no one knew. Did anybody ever mention Mukasa, the spirit of Lake Victoria, the spirit of fertility, with his temples dotted about Buganda? I don't think so and yet, it was their country. Did anybody refer to his main temple on the Ssese Islands where the Kabaka, the King, sent cows each year to guarantee a good harvest and rain? Nobody talked about the shrine at Bubembe where barren women would go to ask Nalwanga, Mukasa's wife, for her husband's blessing. No one spoke of the lubaale Wanga, guardian of the sun and the moon, who has no shrine on earth and who is the father of the most powerful one, Muwanga. People, I have since heard, would once ask Musoke for rainbows to stop the rain so that they could start ploughing or bring in the harvest. They would ask Ddunga for good hunting and Kintinda to bring them wealth. They prayed to Wamala to keep Lake Wamala full. They left gifts out for Kawumpuli to keep away his plagues, and for Musisi to protect them from his earthquakes, and for Ndahura to keep away the smallpox. But nobody thought about telling us about Nabuzaana, the lubaale of obstetrics, tended by priestesses of a different tribe, the Banyoro, not the Baganda. Nor did we hear about Ggulu, the guardian of the sky, whose children included Kiwanuka, the spirit of lightning, and Walumbe, the spirit of sickness and death. I never knew about the shrines, the ekiggwa, nor the mandwa, the priest or medium that could be possessed by a spirit of the place and act as its oracle. I didn't know that there were three temples dedicated to Katonda in Kyaggwe near the Mabira Forest tended by the priests of the Elephant, of the Njovu clan. Perhaps they, the lecturers, the Baganda, the powers that be, whoever they were, didn't want us to know. The Baganda seemed at times to be locked in a cocoon. Perhaps some, perhaps many, did not want to know themselves. Occasionally I heard whispers about the misambwa, the cantankerous spirits of mountains, rivers, forests, and caves, whom one had to avoid, that one had to appease. Perhaps I heard talk of the mizimu, the spirits of the ancestors, with whom one dealt using cowrie shells or beans and, sometimes, with a sacrificial chicken or goat. Perhaps I wasn't paying attention but, as far as I can remember, none of the Mukasas, the Katondas, the Musisis, the Musokes, the Wamalas that I taught at Kitante in Kampala, ever mentioned this. The truth is that all I heard was talk of curses, and how evil spirits had been put on X or Y and how Z would die in exactly one year's time for some petty offence or other and did. Had the missionaries shut the door on all this? Was it I or was it they who were in a bell jar? I just don't know. All I was aware of was a void.

The Pioneer
To Saul Olek

There was something wrong at the university in Kampala. I am not sure what it was. The Professor of Education wrote that staff at Makerere experienced boredom 'due to a complete lack of common interests' when they mixed with students at parties. Well, what the Professor lacked in tact he made up for with honesty. The warden of my hall of residence wrote that there was 'a missing background' on both sides of the equation. One eminent Ugandan writer said that Ugandan students, disguised as Europeans, wearing 'worsted woollen suits, starched white shirts and ties to match,' concealed their private lives. I had a friend, however, who crossed the 'divide', if, indeed, it existed. His name was Saul. He wore Tanzanian shirts and flip-flops, as did I. He was slightly Bohemian. He cultivated a shamba, wielding his mattock proudly, in view of us all at Namilyango. He was a good painter. He liked painting the light he saw reflected on African faces. He saw things differently. He was, in some ways, a pioneer. He used to laugh as he imitated the histrionic gestures of western orchestra conductors. He found it funny and, when he laughed, so did I. He was, in some ways, a pioneer. Some said that students' souls were being 'murdered' in the colonial hothouse of Makerere. His wasn't. Others didn't go so far but they talked of spiritual mutilation. Mutilation could be remedied, they said, by intervention. Mutilated souls. The problem, they said, was that the students lacked resources. They didn't have access to European papers, to the BBC or to public libraries. They had no common knowledge to share with their teachers. I am not so sure. They knew a thousand times more than we did about what was happening in their own country. Most could read Luganda. We, on the other hand, had to really struggle to find out what was going on. The great writer I mentioned said, in his *Secret Lives*, that many Makerere students behaved like aristocrats, snapping their fingers at waiters, ordering taxi drivers to pick up girls for them from the side of the road. Someone wrote that they were ashamed of the agricultural labour that sustained their families. Some changed, they say, when they saw the huddled houses of the north of England and heard the sparrows cough. I think that the problem was slightly different. We, too, from 1960s England, were not on the same wave-length of many of our teachers. Some seemed to belong to a different social class, one that looked down on others. I don't think they even knew that they were doing it. It's just how they were. It was ingrained. Frankly I felt bored when mixing with some of the senior academic staff. They would ask what we had done with the £50 allowance sent to us to buy dinner suits before we embarked in London. One told them he had spend it on a pair of luxury snakeskin boots down the King's Road. I felt too embarrassed to admit that I had spent mine at the 1964 Edinburgh Festival. We didn't seem to have a common background with some of the staff. No one seems to know what happened to Saul Olek. The headmaster of Namilyango where he worked doesn't reply to my mails. He probably doesn't know. Perhaps Saul had an effect while he taught there. I have heard they have erected a twenty foot statue in front of the school which they call 'The Pioneer'. My only hope is that Saul didn't disappear during Amin's purges of the 1970s. Saul, are you still out there?

The Jembe

We were in the Museum Tavern opposite the British Museum. We were talking about KiSwahili. I told my friend about an artist who loved turning the earth over with his mattock on his shamba at Namilyango.

"You mean jembe," he replied.

"No, mattock," I repeated.

"Jembe," he insisted. "They are called jembes. Jembe is KiSwahili for the type of hoe used in much of Africa. It looks very much like a mattock. I think it was used in Uganda, as some wags used to say 'Nini jembe!' i.e. 'What Ho!'"

"Very good," I responded, "Ho- Hoe, I get it."

"KiSwahili was a bit diluted," he went on, "by the time it reached Buganda. They, the Baganda, didn't seem to like it. It was considered to be the language of slaves, servants and prostitutes. I have a book somewhere, *Upcountry Swahili*. They recommended it on the boat. It reached well into the Congo and as far as Oman. Omanis will sometimes use it when they don't want a European to understand them, assuming that a European is more likely to know Arabic than KiSwahili. A friend of mine years ago found himself using it in Marseilles."

"You know that slaves," I added, "were taken to that area, to the whole of Arabia, and castrated. Their number was huge but they had no offspring. I heard some years ago that Swahili was heard in, where was it, in Congo Brazzaville, I think."

"According to Mazrui, NO slaves were ever taken by Arabs to Arabia! The guy's off the scale!" We paused to sip our beer. I had a slight feeling that lèse-majesté had been committed. Ali Mazrui had been one of our lecturers.

"Certainly," he continued, "it is used in the DRC but how far west, I don't know. Oman and Zanzibar were once united, and at times Zanzibar was the capital of the joint country. Can't remember the details. Someone I know, a mzungu, who was brought up in Kenya, was in Oman and called on some high-ranking official. He was shown into the bloke's office by a minion who said to his boss in Swahili, as they entered, 'Here is that fat white bastard, Sir'."

"Brilliant!" I said. "Can I use that in a story?"

"Be my guest," he said.

"Another pint?" I asked.

"I don't mind if I do," he replied. (CM)

Bark Cloth

I lived for a while in a huge house in Buganda. It had the biggest picture window I have ever seen. You could see for miles across the trees. It must have been a supermarket window. It had no curtains. I quite like my privacy. I was in a local market and saw rolls of a light brown material which was very cheap. It was bark cloth. I went back with it and hung it up, not very expertly but it did the job. A feeling of relaxation came over me as I sat, in the evenings, enjoying my privacy, instead of being on view on top of the hill like a tailor's dummy. People started to look at me with sad expressions. They seemed to be keeping away. I wondered if they were sad at missing the evening spectacle. Eventually one of the locals plucked up courage and asked if there had been a death. I looked inside Niall's tent. He had pitched it in one corner of the room. No, he was all right.

"No, no, we're fine, thank you," I replied, puzzled.

"Only, we wrap dead bodies up in bark cloth here," the gentleman explained.

I think the curtains soon came down. I am not sure though, because I left for a flat in Kampala shortly afterwards.

The Egg Sandwich

The atmosphere was becoming tense in the New Life Club on the outskirts of Kampala. Tempers were running high about all sorts of issues. The Baganda wanted to break away and form an independent state. The Kabaka, King Frederick Mutesa the Second, who was still President, had even told the Prime Minister to remove all his things from Buganda. It was not just that. Prime Minister Apolo Milton Obote had given some Bugandan counties - Byuaga, Bugangazi, and part of Singo Buruli and northern Bugerere -'back' to Bunyoro. Tension was rising between the Baganda and the Banyoro. The agony of being a Munyoro but being called a Muganda could be almost physical, I was told. Bunyoro dances had been banned in the counties in contention. Banyoro were expected to become cultural Baganda. They had had to learn Luganda. My friend was enjoying an excellent egg sandwich in a small side bar inside the New Life when he saw an arm rise up holding a bottle above the crowd and come down on somebody's head. Very quickly other bottles popped up in the air and came crashing down on other heads. In films they use bottles made of sugar. I know because I have felt one. It didn't hurt. These were different. They clearly hurt. Like mutually repulsive particles the crowd dispersed in every direction. My friend left in a hurry clutching his egg sandwich and found people streaming out onto the streets all around in fear, perhaps, of another army raid. Glad to get away from it all, my friend strolled slowly back to the university campus through the cool night air enjoying the rest of his fresh egg sandwich, bracing himself for the sound of gunfire which, that night, didn't come. (DS)

Moira's Curse

Moira, our minder, warned us on the boat: "Before the year is out three of you will be dead". Each of us took this on board in his or her own way. I looked at Alex. He looked at me. We didn't say anything. I don't know if he knew what I was thinking. We had known each other well in St Andrews. One night Alex went through the windscreen on the way to the New Life. The car broke in half. He needed thirty-eight stitches and a set of false teeth. When I next saw Alex, after the crash, I remembered Moira's warning. It felt like a curse. Later Caroline and Hugh perished on the Nairobi to Thika Road when a wheel came off a lorry and hit them. (AF)

The Kingu of Sebei

I don't know who he was. His face was vaguely familiar, though. I may have seen him before at the exhibition of Congolese Art in Luton Public Library. Perhaps I had seen him in Uganda. The exchange actually took place in 'The White House' in Luton. The latter is one of my favourite places. Inside there is a balcony like a minstrels' gallery. It is lined with books. You can enter the pub via Manchester Street or from St George's Square. It was built on the spot where The Crown and Anchor once stood, where I used to sit, when I got back from Uganda in 1967, a pile of books and a pint on the table, borrowed from what was then the best public lending library in Western Europe. Ovid and Jung, Freud, Proust, and Whitbread: perfection. The early drinkers had already arrived. I was writing a poem on Milton Obote, Idi Amin and the Kabaka. On my table was *A State of Blood* by Henry Kyemba. The vaguely familiar man came up to me. I read him my poem 'What if?' about the three main actors in Buganda's tragedy. His response was astonishing. I tried to join in with a 'Yes, but' and a 'But, what about?' I couldn't get a word in edgeways. The words just poured out of him in a torrent:

"You have to remember the circumstances surrounding Amin's promotion. When the army mutinied in 1964, Obote could not afford to follow Nyerere's example and dissolve the army and start again. It was already clear that he would need the army in the dispute with Buganda. Rumours at the time suggested that Mengo was organising an army of 6,000 ex-servicemen to respond to the Lost Counties issue. Initially, Opolot, from Teso, was appointed head of the army, with Amin as second-in-command. But as the crisis developed over 1964-65 and Obote felt threatened, not only by Mengo and the Bugandan Parliament, or Lukiiko, but also by the opposition within the UPC. The latter was organised by Grace Ibingira, a Muhima from Ankole. Obote had made him Secretary-General at the 1964 Gulu UPC convention because he felt threatened from the left by John Kakonge. A huge mistake. It emerged that Opolot was siding with the Ibingira faction so Obote had no option but to use Amin, who delivered in the battle of Mengo. As you know, just before that battle, Obote arrested Ibingira, Magezi, Ngobi and two other UPC ministers. In any account of the conflicts within the UPC, the investigation of Obote, Amin and Nekyon's involvement in the Congo is crucial.

You remember that at one point Obote was down to a small group of supporters in Parliament. Also, the Congo involvement probably turned the US against Obote."

"Yes, but ...', I said. He waved my unformed question aside.

"Ibingira received support from the CIA. In this complex story, another issue is how Obote came to be PM in the first place. There could have been a Muganda Prime Minister of Uganda, Benedicto Kiwanuka, if Kabaka Yekka had combined with the DP but the Mengo establishment was firmly Anglican and did not want to have any truck with a Catholic as Prime Minister. Obote tried to handle the Buganda problem by giving a prominent role to Baganda UPC members, by making the Kabaka President and by taking a Muganda wife. You may remember the hilarious parliamentary debate about the wedding. Where was the first Mrs. Obote, they asked? One member protested about the cost of the reception. Another chimed in, pointing out that he had had more than his fair share of the booze. The reply came, "I did not know I was paying for it."

"Obote's other trick was to attempt to debase the currency of the Bantu kingship system by a sort of Gresham's Law, inventing kings for everyone. You may remember the Kingu of Sebei. In the end none of it worked." My new found friend suddenly got up and left with a polite "Kwaheri". I tried to call him back with a "The Kingu of Sebei?" He turned round.

"You know the Kingu, they called him the Kingu, not the King of Sebei, because it sounded silly. In some cases like the Kyabazinga of Busoga, Sir Wilberforce Nadiope, had historical antecedents. Other cases like that of the Kingu, were innovations."

Then he was gone. He just disappeared down the stairs into the gloom. I don't know who he was and I haven't seen him since. I think he lives somewhere in Luton. All I know is that he said that he was from Sebei, from a village near Mount Elgon. (BVA)

Breathless

We had arranged to meet in 'The Hub', a nice little restaurant in Regent's Park, near the Open Air Theatre. I didn't realise that my interview with him, with the former High Commissioner, would be conducted on the run. He was fully kitted out: track suit, trainers, woolly hat and Walkman. I wasn't even dressed for a stroll round the lake.

"High Commissioner, can you tell me about the Congo Affair, you know, the ivory and gold business?" I gasped, as he set off. I was out of shape.

"Obote, Nekyon, Amin were said to have got hold of a load of loot in Zaire," he replied, between what appeared to be puffing-type breathing exercises.

"What was it for?" I blurted out, already beginning to feel a little out of breath.

"It was payment for arms supplied to the late Patrice Lumumba's band of fighters. America freaked. I met Lumumba at Toni Nuti's guest house in the south of Uganda. She was foul to him."

"Who?" I asked, I felt I sounded like an owl.

"LUMUMBA, of course!" he shouted.

"What happened then?" I asked. I felt I was becoming almost monosyllabic.

"Obote psychologically dumped by the Yanks," he replied through gritted teeth.

"As simple as that?"

"Yup." He began to increase the pace. He started waving his arms in circles. My arm was aching from trying to hold my small tape recorder near to his mouth.

"There was talk of people hanging on to the 'cash' or loot. Amin, perhaps. Needed to fight off the Buganda threat? Amin tried to cash bars of gold somewhere in Kampala, Barclays, perhaps, or National and Grindlays." He began to speed up. My heart was pounding.

"Emergency debate in cabinet," he puffed. "Censure motion against Obote. Only Kakonge opposed the motion. Not sure now about Nekyon. Five Ministers arrested. Subset of those, in effect, deserting Obote. Ibingira amongst them. Leader of the anti-Obote faction in the UPC party. Ibingira - Kabaka's Man. Kabaka weakened. Buganda weakened. The Baganda wanted to form a breakaway state." I could no longer form a question. I was falling behind. I just wasn't dressed for it.

"Amin promoted to Army Chief of Staff, instead of being sacked. First nail in the coffin of Westminster-style parliamentary democracy." His phrases were uttered in time with his rhythmic panting. "Shock waves in the City Bar. Atmosphere curdles." That was the last I saw of him. I just couldn't keep up. He disappeared into the mist.

Tremors

A chap I bumped into in The Speke Hotel in Kampala told me that Buganda had always been unstable; that it had had numerous civil wars; that there had been nineteen. It never developed a system, he said, of orderly progression to the throne. Clans often fought with each other to put the crown on their leader's head. Kabakas could have up to a hundred wives from different clans in order to consolidate their power. When a kabaka died, his numerous sons, supported by their mothers' clans, would make claim to the throne. The kingdom was thus ravaged by frequent conflict. By the nineteenth century, he whispered, when the British arrived, most Bugandan kabakas got there by murdering their brothers.

Things Fall Apart

The shrines of Buganda's first King, Sekabaka Kintu, were set ablaze on the night of Wednesday, 14 October, 1995. The fire broke out at 8.20 pm at Kikumbi palace, Bunamwaya, Zana, 8 kilometres down the Kampala to Entebbe road. It reduced the four hundred year old palace to ashes, destroying all the traditional regalia. The palace had recently been refurbished. The fire may have been started by some people brought in from Kyaggwe to work in the palace by Prince Nakibinge Mutebi. He is reported to have abandoned them without paying their wages. I don't know if this is true.

Hornbills

The first thing I heard each morning in Kampala was the sarcastic laughter of hornbills in the jacaranda tree next to my window.

The Frogman

I have often wondered if I should write about it. I was walking down the main road in Kampala with a colleague from work. It was a beautiful day, as usual. Everybody was smiling. It felt good. It felt like the place to be. Suddenly he was on my back. His hands were around my neck, squeezing. Fortunately, I was fit. I was a second row forward for Kampala. His hands had no effect. The problem was, what should I do with this strangler? My colleague was upset. He was still strangling. His feet were off the ground. I was taller than him. "Black with white no," he kept bellowing. "Black with white no." His voice was getting weaker. I weighed up the options. I saw the welcoming open door of a bar that I didn't usually frequent. It was dark inside.

"Follow me," I said to my colleague, who was trying to pull him off. "What would you like to drink?" I asked.

"A Coke," came the reply.

"A Nile for me," I said to the barman. "Oh, and a Fanta for the bloke on my back". I could feel my strangler's grip loosening.

He slipped slowly down to the floor.

"Please sit down over there," I said, taking charge of the situation. "I'll bring the drinks over".

I then began my tirade about racism. I really tore him off a strip. I asked him what on earth he thought he was doing.
"Black with white no," he kept muttering, feebly by now. I lifted my glass.

"Cheers! Maisha marefu," I said.

"Afya" he replied
"Asante. Vifijo," my colleague added.

He told me he was a frogman with the Uganda police and that he worked in Lake Victoria. I told him he should be ashamed of himself, that he had a good job. We slowly began to warm to each other. He was quite a nice young man. I felt bad that I had used sarcasm to get out of the scrape. We finished our drinks, shook hands and left.

"Turn the other cheek," my vicar used to tell me, "Matthew 5:39: But I say unto you, That ye resist not evil: but whosoever shall smite thee on thy right cheek, turn to him the other also." I wasn't so sure, at the time.

"Kill them with kindness," my mother used to say, when I asked her how to deal with difficult people.

"Yes, kill them with kindness," my father would nod. "It's not that hard and it works". My approach was slightly different. I used some sarcasm as well as kindness. I felt a bit bad. I never saw him again. Perhaps he kept out of my way. I think he was Mugandan.

"Did you know him?" I asked my companion.

"No," she replied, rather sharply.

The Spy

I can't remember where I had first seen him. He came into focus gradually. I had been dimly aware of his presence for a number of days. He was often sitting near us, on the veranda of the City Bar on Kampala Road. He looked lonely. It was as if he wanted to join in our conversations. I never actually caught him looking directly at us but I had a feeling that he was watching us, out of the corner of his eye.

Suddenly I became aware of him sitting there at the next table. He was immaculately dressed, in an aristocratic English style: brand new sports coat, matching tie, trousers perfectly creased, beautiful brogues. He spoke with the accent of the English Home Counties. No, it was more than that. It was upper class, Eton or Harrow. I had always prided myself on my clear accent, but his, in comparison, was 'cut glass', Waterford cut glass. His was the English of an Oxford-trained Anglican bishop. In reality, he turned out to be far from that. He unnerved me a little but, because of the voice, I felt safe.

He said his name was Toby. We exchanged pleasantries. It was all very civilised. At first he let me speak. He asked me how I was. I don't know how we got round to it but I found myself telling the story of a silly incident that had happened earlier that week in a lake, near Masaka. I thought it might amuse him. I told him the story of Mukasa. He didn't to know who Mukasa was.

"How would you like to have a big house?" he asked me, out of the blue, going for the jugular. The image of a crocodile's opening jaws flashed across my mind. I felt that the metaphorical canoe that I had been paddling gently through life, up to that moment, was about to be rocked.

"I beg your pardon?" I replied.

"Yes, a big house in its own grounds, with six bedrooms, on top of a hill, away from the mosquitoes, with your own servants and spacious servants' quarters, a double garage, manicured lawns, mature flower beds, honeysuckle, hibiscus, gardenia, shamba boys, everything you need."

"But I have a flat of my own on a hill already," I stammered, "next to Lugard's Fort."

"Yes, I know," he replied. How did he know that?

"Yes, a mansion with a swimming pool surrounded by trees, cleaned everyday," he went on, upping his offer. "How would you like that?"

"Who wouldn't?" I responded, trying to sound cool, blasé but, underneath, feeling bewildered. I felt that he felt that I was beginning to lose interest.

"How would you like a swimming pool filled with beautiful girls?" he said, adding a note of urgency to his voice and leaning closer towards me. He had by then moved his chair up to my table.
"With w-wh… what?" I stuttered. My reaction was one of indignation tinged with curiosity.

"With girls, yes, incredibly beautiful girls, hand-picked for you". He emphasised the last part of his sentence. His eyes, I thought, were beginning to look slightly febrile. I tried to picture a pool, full of beautiful girls, surrounded by palm trees. He had found my weak spot but then I began to wonder where these pretty girls would come from, the Gardenia, the New Life, the Crested Crane, the Susannah, the Imperial Hotel? No thanks, I thought.

I felt my heart begin to sink. I shook my head, trying to clear it. What on earth was I thinking? What would my family in Luton say, if they heard I had acquired a pool brimming with bikini-clad beauties? I knew that my brother was in constant touch with clergymen in Uganda who were fellow Oxford graduates of his.

Would the girls even have bikinis? How could I let all this seduce me? "All these things I will give you, if you fall down and do an act of worship to me" - the words Satan uttered to Jesus, in the Wilderness, ran through my mind.

What was all this about? Was it to do with Obote? In my mind Obote had been a fairly all right sort of chap, more or less, with some reservations, up until then. He was a friend of Nyerere who, to many young Britons, then, was more than just all right. He admired Kwame Nkrumah who for us could do little wrong, and Sekou Touré and Modibo Keita. That's how I was then.

The beer, the sun, the heat, the strange temptation: my head was beginning to spin.

"Go on," I said, drawing my chair nearer but distancing myself inside. By now curiosity was beginning to take over inside me. "And what do I have to do to get all that?" I was struggling to avoid a hint in my voice that I thought it might be a wind-up.

I suddenly remembered the 'Tank Hill Gang' and the ripples one of them had caused with a remark he had made just after Uganda's Independence. He had found himself on the next plane home. The reply that came surprised me.

"All you have to do is tell the Minister who in Uganda is anti-African." He smiled like a doctor reassuring a patient about an unwelcome course of chemotherapy or a dentist recommending a programme of deep, under-the gum, periodontal treatment.

"I beg your pardon?" I spluttered again.

"Yes, just tell us who in the European community has negative attitudes towards Ugandans," he explained, showing the palms of his hands. The words sounded terrible. I was passionately anti-racist. I had just turned down an invitation to go to Rhodesia, as Zimbabwe was then called. Something shrank inside me. I felt physically sick. How could even he think that I could even contemplate doing a thing like that? And, anyway, I would avoid such people like the plague, if they still even existed, that is. It is true that I had said on more than one occasion that I felt more at ease with educated Ugandans than with poorly educated Europeans, but surely that was unremarkable? I had a huge number of English and American friends at the University. I felt that I was drowning. I came back to reality. How could I get out of this? I felt almost hypnotised by him. He was beginning to make me feel dirty. Questions swirled around in my head. He was staring into my eyes, trying to read my thoughts. I remembered the man who gone out into the night outside the club in Kisumu only to be literally flattened by a herd of panicking hippopotami. A feeling of shame started to become unbearable within me. One category of human being I had always despised was the informer, the 'grass', in any context.

"I'll let you know," I said, getting up abruptly. He looked hurt. "Yes. I'll let you know," I repeated, as I made for the steps that led down to the pavement. I didn't see him again in the City Bar for ages. Our eyes didn't meet. I never found out his name. I didn't want to know it. I often think, when I remember that incident, that you don't know what freedom is until you feel you are starting to lose it.

Years later I was recounting this to a friend from those times. He asked me if my temptor was MI6. He had been offered £1000 a year to report on rebellious elements in the 'White Highlands'. He had declined the offer. I told him that the man in question was not MI6. He was Ugandan. I couldn't work out his tribe. Was he from Buganda, Lango or from somewhere in between?

Bodies

"All it takes for evil to succeed is for a few good men to do nothing..."

–Edmund Burke (1729-1797)

People were coming into Kampala with stories of bodies lying on the roads out in the bush. They said that the lorries in which they were travelling were riding right over them. People fell silent and went numb in the City Bar. No one knew what to say. No one pronounced the words 'human rights abuse'. It was a conspiracy of silence, the default position being not to criticise the government. "None of our business now," I heard someone mutter.

The Future Dictator

I have a friend who was a pupil at 'the Prince of Wales', now called Nairobi School. It happened, he says, during the Bugisu and Bukedi riots in 1960, two years before independence. People were protesting against the colonial authorities about taxation and representation. Some chiefs had been sacked from the council in order to save money. My friend was on his way with his father, the headmaster of a local school, to pick up someone who might be in danger. They were stopped at a road block where a certain Sergeant Amin flagged them down. He told them it would not be safe to proceed and promised to collect the person in question and deliver him safely to Tororo. It's strange how, even then, the future dictator's soon-to-be familiar shape was beginning to appear in public. (CT)

The Rock

One of my plans, while I was living in Tororo, was to scale 'The Rock'. Tororo Rock is a volcanic plug, the hard inside of a volcano that was left when the sides were eroded away. There's one in Soroti that was destroyed by an earthquake and is now a heap of huge rocks. I would sit there in my garden planning the ascent, which side to go up, which side to come down. The weeks went by. The Rock stood there, defiant, challenging me with a "Come on, then". Meanwhile, the radish seeds I had planted in the rich volcanic soil were ballooning like beef tomatoes. The end of my stay there was approaching. I still couldn't stir myself. But why? Someone had told me that it was a great rock to attempt and that when he had tried it, he was half way up when he put his hand on a ledge to heave himself up and found that he had gripped a poisonous snake instead! He didn't know how he had escaped without a bite but had beat a hasty retreat and had never reached the top. The snake was sunning itself, he added, when he disturbed it. My plans to scale the plug began to crystallise around a route in the shade, away from the sun. My original plan, before hearing of the snake, had been to treat it like a helter-skelter and climb up it by going round and round, spiraling upwards. That idea was abandoned. The second plan failed because with the sun overhead and moving round, where would there be shade? The time came to go back to Kampala. The Rock remained unconquered, at least by me.

The Club

They didn't stop asking me the same question, as soon as I arrived. I remember a room that seemed never to have enough light. 'Europeans' used to come up to me and stare into my face, look into my eyes, as if they were searching for something, some tell-tale sign, of what I didn't know. I could hardly make out their features. There was one, in particular, the secretary perhaps, who wore a wide-brimmed hat, indoors. "Are you coming back?" he would ask me screwing up his face. That was the litmus test. Was I coming back? I had only just arrived. I felt ill at ease in the claustrophobic club. I took to sitting, alone, on the balcony of the Rock Hotel in Tororo overlooking the plain to the north. There seemed to be no horizon. The light of the setting sun would light up the dust rising from villages I couldn't see.

The Prisoner

I am not sure when it actually happened: some time between 1965 and 1967, I think. He boarded the Soroti bus at Tororo. His Saab was being repaired, after a nasty lawyer had had some one fill up his tank with sand. A prison officer climbed aboard, manacled to a prisoner. The guard asked if his prisoner could sit down beside him. My friend agreed. The manacles were unlocked. The prisoner sat down. The bus stopped in the next township. The passengers got out for a cup of tea. The question came up about what the gentleman was in for. Murder, came the reply. He was serving fifteen years. He was, it transpired, a model prisoner. Every now and then, every few years, he was taken from Soroti prison to a prison in his home area so that his relatives could visit. The policy, it seems, was to keep convicted criminals away from their home area to discourage them from trying to escape. It reminded my friend of the German prisoners of war who baby sat him in Colchester during World War Two. He lived next to a bakery where a lorry load of POWs were dropped off every morning to make bread. Two were co-opted to look after him while his mother and grandmother went shopping. They spent the time making him wooden toys. (CM)

Rebels versus Assassins

It's strange how little we saw of Idi Amin. I mean, he was always popping up here and there, now and then, like a Will-o'-the-wisp, an igneus fatuus or foolish fire, but not for long. He turned up, for example, at a rugby match in Namilyango in 1966, just after the Battle of Mengo, in which Amin had deposed the President, the Kabaka, or King, of the Baganda. 'The Namilyango

Rebels will now take on the Namilyango Assassins', a voice announced over the tannoy system. The agreement had been that they would be called Teams A and B but the pupils were mainly Baganda and chose inflammatory team names. The heads of Amin and his henchmen, looking like tontons macoutes in their berets and black glasses all swivelled round to eyeball my friend, the school rugby coach. Amin, in particular, had a menacing grin. My friend thought that he was done for. The Rebels beat the Assassins but, even so, Amin, slapping his thigh and guffawing, seemed to enjoy the joke. (NH)

The Night Watchmen

It was an awkward situation. We weren't really supposed to do it. We even had to hide when certain 'officials' came round. Uganda, I suspect, was trying, at the time, to stay neutral in the conflict between the North and the South of Sudan. The camp was bursting at the seams. It was full of bright young Sudanese boys hungry for education. We managed to cover most of the disciplines. All we had were mud huts. Against the regulations, my friends tried to find employment for some of the refugees. The young men were tall and strong. The only job they could get was that of askari (night watchman). For this they had to have shoes. Some of the Dinkas had very long feet which meant getting cobblers to make one pair of Bata Safari Boots out of two discarded pairs. (CM)

The Kick

I had better not use his name. He may well be still alive. He was, I have to say, very friendly. He had lost the key to the hut where we were going to sleep. We all tumbled in through the open space of the glassless window. At dawn he appeared to show us the farm. It was already hot when we walked up to the fields even though we were in what they called the White Highlands. A row of women hoeing, some with babies on their backs, came into view. He was muttering something about lazy people. They all seemed to be working hard to me. Then it happened. It felt like an act of insanity. Even now, I am not sure why he did it. Was he mad? Did he do it to shock us or was he just not thinking? "I'll show how we solve this," he muttered. "What?" I asked. "This," he replied. Perhaps he thought they had not done enough hoeing. He went behind a young lady who was scratching the surface around a young coffee bush. I caught her eye, she was a good-looking woman. He had a stick in his hand but I had no idea what he was going to do. He took a step back and then lunged at her backside with his boot. "Stop. You can't do that!" I shouted. He laughed and shrugged his shoulders. I realised in that instant why I had not wanted to be posted to Kenya and why Obote had not wanted to join the East African Federation. I was glad to get back to Kampala. Uganda felt so safe, in comparison, in 1964.

Mountains

I was hopeless with mountains when I was in Africa. As you know, I tried to summon up the courage just to scale Tororo Rock but was put off by the story of one of my friends. I set off once to climb Kilimanjaro but got no further than a cool pool at the foot of the mountain and a ramshackle bar which served peanut beer and where the 'craic' was in Swahili. I once nearly joined a Frenchman on his journey up the Ruwenzoris. I am glad I didn't. He came back with a coat made from the fur of the hyraxes that he had shot and of which he was very proud.

The Crooked Path

There's a crooked path in the field just opposite my house in St Albans that always reminds me of something I heard in Africa. There's another one that meanders this way and that through the bluebells in the wood on top of the hill. They make me think of a character in Tororo Club who used to stare me in the eye and say, without a trace of irony, that Africans couldn't walk in a straight line.

"You what?" I would reply, bursting out laughing at his theory.

"No, no," he would say, with a look of seriousness. "Next time you are in the bush just have a look," he would insist.

"I need this like a hole in the head," I would say to myself. It was about then that I started going, by myself, to the Rock Hotel. I still hear stories, I am ashamed to say, about crooked lines in Africa.

The Termite Eaters

Today, lying wounded by the river in Patagonia, I remembered, as clearly as if it were yesterday, those children sitting around a termite hill in the grounds of the school on Kitante Hill, sticking twigs into holes and pulling out workers, soldiers and the occasional nymph that grabbed on to the stick. I knew that I wouldn't die of hunger. (*Poemas a la Patagonia*, 2004)
Johnny

Whatever happened to Johnny? He was part of the crowd in Kampala. He was, it is rumoured, the first person to be seen in Kenya with a windsurfer on his car. He had a flat in Marchmont Street near Russell Square tube in London. We used to meet for a jar in 'The Lion's Head'. One of the last times he was seen was when he got out of a car in a traffic jam on the Brentford-Chiswick flyover and strolled calmly away into Central London. They say that he knew the sister of a Kenyan minister called Bruce MacKenzie and that he eventually landed a high-flying job in Nairobi. The very last time he was seen was at the house of MacKenzie's sister round the corner from where a mutual friend lives. That was just two years after her brother had died in his aircraft, blown up by a time bomb. Some say it was inside a stuffed impala, a present from Idi Amin. Others say no, it wasn't inside a stuffed impala, it was inside a lion's head. (CM)

The Sixty Second Friend

There he was again, sitting there in The Hollybush with his wife, smiling and nodding at me in a friendly way. "Carpets," I said, pointing at him as I went past with my drink. He looked hurt. "No, steel," he replied indignantly. I sat down. He explained. He had had warehouses in London and Liverpool from which he had exported steel to every part of the world. He knew the country's steelworks like the back of his hand. Other countries, he sighed, had, alas, taken over. It was all very interesting. We moved on to Africa to where he had also exported steel. His face became sad as he talked about corruption. "But Nyerere was all right," I interjected. His face froze. "His Ujamaa policy was interesting," I ventured nervously. "Bankrupted Tanzania!" he muttered. I tried to rescue the conversation: "But he did step down from being president in 1985. That's quite rare". "Harumph!" came the reply. The hole I was digging for myself was getting deeper. I decided to beat a retreat and return to my table. I can see now, in retrospect, that he had me down as a communist, which I am not. They say the same thing now in Argentina about my friend, the poet Juan Larrea, who was, in fact, the target of Marxists in the 1960s, some of them now very important, when he was living and lecturing in Córdoba. I remember conversations like that in 'The George' in my home town of Luton. With a certain type of right-winger you just can't examine more than one side of a question. There are lines that you cannot cross. Certain topics are taboo. The shutters come down. My sixty second friend now looks the other way when I walk into the pub. It's sad as I quite liked him. It wasn't like that in the City Bar in Kampala. I miss it.

Burn's Night

Amin was always proud of his Scottish connections. To celebrate, he decided to take over. The night before Burn's Night, Sunday, the twenty-fourth of January 1971, academics at Makerere were kept awake by the sound of gunfire and the crash of mortars. The coup had started. Radio Uganda was playing music. Only half the students turned up for lectures the following morning. Half-way through a lecture on rising public expenditure and the increase in spending on defence, guns and mortars could be heard again in the background. My friend decided that enough was enough and sent the students home for their safety. It was early afternoon when Wanume Kibedi announced on the radio that Idi Amin was now in charge. People at the university had been worried for four or five years about Obote's secret police, the General Service Unit. Lecturers had been called in for questioning. Staff were worried about being overheard in bars and misinterpreted. They were always looking over their shoulders. Tension had been rising. The coup broke the tension. It was as if a boil had been lanced. There was a feeling of relief but, as the normal afternoon storm broke over Kampala, muttering began in certain quarters. There was a feeling of apprehension amongst those who had an eye to the long-term future of Uganda.

The Saviour

It's strange how quickly things in life can change. Nearly all the Asians and the Europeans in East Africa thought that Idi Amin was the best thing since sliced bread when he deposed Obote. The Kenya-born English were 'over the moon'. Obote was getting too close to Russia, they said, and was best out of the way. Much of the press in England was effusive with its approving clichés. I am told that more than one ex-soldier came forward to claim he'd been Amin's commanding officer. He was a good chap, they said, played rugger, boxed for the regiment, one of us, 'as solid as a rock'. A rumour even started that he had been to Sandhurst. Well, the honeymoon was soon over. Soon everyone felt 'as sick as a parrot'.

The Bullet in the Neck

We were in the smallest pub in London. It felt like being in a confessional. I couldn't see my inquisitor. The light was too dim. I could see his shape but not his face. He asked me why I lost my faith, my faith in the UPC. I told him that I couldn't answer, that some of the protagonists of that time were still active in the party. He asked me what on earth did I mean by suggesting that they introduced a culture of violence? I told him the story of a young athlete I was training in Kampala. He was giant of a lad with a tremendous throw. He showed an interest in my favourite event. I knew he was capable of winning a medal. Little by little, further and further, he threw the javelin high into the sky above the football pitch at Kitante Hill School. I was beginning to think we would have to move to Kololo airstrip. One day there was a knock on the sports room door. It was Mukasa. He asked me if I had a spare plaster. He pointed to two holes in his neck. He had got them, he said, whilst walking to school. A lorry load of soldiers had passed by. A shot had rung out. The bullet had passed right through the muscle above his right shoulder.

"How did you feel after that," my friend asked.

"Beg your pardon?" I asked.

"What were your feelings?"

"Outrage, horror, disbelief, disgust, anger, helplessness and then a growing state of mindlessness morphing into anaesthetised mental catatonia."

He stared at me at me in disbelief.

Rule by Helicopter

I was always in two minds about golf courses in Uganda. There was one that I used each day on my way to work and back. It lay in a valley between two hills, Nakasero and Kitante. It was nearly always empty when I crossed it at midday. I had it to myself. Sometimes I found myself humming Noel Coward's "Mad Dogs and Englishmen go out in the midday sun," as I strolled from tree to tree. Some days I would get a sideways disapproving glance from a solitary player. Some clubs frowned upon being used as a short cut. To them it was an act of desecration to walk uninvited over their hallowed turf. No, I have never really taken to golf club life. They always seem a bit cliquey. Idi Amin saw them in a similar but slightly different way. To him they were symbols of colonialism. They say that is why he used them as part of his way of governing the country. He ruled by helicopter, landing on greens in Tororo or Masaka to the cheers of small but rapturous crowds that he had paid to be there to greet him. Momentous decisions would be announced on golf courses. Down he would come, out of the sky. Out he would get, onto a stage that had been specially erected a few hours beforehand. The cameras would roll. The country felt his presence. He seemed to be everywhere at once, like a medieval English king doing the annual tour of his kingdom. Things normally went well, except on one occasion, when he landed on a dry patch, one that hadn't been watered for over a month. The crowd was sent flying in every direction, stumbling into bunkers and tripping over in the rough, as they tried to escape a cloud of choking red dust.

A Perfect Storm

I can't remember who first said, "He may have been a son of a bitch but he was our son of bitch". It may have been Roosevelt talking about Somoza or Trujillo. It became a cliché of the twentieth century. I heard it said again about Saddam Hussein. I have also heard a theory that Idi Amin suited a particular country because of some problem it was having with Khartoum. I have heard a rumour that he appealed to another because they liked the idea of an amusing figure being in charge of an African country. I have heard it argued that he suited certain other powers in Africa because, they claimed, he wasn't a 'commie'. There is even a theory that he was supported by some countries because of his religion. Some people have thought that he was welcomed by a certain block because he was viewed as a destabilising factor within the status quo. Even Gadaffi from March 1972 is said to have sent soldiers to help him. He wasn't, it turns out, the only one. You could say, that all in all, it was all a perfect storm.

Guardian Angels

"Those who don't know history are destined to repeat it."

Edmund Burke (1729-1797)

Some stories are just too bad to be told. Some stories, perhaps, should just not be written. This may be one of them. But, then, there are worse, I suppose, that definitely can't be published. I have always believed that a text, once written, should leave the world a better place. How can this one do that, unless, in the telling, it cautions us never to hand too much power to any one person? On 12 April 1978, I have heard, soldiers loyal to Amin entered a church in Kampala and started firing above the congregation. Pentecostalism had been banned. There were six hundred people in there, men, women and children. The soldiers, they say, were 'wild-eyed'. I can believe it. I saw it one night, with my own eyes, in a club in Mengo twelve years earlier. The assistant pastor sank to his knees. Hundreds more did the same. The red-brick church echoed with the deafening roar of gunfire and prayers. A man in the orchestra raised his trumpet to his lips and blew it loudly. The soldiers panicked, thinking it was a Christian counterattack and fled the scene. Four hundred escaped at that moment but two hundred stayed. The soldiers returned and began to spray more bullets at the roof and the walls. They took Joseph Nyakaru's trumpet and threw it on the ground. They fired at it until it was just a piece of twisted metal. The congregation was taken to the State Research Bureau on Nakasero Hill, to Lugard's Fort, next to where I had once lived. General Mustafa Adrisi, Amin's second-in-command, signed an order that they were to be burned alive. They prayed hard. It seemed to work as Adrisi's car was involved in a crash. His legs were destroyed. He became wheel chair bound and turned on Amin. Many of the congregation were badly tortured in Nakasero but, somehow, they survived. It is said that George Santayana wrote: "Those who ignore history are doomed (or bound) to repeat it". He didn't say that. He said, it appears, 'Those who cannot remember the past are condemned to repeat it." He was echoing Burke's words. But whichever way you say it, it is true. That congregation must have had a guardian angel. Ours is History. The History Department of the university in my home town has just been closed down.

Amin's Eyes

Funny things could happen in Mbarara. One day, in a shop, in either 1972 or 1973, a teacher inadvertently handed over a twenty shilling note from which someone had removed Amin's eyes, leaving just holes. He was immediately expelled from the country, leaving his wife and children to get out as best they could. (LH, MC)

Light and Shade

> Our youth-time passes down a colonnade
> Shafted with alternating light and shade.
>
> *O Dreams, O Destinations*
> *A Sequence Of Nine Sonnets*
> Cecil Day-Lewis (1904-1972)

It's strange how I remember much of my childhood in Luton as a world filled with light even though the sky was no doubt grey for much of the time. And it's strange how my memories of Africa are often suffused with darkness even though the sun must have been blinding most of the time.

Newton's Cradle

I used to drive through Namanve Forest on my way each day from Namilyango to Kampala. Back and forth, back and forth, as regular as any other commuter. It felt safe then. I even slept there once, on my way back from the city but that's another story. Later it became one of Idi Amin's favourite killing grounds. Real or imagined opponents would be taken there in pairs and made to club each other with massive sledge hammers. The winner would be rewarded with a bullet in the back of the head. Unwilling participants would be shot in the stomach and left to die a slow death under the sun. I often think now of an executive game in which swinging ball bearings strike each other rhythmically, whenever I remember Namanve.

The Nightly Ritual

My room, on top of Nakasero Hill, far above the malarial area in the valley below, had a fine metal mesh covering the windows but still the mosquitoes came in. The trick was to fling a pillow as hard as you could at the space in front of the spot where the insect was perched. Each night I killed between six and ten, leaving blood stains on the walls. After a year the wall was turning red with my blood and with that of others whom I didn't know who lived down the hill.

The Diaspora

A friend in America sent me an e-mail today. In it he talked about a good friend of his from the past, Benedicto Kiwanuka. He said he always thinks of that 'trio' - the Kabaka, Amin and Obote - whenever he sees the New York Giants play football. The Kiwanuka in that team, Mathias, an American hero, is, he says, Benedicto Kiwanuka's grandson. He seemed angry when he said it. He appeared to be implying that the 'trio' ruined the Uganda of the sixties, a fate that Benedicto would have avoided.

Obote and Nyerere

> Life's but a walking shadow, a poor player
> That struts and frets his hour upon the stage
> And then is heard no more. It is a tale
> Told by an idiot, full of sound and fury
> Signifying nothing.
>
> — *Macbeth* (Act 5, Scene 5, lines 17-28)

It's strange. Writing this book feels like constructing a puppet play of the sort that delighted Federico García Lorca when he was a child. The characters come and go, strutting and fretting, 'seeking the bubble reputation'. Some characters are just left in the box. Obote and Nyerere are always out. Both very different, they both loved Shakespeare. Nyerere translated *Julius Caesar* and *The Merchant of Venice* into KiSwahili: *Julius Kaisari* and *Mabepari wa Venisi*. Obote was even fond, they say, of quoting Shakespeare in Cabinet. I was told that he acted Julius Caesar at Makerere and that he was a good actor who, on the stage of Mwiri College, could reduce his audience to tears of laughter without saying a word. He, too, was a cultured man. Some say he initiated a culture of violence when he sent in Amin to attack the Lubiri and dethrone the Kabaka. As Mark Anthony says: 'The evil that men do lives after them. The good is oft interred with their bones'. (BVA)

Respect

I didn't really know what to make of the Kabaka back in the sixties. I mean, in my group, back then in the sixties, monarchism was not very fashionable. I don't think I ever knowingly saw him but I have a friend who did. He did not personally shake his hand, but occasionally, such as on his birthday, the King would be slowly driven through the school grounds in one of his five Rolls Royces. The staff and pupils of Lubiri School, which was inside the palace grounds, were notified in advance of these events. My friend saw him up close and felt he was expected to genuflect in his presence. The first time it was new to him, of course. Someone noticed his hesitation and immediately pushed him down, politely, from behind. He didn't know the Kabaka personally but he knew one of his cousins, from their Makerere days. (CG)

The Other

We knew it was there, beyond the balcony wall of the City Bar in Kampala. It's just that many of us didn't want to know it. We knew we were surrounded by unknown knowns as well as known unknowns. We didn't want to know, for example, about the talking cockerel of Misindye village. We didn't really want to hear it say, in Luganda, that anyone who killed it and ate its flesh would surely die. We didn't want to know about animals possessed by evil spirits. "Not today, tomorrow perhaps," we would say. We preferred to allow a sepia screen, like a comforting veil of bark cloth, descend around us. Inside our cell we knew what we knew, which wasn't much at all.

La Révolution

"What was it like in Bujumbura?" I was asked by my friend from Soroti in 'The Marlborough Arms' in Torrington Place, in London. He said he had always wanted to visit the capital of Burundi.

"I can't tell you what it was like," I confessed. "It was dark when I was there."

"But what do you remember?" he insisted. "You must remember something."

"That's it, the darkness, the emptiness, streets without lights, without people: a deserted city."

"That's all?" he gasped.

"Oh, I remember asking the manager of La Liberté hotel what on earth was happening, 'Que se passe-t-il?' 'C'est la révolution,' he replied. It was the quietest revolution you could imagine. Hardly anything moved, apart from the bedbugs. We did see a brightly-lit bar on the other side of the road. Absolutely exhausted, we staggered across. They were serving gorgeous French food. I ordered *escargots*, my friend *boeuf bourguignonne*. We both had *tarte tatin*. Sitting there in the light, we seemed to draw people out. We seemed to give them confidence. They started walking up and down outside, looking in at us. My friend smiled and relaxed.

'Do you hear that?' he said, stretching his legs. 'They are saying we are 'missionaires'.'

Sipping my wine slowly, I nonchalantly replied, 'No, no. They are not saying, "Ce sont des *missionaires*". They are saying, "Ce sont des *mercenaires*". They think we're mercenaries.' He went pale, choked on his beef and nearly fell off his seat. We went back out into the pitch black night, crossed the road to our sleazy hotel and spent the rest of the night feeding the local insects. Our bodies in the morning were covered in bites."

"Is that all you remember about Bujumbura?" my friend asked, looking disappointed.

"Just about," I replied.

Frogs in Bujumbura

We were in an exquisite French bar-restaurant in the centre of Bujumbura. I ordered the snails. My friend was still hesitating. I could see him eyeing the *cuisses de grenouilles*, the frogs' legs on a nearby table. They looked strangely erotic. While he was deciding, I felt an urge to discuss frogs.

"I am blissfully unaware," I began, "of any frogs here in East Africa. I feel bad about this because I know there must be some out there. Tree frogs, for example. Have you come across any?" He was still engrossed in deciphering the menu.

"I mean," I went on, "are they out there but hidden? Tree frogs must be difficult to see." He didn't look up.

"Are they more predated in Africa than in England?" His eyes were moving around the restaurant from plate to plate.

"Are the swamps full of frogs?" I continued, trying to catch his attention.

"Umm." He wasn't rising to the bait.

"Did we drain the swamps in Kampala depriving them of their habitat?" I insisted. He looked up.

"Is there a frog chorus at night in Buganda?" I asked.

I felt he was beginning to formulate an answer.

"Does it fall silent when the moon comes out and owls can see them?" I threw in, alluding to a poem by Lorca that I knew he hadn't read.

"Sorry," I said, "Lorca's Andalusian poetry has filled me with many strange questions." Without looking up from the list of French dishes, he suddenly burst into life.

"Tree frogs are very vocal but may not be easy to see. Swamps are full of frogs. Lots of predation, but lots of frogs. Frogs do chorus at night, but I can't remember if they go quiet at full moon. Lots of swamps were drained as an anti-malarial precaution and for development, but plenty remained. *Boeuf bourguignonne* and *tarte tatin*," he said to the waiter who had been waiting patiently for his order. (CM)

The Fuse

You could buy anything in Kampala market. The fillet steak was just as good as anything in the supermarket and one tenth of the price. If you needed false teeth, there was a stall for that. If you needed new glasses, there was one for that too. You just had to disentangle them from an intertwined heap and try them on until you found a pair that worked. A chap I know, who was teaching at Makerere in 1993, needed something for his portable computer. A fuse had blown. Computer accessory shops were opening up in Kampala but none of them had one. He and an assistant set off for the local market. They arrived in front of a shop festooned with brightly coloured material for ladies' dresses. At the back of the shop there was a large case filled with every fuse you could imagine, including the one that was needed. They bought three. Back at Makerere Guest House the computer was running again, before you could say Heath Robinson.

The Sea Venom Pilot

(In memory of Group Captain Robert Olding, DSC, 1932-2012)

I didn't know Robert Olding. I didn't know that he went to Colchester Royal Grammar School. I didn't know that he had flown Sea Venoms from an aircraft carrier called *HMS Eagle*. I didn't know that he had led a formation on 1 November 1956 to destroy aircraft on the ground at Bilbeis airfield in Egypt. I didn't know that on the following day he had gone on to attack with cannons and rockets Egyptian Air Force aircraft on the tarmac at Almaza. I didn't know that the anti-aircraft fire was accurate and heavy and that his cockpit floor was holed and that his legs were filled with shrapnel. I didn't know that he landed his jet on the ship without flaps and with his undercarriage up. I didn't know that they had to amputate his leg in Cyprus but that later he went on to fly Javelins. I still don't know if my brother John, a Vampire pilot, was asked to get ready during the Suez Crisis. What I do know is that I suddenly became more than just politically aware on that first day in November when I heard on the six o'clock news "Today British bombers bombed airfields near Cairo," while learning to drive the Bentley that I cleaned for ten shillings for a wealthy Luton hatter. I also know that that is one reason why I was spat at in the street in Port Said on my way to East Africa in 1964.

The Car-Wrestling Snake

I was driving east from Kampala towards the Kenya border when I saw, ahead of me, a gigantic snake lying across the road, as long as the road was wide, longer, in fact. It wasn't clear if it was dead or alive. It looked like a fireman's hose. I was going fast. A split second decision had to be made, whether to slam on the brakes and risk a dangerous skid or whether to press on and run it over. You don't have much time for ethical considerations when you are doing ninety. The car went over the snake. In my rear view mirror I saw it lying there, motionless. It must have been dead already when I hit it. Had it been alive, an expert on snakes has told me, it would have writhed and thrown itself around in the road. Down in Wales, where we used to spend our summer holidays, I found myself in the evenings telling African stories to a crowd of small boys and girls. They hung on my every word. I tried to stay truthful but on occasions the raconteur in me would take over. I embroidered things a bit. In the case of the big snake I decided to add some drama. I told them that the snake wrapped itself around the car with which it was locked in mortal battle. I told them that the python tried to crush the metal as well as me, the driver, inside, as the car hurtled along lurching from side to side. The children sat wide-eyed. This mighty tussle, I said, went on for quite a while, until the snake gave up and fell back, exhausted, onto the road. I realised I had gone too far with the story but, I don't know, it made the evening seem, somehow, more interesting and the children, I felt, were egging me on. I was sure that they must have taken the story with a large pinch of salt. Even a Rock Python, which this probably was, couldn't wrestle a Ford Zephyr 4 going flat out. "Tell us more, tell us more," Bunty would cry.

It was twenty years later when the father of the six girls said to me one night, very seriously, "Bunty has something to say to you".

Bunty stepped forward. She seemed slightly embarrassed. She said that she had been on a safari holiday in Kenya. She then fell silent and looked down at the ground.

"She wants to tell you that she doesn't believe your stories, especially the one about the snake," her father blurted out.

It was like a smack in the face. I was literally gob-smacked. I thought of all of those long evenings telling stories, keeping the children entertained, wasted, down the drain! What a reward, after all that effort expended keeping his kids and mine happy summer after summer with my post-colonial tales! There must be a moral to this story. No, it's not what you think it is. If it hadn't been for (eventually doubting) Bunty and the rest of the gang, this book may never have happened.

The Scramble for Africa

It's a long story. I was writing a book about Africa: this book, the one you are reading, in fact. I was trying to imagine what it must have felt like to have been colonized by a people from a distant culture. A friend of mine, with whom I have lost touch and who edits a poetry magazine in Wales, compared the loss of his language to losing one's house to a stranger. I imagined being thrown out onto the street and looking sadly at the family house now occupied by someone with a different language. In fact it had had happened to me. My Welsh friend's theory seemed not to apply to Uganda where languages remained generally healthy and intact. My head was spinning with the problem. How could I possibly write this? How could I include that? Would this be seen as 'racist'? Would that be seen as bawdy, 'superior', condemnatory, condescending, patronising? How I could achieve an acceptable balance, one that would appeal to all possible readers? I was finding it impossible to make decisions about what to include and what to leave out, about what was politically correct and what was not. What was it like to have been taken over by the English? Some Ugandans told me it was all right, that it could have been worse. My 'house boy', Jean, told me sorrowfully in French: (it was against his self-interest to say so): "Go home, monsieur. They don't want you here." He was from near Goma. We were in Buganda. Then, later, back in England, a Ugandan student of mine at Trent Park, in the north of London, told me off, quite severely, saying that we had just walked away and left them holding the baby. He said it had not been right. He was from Toro. I suspect he was from a royal family. Did it depend on where one was or to whom one was talking? Did the Baganda feel we had already let them down by supporting Obote and therefore should go? Hadn't Obote won the election? I had heard that the imperial authorities had begun to get a little nervous before Ugandan Independence about the gathering chaos in Rwanda and the Congo and had concluded it wasn't worth the candle to try to hang on.

My mobile rings. My daughter-in-law is learning to fly. North London Flying Club at Panshanger Aerodrome, near Welwyn Garden City, is phoning her up at the last minute to say that the conditions are right. My son cannot look after their baby, Alban, as he booked golf at Luton Hoo with his younger brother a couple of weeks ago. I am left literally holding the baby. It is cold outside so we sit in the club house. It is full of children. It keeps Alban amused. Little girls come up to him and pull faces. He smiles back. A large fish tank with tropical fish and the model of a wrecked plane on the bottom holds his attention.

I feel very comfortable inside Panshangar clubhouse. The truth is I have always wanted to be a pilot. As a child I cycled to Panshanger regularly from my home in Luton just to peek inside the hangars. Even the name was charged with magic. Everything about the present-day décor of Panshangar reflects the flying theme. There is a giant chromium-plated propeller standing in the corner, propping up the bar. A video is playing of an aircraft doing the loop the loop. There are photographs on the walls of autogiros and old biplanes. Even the menu uses aeronautical terms: Duxford Pie, Gatwick Gammon, Stansted Steak and Heathrow Hamburgers. I feel very much at home.

I couldn't have been happier if I had constructed the place myself. Inside the menu it tells the tale of this unique airfield. It had been built as a decoy aerodrome during Word War II to divert enemy bombers away from Hatfield where Mosquitoes were being built. It had dummy aircraft, smoking chimneys, cars and "black-out leaks" which were controlled by an automatic time switch varying the chinks of light offered up to prowling German aircraft. The whole thing was a trick to deceive the Nazis and had been put together by the best brains of the British film industry. It could have been compared with the line of cardboard tanks a friend of mine, a top Kampala silk, had strung out across the horizon which sent the Italian army fleeing back into Abyssinia during the very same war. It was perfect. Alban was asleep. Alison was over Letchworth. I could sit and gaze fondly through the window at the light aircraft coming in, touching down and going up again like House Martins gathering mud for their nests from puddles on the sea front in Port Eynon in Wales. I was in my element. I was completely *en casa, chez moi.*

It was then that it happened. The door flew open and there they stood like a small army of aliens. They had large, strange-shaped heads, like Dan Dare Mekons, except that their skulls were more like rugby balls about to be kicked for conversion. They wore glowing yellow tops, like the fluorescent jackets that the police wear at motorway accidents. But it was their lower halves that were the most peculiar. They were wearing black tights. Inside these very tight tights they seemed to be sporting Shakespearian codpieces but it wasn't that that drew the bar's attention. They all had very knobbly knees. They came in and sat down, colonising, without a thought, the best parts of the club house. The whole atmosphere changed,

Suddenly it dawned on me how the people of Uganda must have felt when English Victorians, pith helmeted, descended on them from up the Nile and from the Swahili coast. It couldn't have felt very comfortable. My grandson woke up with all the commotion. His face was a picture. His mouth was wide open. That's not the worst of it. They began to peel off their day-glo tops to reveal chest-hugging tee-shirts sporting a message. I couldn't believe my eyes, it said "Luton Cycling Club". These invading 'aliens' were from my home town! One couple was using French. I had a feeling they were from Rwanda. My mental comparison of the Panshanger club house invasion with the Scramble for Africa was, I realised, already beginning to break down.

The Philosophers

We had come together in The Museum Tavern in London, after many years of not having seen each other. It was Brian who began the conversation.

"One reflection on all this is why are we all evidently so into Uganda reminiscences? Was it something about Uganda before the Fall (i.e. before Amin) which was particularly magical? Or is it just that we are responding to memories of a particular time of our lives? Personally, there are other periods of my life which speak to me in memory with an equal intensity. Certainly Berkeley at the beginning of the 1960s (hence my frequent return). Tanzania after the Arusha Declaration drew a lot of interesting people to Dar but the 'building the revolution' atmosphere made it a bit too heavy and, in the outcome, it was a bit naïve - and not in the fun way we were naïve in Kampala. For me, another period of exciting memories is Hanoi, where I went in early 1989 and have returned to ever since."

Clive went for a tray of drinks. He came back.

"Kampala," I responded, "was very colour-blind in many ways. It had not been a colony. The protectorate atmosphere was qualitatively different from that of Kenya. I could feel the difference as soon as I went through the border on my way to Eldoret and Kisumu. There may have been a weakness in the structures in Uganda which made life feel freer, less controlled, less socially conservative. Those institutional weaknesses, if they can be called that, led to its downfall, perhaps. Having been less 'colonised', mentally, in spite of everything M7 [Museveni] says about the terrible burden of colonialism that Uganda must shake off, it was less 'Victorianised', perhaps. Hedonism was not *verboten*. Everyone was very relaxed, then, about their sexuality. It was, of course, a land of milk and honey, at least in Kampala, with the rich surrounding agricultural infrastructure of Buganda. The British were very keen to take visiting parties of Russians around a show-piece protectorate. "Look, we are not so bad," they would say to both the Russians and the Americans who were breathing down our necks. Mulago was the best hospital between Cairo and Johannesburg. You could drink the water from the tap (thanks to Harry Harbottle). Wages were high because of the country's favoured status. Quality of life was high."

It was my call for a round.

"I felt more relaxed," Clive interjected, and more at home there than I had ever done in the UK but then I was young! I was never as happy in Kenya (1969-76), and certainly less so in Brunei, (1981-1991), although the latter gave me huge opportunities for travel around Asia and Australia, all paid for by the Sultan. I constantly think of Uganda now that I live in London, which I've never grown into."

Brian went for the next round.

The other Clive, 'Japan Clive', chipped in: "Referring back to Brian's question, I think it WAS "particularly magical, partly simply because we were young, privileged and open to the stimulation of encountering a totally different society to the European one. The magic also sprang partly from the timing, as you suggest. We were lucky enough to see a very interesting and beautiful part of Africa on the cusp of enormous change. I'm not sure when you first arrived there, Brian, but I get the impression it was before most of us did. We were the 1964 wave. If so, you might have seen more of the colonial Africa. But it hadn't disappeared, even in the mid-sixties. In Uganda, you also witnessed some of the worst excesses of Africa turning its back on democracy. For those who survived it, a very rich source of adventure stories! In Tanzania, we were spared the excesses of dictatorship, but were able to witness the interesting idealistic efforts of Julius Nyerere's African Socialism. That, too, ended in failure, but as far as I know, didn't result in lawless chaos."

"Same again?" I asked. (BVA, CM, CL)

The English Pope

We had been trying to get together for over a month but the snow kept coming down, stopping our meeting. He had just got back from five years of lecturing in a Catholic College in Jinja, near Kampala. He had students from all over, from East and Central Africa: from the Congo, Burundi, Rwanda and Kenya. Some were even from the UK. It didn't start too well. First, he confessed that he had not voted for me in the election for Dean at the university at which we had worked together in London.

"Fair enough," I replied. Men had probably died at Makerere, in the Amin years, I thought, over such a remark but I was not bothered. I hadn't really wanted the post. The EFL group, with hardly any serious academic qualifications, other than their knowledge of their own language, had wielded enormous power in elections.

He told me that he had worked for fifteen years in Africa: in the Sudan, Malawi, Uganda. He corrected my aspirated h in Mehta and told me it must have been the Madhvanis, not the Mehtas, who were involved in the recent anti-Asian riots in Uganda over the felling of trees in Mabira Forest, to make way for sugar cane. I kept saying, no, it was the Mehtas. No, he would reply, it was the Madhvanis.

I kept saying "MeHta". He kept saying, "No, Meta".

"Mekta" - "Meta," "Mechta" - "Mater": we were pushing each other to extremes. People were looking.

In the end I gave up and, for the sake of peace but not believing it, said, "You are probably right". I am sure you have met people like that. They just won't give up. Life, for them, is one long game of one-upmanship. I checked later. He was wrong on both counts.

No, it didn't go too well. I had decided to take him to a very special place, past which the only English Pope, Pope Adrian IV (Nicholas Breakspear) used to walk on his way to school in St Albans at the beginning of the twelfth century. That's how we found ourselves in 'The Hollybush' in Potters Crouch. It has been my 'local', on and off, man and boy, for fifty-eight years. He told me he had seen the plaque on the side of the road in Bedmond marking the place near where Pope Adrian was born. I asked him to imagine the future Pope walking down Bedmond Lane from Breakspear Farm near Abbot's Langley, across Roman Verulamium, crossing himself, as he passed the ruins, to ward off evil spirits, and going across the Causeway that crossed the swamp and up the path that is now Abbey Mill Lane which was then inside the monastery. He did and I could see that he was enjoying a mystical experience.

I then dropped the bombshell. I told him that Nicholas Breakspear had been rejected by the Benedictine Monastery of St Albans and had been told to come back later when he was more 'prepared'. I added that people were a bit rough in Bedmond in those days. To my shame, I found myself saying that Adrian was not the sharpest chisel in the bag.

"Probably in a fit of pique," I added, "Nicholas went off to the continent and eventually became Pope Adrian IV."

My friend did not like this story at all. Neither did he like my further remark that Pope Adrian IV essentially agreed to Ireland being given to England. (He has Irish connections.) Adding insult to injury, I added that they never asked an Englishman to be Pope again after that. I didn't tell him that to make things worse, Nicholas's father's application to become a monk in St Albans had been successful. That would have been rubbing salt into the wound. No, it didn't go well, that reunion. Some reunions are like that.

Reality and Desire

We hadn't met for over a decade. He used to repeat the story about how he had sat at Fidel Castro's feet listening to his long speeches. He asked me how, in retrospect, I viewed our experience at the Poly.

"Last night I had a dream," I said. "It was very vivid. There was a python under the fridge. I had to get it out. I managed to get hold of it but it fought back. Holding it by its neck only encouraged it to spit out its bacteria-filled saliva. Two of the issues of the twentieth century with which some us wrestled remain unresolved and will, perhaps, always stay so. They are reality versus desire and egalitarianism versus elitism. My hopes for Africa in the nineteen-sixties were quixotic. Back home, open access to all in higher education was like the cow that was swallowed by the python. The snake took on the form of the cow before returning to its normal shape. I always found it astonishing how even the loudest egalitarians struggled to scramble aboard the elitist gravy train." He looked embarrassed and shifted on his chair.

"No politics in the mess!" he replied with an awkward laugh.

The Explosion

Seeing the meteor that crashed with a huge flash and a bang in Russia yesterday made me go back to an explosion that took place in London years ago. Let me explain. I had a terrible row with a friend from Uganda in about 1970. I was working at a Polytechnic. Starting in the sixties, the Polytechnics were a new idea in Higher Education. They seemed like a possible way of breaking the grip of the Establishment on society and opening up education to all. Some of us went even further and set up open and free universities in London, Paris and America. The explosion took place two years after 'the events' of 1968. I began to notice that the traditional universities were looking at us askance, as if they viewed us as something the cat had brought in. We were not made welcome at their conferences. One response was to set up rivals. One of our tenets was parity of esteem between utilitarian and non-utilitarian subjects. No subject was, thenceforth, to be considered superior to another. It was very democratic. Single subject departments were to be dismantled. Disciplines had to reach out to each other. Interdisciplinarity was the key note. The list of new demands was long. I launched The Conference of Hispanists in Polytechnics and Other Colleges. It went well to start with but then some of the 'politicos' I had allowed on to the steering committee began to flirt with emissaries of the old universities with a view to mergers. "Sleeping with the enemy" you could call it. At that point there were four Hispanists' conferences. A partial merger of two was made, in secret, by two of the characters on the committee. At that point I withdrew from the conference I had created and refused to have anything further to do with it. That's part of the background. I then did the unforgivable, something I totally disagreed with. I pulled some strings to get a job in Environmental Science for a friend from Uganda at Middlesex. To my astonishment he suddenly turned round and said he didn't want it. He turned his nose up at the offer! Later I learned that he had gone to Durham. This sparked a furious response from me in a pub called 'The Greyhound'.

"I thank God I work in a REAL university," I shouted and stormed out.

Since then we haven't spoken. Like all things in life, it was more complicated than that. We had lived in each others' pockets in Africa. I needed to go my own way. Nuptials were in the air, as happens. His girlfriend, a Muganda, had taken to stubbing her cigarettes out on the back of my hand in a pub down West End Lane. Different futures were taking shape on the horizon. A friend told me the other day that that friend had always been considered right of centre. I had always felt that he was the epitome of radical chic. Things are not always, it seems, what they seem to be.

Heat 2

We met again in the Museum Tavern just opposite the entrance to the British Museum. We had all ordered fish and chips and a pint of bitter. It was all a bit cramped but it didn't seem to matter. We had just finished eating. Somehow we got on to heat and the hottest places we had ever experienced. I had just told the group that the night before I had woken up, because of the cold. Brian was there from Cambridge. He'd been in Dar the day before. He began by saying that recent weeks in Dar-es-Salaam had been the worst combination of heat and humidity he had ever known in Africa.

'Climate change,' I said. I told him that I remembered the rain that fell like fat drops of sweat on a tin roof in Moshi. I mentioned a heat like that which greets you when you open an oven door, whenever I stepped out into the valley that lay between my flat and the school at which I worked in Kampala. T.E. Lawrence's phrase 'The Devil's Anvil' would often cross my mind during those walks. I added that I remembered gulping down salt tablets in the shade of the life boat on the Rhodesia Castle as we sailed down the Red Sea.

Clive intervened. "The hottest places for me," he said. "were on the Red Sea coast of Sudan and Ethiopia (now Eritrea). In East Africa it was Dar-es-Salaam. The eastern side of Lake Rudolf was potentially very hot, but there was always a fierce wind. Out of Africa, lowland Brunei was the most uncomfortable climate I have ever been in. Although the temperature rarely got above 35C, it was 80-100+ % humid for much of the time. Three showers a day were the norm. Trying to sleep," he added, after a long sip of his beer, "in an Arab house in the centre of Lamu was an enormous challenge."

Lilian joined in. "The Lamu guest house," she explained, "Mahrus Hotel, small, square, humid rooms with tiny windows. It had a flat roof where you could lay out your mattress and have a sleep. The rooms below were very hot and stuffy. We ate goat curry on the roof," she said, getting carried away. "Quite delicious and curries were always somehow cooling. They were even better when a stiff breeze was blowing in off the water. I remember," she continued, "sliding in my own sweat drops at the Makerere Squash Court." The group fell silent allowing her, politely, to stay for a moment in the limelight. "Seeing and hearing heavy tropical rain on hot tin roofs, a curtain of water cascading from the roof corrugations past the window. You could trace a row of perfectly circular depressions in the ground from the fall of heavy raindrops from the roof edges."

Dave went for some more beers. There was a pause. He came back.

"I remember keeping cool," he said, "by lying in the pool, at night, on the Rhodesia Castle in The Red Sea. They kept changing the sea-water to keep it fresh."

No-one responded. Their eyes were on Lilian. "I remember my eyes," she went on, "irritated by melting sun block, sweat–blinded, in fact. I discovered that solid zinc oxide cream didn't melt so fast, but left you looking as if you were using Ambi-Extra, the whitening cream that Ugandan women used to use a lot and still do, by all accounts." The group was now fascinated by these glimpses of a woman's world in Africa. We all nodded, willing her to go on.

"Pictures of tall, full length wooden louvre doors and windows, plus those fabulous Raffles ceiling fans conjure up tropical heat for me. The cicada insect scream, joined by more and more as the heat increased until it became a deafening noise in the bush. Then it would stop as abruptly as it had begun. Hotpants and miniskirts in the nineteen seventies worn by expat women watching rugby at the Kampala Club. Flip flops to keep our feet cool, closed in shoes being impossibly hot and sweaty. The trouble was your feet would expand with the freedom, so the next time you had leave and a ticket to travel back to Blighty, your feet wouldn't fit your closed-in shoes with any comfort. All right when you were in a cooler climate, because your feet shrink."

We were now mesmerised by this female vision of the experience of heat in a faraway land.

"Of course," she went, "alcohol and coffee dehydrate and are a hopeless but constantly sought-after panacea for the heat."

"Eating salt tablets when doing rugby training, no matter how hot it was," her husband Mike interjected.

"Being invited to beat the heat," she chimed in, "by sailing on Lake Vic, but declining because of the freshwater Bilharzia parasite – the only cure being injections of heavy metals like mercury and lead into the abdomen – a killer if there ever was one – a horrible treatment."

We sat there, dumbfounded, but she went on in full spate: "The hottest day I have ever experienced was on Durban beach in December 1968. My bare feet cooked! I ran for shade!"

I looked round and saw that some of the group were misty eyed, lost in their imaginations. Her husband sat there, smiling, in admiration.

"Last orders, please!" a voice boomed out. The spell was broken. We got up to leave, putting on our thick coats, each making a point of air-kissing Lilian goodbye, before we made our separate ways home through the falling snow. (LH, MC, BVA, CM, DS)

The Marabou

We had arranged to meet once more in the Museum Tavern.

"Marx must have drunk here," I suggested. I wasn't so sure. Brian looked around at the décor. He wasn't sure either. It was a great reunion. There were biologists and economists and a Hispanist, me. I have always relished their company, even though, at times, I have to concentrate hard, especially when it's economics. Sometimes I don't bother and drift off into a dream. That's how it was half a century ago in the City Bar in Kampala. You could opt in and out. Nobody cared that much. It didn't matter. My attention was pulled this way and that, by the names of famous economists I had never heard of before, as well as to experiments conducted on the biology lab floor. I was torn between one David Ricardo, at one end of the table, who had opted out and lived in a cabin on the beach in Tanzania to talk, at the other end, of wrestling a Marabou with a fifteen foot wingspan.

"Fifteen? Do you mean ten?" I asked, trying to join in but wishing I hadn't.

"One was brought in, with a damaged wing. Nothing could be done so we dispatched it with chloroform," said Trev. It fought like hell, pecking and flapping. Its powerful wings stretched from one wall to another. It had to be strangled. We put the body on a termite hill to collect the bones. We didn't have a perfect skeleton, you see, to show the pupils. It didn't work. Termites pulled its legs down into the hole. They just disappeared."

"Are you sure it wasn't a stray dog?" I asked.

"No, no," Trev said. The same thing happened to our dead monkey. We lost the legs. Well, yes, it may have been the local leopard, not the termites."

"The most maribous I ever saw," said David, who had just come in, "were on the shores of Nakuru, when Charlie, I and some others, walked round the lake. Their genus name *Leptoptilos* comes from the Greek and means 'thin wing'. Their species name *crumeniferus* means 'carrying a bag', the long sack between beak and thorax, used in display and to enhance what little sound they make. The bag hangs down like a long pink sausage and adds to their grotesqueness. Derek Pomeroy came in.

"I can't remember," I said to him, "many or any Marabou Storks in Kampala when we were there in the sixties. Now they seem to be everywhere in the city. Am I right or is it just my bad memory? Are they attracted, I wonder, by road kill or plastic rubbish bags?"

"They call them the "Undertaker Birds," Derek replied, "because they look like an undertaker from behind and when scavenging carcasses. Some say in Uganda that their number increased under Idi Amin when they fed on the bodies of those he had killed. They have had a press."

"Marabout. C'est un mot arabe, qui signifie un Religieux; qui a été formé du verbe rabar, qui signifie mener una vie retirée," a French tourist said from a neighbouring table.

"Like a hermit, because they are not very vocal?" asked Clive.

"Précisément," the Frenchman replied with a smile.

"Their numbers have increased from the late 1960s," said Derek, "when they first nested in Kampala, to the mid 2010s, when there were more than a thousand nests, mostly on the Makerere campus. Since then there has been a slight decline. Hooded Vulture numbers have also gone down, as they have all over Africa, due, in all probability, to better methods at abattoirs and better rubbish collection. Absolutely nothing to do with Idi Amin!"

Mike had just walked in. "The steady increase," he added "in the number of Marabou in Kampala was related to the complete collapse of the refuse collection system. When I was there during the 1990s - my most recent visit was in 2000 - Marabou were everywhere. Sitting in an office in the Ministry of Finance, I could always see them out there perched on the street lights. They were all over the roof of the Sheraton (Apolo) Hotel ballroom. Absolutely everywhere. From a distance the Marabou and vultures, I suppose, as well, wheeling over the abattoir in the industrial area looked like a swarm of flies."

I shuddered, hoping that my friends hadn't noticed.

Dave Smith came back with a tray of London Pride: "There were masses of them on the rubbish dump opposite Kololo School," he said. It was time to change the subject. (BVA, CM, TM, JW, MT, DP, DM, DS)

Magpies and Marabous

> My father named me Autolycus; who being, as I am, litter'd under Mercury, was likewise a snapper up of unconsider'd trifles.
> *The Winters Tale*, IV, ii.

In Gower they call magpies 'chatterpies'. Not far from Port Eynon there's an isolated house called 'Chatterpie's Nest'. I used to see myself as a magpie fluttering down, snapping up anything that shines, rings and things through open windows. Then I heard that shepherds were shooting magpies for gouging out the eyes of their new-born lambs and stealing eggs from the nests of blackbirds and blue tits. Writing this book on Africa, I sometimes feel more like the Marabou that feeds off carrion at the abattoirs and dumps in Kampala.

Dying Vultures

Having bewailed the fate of vultures in Europe, my friend fell silent. He stared into his cup. He seemed to be trying to read the tea leaves. I didn't know what to say. He was clearly upset but I was finding it hard to empathise. I have never really liked vultures, if truth be told. They give me the creeps. I find them revolting, although I would never admit it to my friend. In the cowboy films I watched as a child, their circling overhead meant someone was dying. But my friend was upset. All I could do was listen, without making any comment.

"Vultures are disappearing all over Africa," he went on. "It's not as bad as in the Indian Sub-continent, where, over the last decade or so, ninety-nine per cent of three species of vulture have disappeared, their place in the food chain being taken by dogs. Hence rabies is much more widespread. Dead cattle are not eaten in India, because they are holy and vultures got rid of the carcasses taken to huge dumps. Parsees in India now have to bury their dead in concrete tubes because there aren't any vultures to service the towers of silence. The killer is diclofenac, an anti-inflamatory, administered to cattle which destroys the vultures' kidneys. Diclofenac is beginning to be a problem in Africa but not on the scale (yet) of India. Another problem that vultures face in Africa is deliberate poisoning and trapping for body parts for muti/'medicine'/juju and so that they do not give away the position of poachers. Poisoning of birds in general is occurring in various parts of Africa, including at some rice schemes such as Ahero in Kenya, not because the birds are a pest, most are very useful, but to EAT! This is documented on film. I wonder how many people have been killed, or at least become ill, from eating such birds."

"Let's go, Clive, they are closing," I whispered. "We can't solve all the world's problems." (CM)

The Post-Mortem

We were the last ones left, in the Museum Tavern. I suppose we had stayed behind to have a post-mortem on the reunion.

"Successful?" I asked.

"Successful," he replied.

There was something else, though, that was preoccupying him. The talk of Marabou Storks seemed to have unsettled him. Brian had asked if vultures had once lived in the north of Europe. I had quoted Chaucer, Shakespeare and Ovid. It hadn't gone down well. It was then that he began. I couldn't believe that he still had the energy.

"Vultures," he said, "were once widespread in Europe, but perhaps not further north than Denmark. Even today, the odd few turn up in Holland, Germany and Denmark, probably because food is difficult to find in Spain. As Europe became more 'hygienic' and carcasses were no longer left around, the vultures disappeared. Spain still has a goodly number, but they have disappeared in some parts."

He took a sip of his London Pride.

"In 1961," he continued, "I remember a big roost in Arcos in Andalusia, but there are few now left in the south of Spain. Perhaps they linger on in Ronda. In the Pyrenees and south, in Extremadura, you can see a number still."

"I remember the storks in Cáceres," I said, trying to join in. I much prefer storks but he wasn't having it.

"Now carcasses are put out in places called 'vulture restaurants'," he went on, "to halt the decline before it's too late. Because they breed very slowly 'captive breeding' is now carried out in Nepal and India. It's of limited value, but better than nothing." We both fell silent and stared into our beers, each for a different reason. (CM)

The Secretary Bird

I have always wanted to write something about the Secretary Bird. There was something pompous about the way it walked, as if it owned the place. We all know people like that. They say that its feathers were once used as quills by secretaries. It has head feathers sticking out that look like old-fashioned quills. The ones I saw in Kenya were almost four feet tall and looked like a cross between cranes and eagles. I have been told they walk for miles, self-importantly, on their lanky legs, as they search for their prey. I suppose the way they walk is to avoid sudden movements. Their favourite dish is snakes, although I have heard they can take trout. I have often wondered why I have wanted to write about them. Do I identify with them in some way? Is that why I haven't been able to put pen to paper? Do I come across as pompous? I had been explaining all this to my friend from West London, about my fascination and my writer's block. His reply gave me a shock. He told me that he had found a freshly dead Secretary Bird in good condition near Eldoret. He had taken it home to Kabarnet, wrapped it tightly in chicken wire and buried it in the back garden. He knew, he said, that the Natural History Museum in London didn't have a skeleton. After a few months, at Christmas, he went off on holiday. His gardener decided to do some gardening. He dug it up and because it smelled, threw it onto a bonfire. The remains were broken up and dug into the ground. It's strange, I no longer feel a need to write about the Secretary Bird. I don't know why. Picasso loved to observe the elegant *midinettes* in Paris, the secretaries who emerged from their offices at midday. Perhaps I did too. (CM)

Secretary Birds

I suppose secretaries can change from century to century. Now, with the arrival of computers, they are a dying breed. When I first started work in London, at the end of the Age of Deference, they were still there to be respected, in some cases, to be feared. If you crossed the college secretary, your days could be numbered. When I first saw Secretary Birds in Africa, I was amazed. "I'm the King of the Castle and you're the dirty rascal" was the message they seemed to be emitting. You could feel the link with the ones back in London. But there was something wrong. They didn't actually look like secretaries. There was nothing shapely about them like the one all the boys fell in love with at school. They seemed gawky. "It's the feathers behind the ears," I was told. "They look like quill pens." I wasn't convinced, until, one day, I saw a picture of an eighteenth century clerk. He was a man and he looked rather servile. He had a quill stuck behind his ear, with the plume pointing backwards, just like the bird's. The penny dropped. Then I heard that, like those of other birds, its name could have come from Arabic: 'Saqu ettair' or 'saqr-et-tair', that translates as 'hunter bird'. The French didn't hear 'saqu ettair' or 'saqr-et-tair', they heard 'secrétaire'. Hence the name, through a false derivation. It's strange that in Latin it's called *Sagitarrius serpentarius*: 'Snake Archer', from the darting way it catches its prey. Some thinkers even link it with a constellation. How on earth has it survived? It looks so vulnerable, out there in the open. I have heard that it's because some people in Africa call it 'the Devil's Horse', perhaps because of its close connection with snakes and refuse to go near it but even this belief, it seems, is dying. Soon, I suppose, you may only see one on the Presidential flag in Sudan.

Insects

We were in The Baron of Beef in Cambridge. I think it was Mike who first raised the subject. He said that what he was going to describe had happened in the late 1990s. Some insects were circling around the light over the Scrabble table at the Kampala Club. When they dropped, say, down the back of the neck inside the shirt, or into the folds of a short-sleeved shirt, they became alarmed by the victim's efforts to remove the irritation caused by the uninvited visitor and squirted some form of acid as a defence mechanism. They gave a nasty burn. They had black and red stripes. Mike said they called them 'Nairobi flies' although they were a type of beetle.

"I am not big on bites in Africa," Brian said, "but one specific Uganda memory was the lake flies in Entebbe and the electric burners that continually and noisily fried them, as one took drinks at the Lake Vic Hotel in the evening."

Yes," I agreed, "there was something pleasant about sitting there enjoying the evening lake breeze and supping a beer under that blue electric burner in the Lake Victoria."

"In some places," Clive added, "the locals sweep up these flies and eat them. There is one place I've been to in California - I think it's Mono Lake - where there is a different type of fly, about twenty times bigger than African lake flies and even more numerous. It is quite impossible to walk through them, and the noise is deafening."

"I had to dig the dreaded jigger larvae out of Smithy's foot," muttered Trev. "Not pleasant!"

Lucinda and Clive

There were so many relationships in Kampala that didn't quite work out. The city was relatively, some say completely, devoid of racism. I have in front of me a photograph of Lucinda sitting alone, on a stone, barefoot, under a sky that could have been borrowed from Millais' *Boyhood of Raleigh*. It was taken by Clive on Soroti Rock. She taught Geography at Kitante, alongside me. She and her friends, Catholics whose antecedents were from Goa, were really kind. They felt strangely vulnerable, like fish out of water. I can't remember their names now, apart from Lucinda's. They worried a great deal about me and with good reason. I was often worried about myself. The other day I told the tale of Lucinda and Clive to Harish from Soroti and how she had caused quite a stir in that mainly Asian town, when she rode side-saddle on Clive's bicycle carrier from the school to his house. "You English teachers had a great time in Uganda," he replied with what sounded like a note of envy. Next time I see him, I shall ask him what he meant, although I think I know. We were free. They weren't. He was in the cage of his culture, even though the door was open. He was inside, looking out. We were outside ours, looking in at his. Clive and Lucinda's friendship only once caused a bit of a commotion in the cosmopolitan culture of Kampala. On coming out of her house on Kitante Hill, Clive hit a concealed tree-stump. His exhaust pipe ended up pointing forwards. His Saab sounded like a motorboat as they drove down the drive. When they parted in London, they came to an agreement. If they were not married to another in ten years' time, they would marry each other. Clive married his first wife in Bangalore three years later. Kampala may have been relatively, or even completely, devoid of racism. The trouble was the outside world wasn't, then. The other day Clive heard that she had just died after a long illness. She had never married. (CM)

Jiggers

Makerere, at first sight, was the Garden of Eden. Exotic trees rose up in every direction. You could pluck ripe avocadoes straight from the tree in Gene Geissler's garden. The temptation to walk barefoot across the dew-laden grass on the way to lectures was immense. Most of us settled for flips-flops. Then we had heard that there was a fly in the ointment. The word 'jiggers' began to be heard. This was an insect that gained access to your blood by burrowing under your toe nail. The sign was a blister with a black dot at its centre. With a magnifying glass you could see that the dot was the flea's hind legs sticking out, plus its respiratory spiracles and reproductive organs. Later we learned that jigger infestation led to ostracism and stigmatisation and were viewed by some in Uganda as a type of curse and an excuse for vilification. Even later, we learned that some of the pins that people used to get the insects out were not sterilised after use and passed HIV/AIDS on to others.

The Howl

I have a book somewhere that I bought in Kampala. On its cover it shows a termite hill. I was always curious, when I was there, to open one up just to see what it was like inside. I just couldn't do it. It may have been the book cover that stopped me or those boys at the school in Kampala who sat down, at break, clutching thin twigs which they poked into the many mounds on the school field. They were supplementing their diet with extra protein. I just couldn't bring myself to damage those termite palaces. In fact, I can't even spread a mole hill without feeling guilty. It was easy, perhaps, for the biology teacher, to dig them out. A metre below the ground surface powdery dried leaves and tunnel linings led to the queen: six inches long and sealed in a mud chamber. The school gardeners were keen to eat her. They also asked for the masticated soil as a compost for their maize and matoke. When the wet season arrived, males and females would rise up out of the mounds, start mating and move on to establish new colonies. Standing next to a termite hill on Kibuli Hill, my friend compared the emerging insects to a vertical plume of smoke and the eerie sound of their clattering wings to a howl. I have heard people talk of massive termite mounds in Karamoja, some almost as high as the chimney stacks of my home town's old factories. (JW, CM)

Wings

Balconies are great for an early morning cup of coffee. There were wonderful ones in Kampala where you could savour the air before the heat of the day. One day a friend of mine, smelling the coffee, stepped out onto his, only to find he was ankle-deep in wings. They had been discarded during the night. The strange thing was, there wasn't a sign of a single termite. The space was two metres by three. Doing the maths, those wings must have belonged to more than a million termites. (JW)

Seeds

Sitting outside, on the side of Kibuli Hill, reading a book in the warm sunshine, could be a special experience. A couple of plants growing up the balcony were permanently in flower and were the perfect home for geckos and other lizards. Up there, in the sunshine, the pods of fruit, tiny structures, twisted, as they dried out, and, with a clear crack, scattered their seeds over one's book. (JW)

Small Beer

I have never attended a three day drinking session in Buganda but I know a man who has. The beer, he says, was served in a pot. It was drunk through a long pipe the end of which was covered with a plaited grass device to keep out the straw and bits of soil at the bottom of the pot. They would sit there, five or six of them, for up to three days, talking and sucking on the straw. The beer, my friend says, was incredibly weak.

The Fox and The Python

Things are hotting up in Potton in Bedfordshire. It must be the cold. A fox appeared in a garden and stared at a Potton man's wife. She stared back. There was a stand-off, until the fox slowly turned and walked across the field towards

Potton Woods. The man's free-ranging chicken disappeared at about the same time but reappeared later from the undergrowth, where it had been hiding. High drama indeed but not as dramatic as the news I received in an email today about a huge python that had got stuck in a drain in Kibuli in Kampala.

Cashpoint

It's one of those places that doesn't look much. You will find it at the back of an industrial estate in Potters Bar. Whenever you go there, you will hear the most incredible stories about East Africa. Today I heard one about a young man who had come to England from Uganda with hardly a shilling in his pocket. Stacking shelves one day, in a Tesco supermarket, the thought crossed his mind, "There must be more to life than this" so he started mini-cabbing in Blackpool and then, when Museveni deregulated, returned to Kampala where he launched a new idea of cash points that convert any currency into shillings and vice versa. He is now a multimillionaire. Contrast this, my friend said, with the family who came here from Uganda at the same time, in 1972, who lived at first in luxury in Mayfair but were seen the other day, sitting penniless on a bench in Northwood, near Watford.

The Dreamliner

We were sitting near the check-in counter at Beijing International Airport, eyeing the arrows on the red carpet that led to the VIP lounge.

"What is it about the colour red?" I asked my fellow traveller. "Why do we give it such importance?" He shrugged his shoulders. To try to get a conversation going, jet-lagged as we were, I encouraged my addled brain to follow a stream of consciousness thread about the colour red.

"My flat," I said, "in Kampala, had a shiny red floor. I remember red floors elsewhere in the old empire. Did we paint floors red throughout the world? A friend of mine's houseboy even painted his balcony red in Kibuli to stop snakes crawling across it into the house. It had a shiny surface that made it impossible for them to slither across." My new friend nodded. I thought he was going to say something but he didn't.

"Is this why," I continued, "we painted our floors red across the world, to stop snakes getting at us? I seem to remember our floors could be slippery. I wonder how many brave young men and women we lost in the imperial venture owing to this dangerous surface? At school we were taught that much of the world was red and that it was British. Was it red polish that made us choose that colour?" My friend opened his palms with a gesture that signified 'Who knows?'

"It became an awkward choice," I continued, "during the Cold War, when people used to talk ominously about a 'red corridor' forming between Egypt and South Africa. This was one reason that was offered for dumping Milton Obote. He was felt by some to be flirting with Communism."

"CARDINAL!" my companion suddenly blurted out, breaking the silence. "That's what we called it! It's a reference to the red gowns of cardinals in the Vatican. There was a picture of a cardinal on the tin." He had suddenly burst into life.

"I had to put rough-textured sticking plaster," he went on, "on to the hooves of an orphaned antelope that I looked after in Kenya, so it wouldn't do the splits every time it stood up. My servants in Kenya used to strap pieces of sheepskin to their feet and skate across the floor to give it a surface like an ice-rink. I couldn't walk in socks! I was once given a surprise birthday party in Kericho. Having had a few jars in a bar, I entered this house to the sounds of 'Happy Birthday'. I clapped my hands in surprise and somehow raised my right leg, as if kicking a ball. My left leg went from under me and I shot across the room horizontally and my right foot connected with one of the two trestle tables laden with food and drinks. The spread went everywhere. My friends were much more concerned that I had injured myself, whereas I was worried about the lost food. I ended up laughing hysterically on the floor. Yes, I'm sure it was called Cardinal because of its colour. I guess it would have been called Bishop or Archbishop, if it had been purple. Surely it is only a coincidence that it matched the red on the maps.

He paused to allow us to decipher a message being broadcast on the tannoy system about our flight.

"I hadn't thought," he went on, "about it being a barrier to snakes. Quite possibly. Incidentally, there's only one surface that geckoes can't cope with: teflon." Half an hour later we were in our seats on our way to London. I never saw him again. Sitting next to me on the Dreamliner was a Ugandan economist who had worked at Makerere who now lives in Tanzania and was on his way to California. I told him my story about Cardinal Red.

"Yes," he said, "in the nineteen sixties the red polished floor was ubiquitous in

East Africa but has since more or less disappeared. End of your Empire?" was his final comment before he fell asleep. On my other side was his colleague, another economist, who was also, he told me, ex-Makerere.

"I see that it is possible," he said, joining in with enthusiasm, "to buy a 250 ml tub of Cardinal Red Floor Polish from Amazon for £7-71!! Today even!!"

"Was the red floor polish." he asked, "simply something which represented the dead hand of imperialism by default? In other words, people had always used red floor polish at home, so they used it wherever they went! We love these references to Empire in Buganda. Have you tried the 'Imperial Experience' at the Imperial Hotel?" I said that recently I hadn't.

"I seem to remember," I said, "it being used in old Victorian houses in the UK."

"Alternatively, he added, with an enigmatic smile, "would it disguise the blood stains on the floor?" (CM, BVA, MT, DS)

The Kampala Club

There was often talk of death in Uganda. Indeed, it even got into tea-time talk. I overheard two pretty, if rather mature, well-dressed English ladies in the Kampala Club talking about a man who had spent three days with his friends drinking weak beer from a huge oil drum. He had staggered out, it seems, into the night and had simply passed out. The following morning his dead body was found by passing school children. I couldn't help overhearing, above the noise of the fan, the two ladies discussing how the man might have died. One asked if he had died though constriction or dilation. My ears pricked up. "It gets cold at night in Kibuli," one of the ladies argued. "When we are too cold," she went on, "the blood vessels supplying warm blood to the skin become narrow or constrict: vasoconstriction. This reduces the flow of warm blood near the surface of the skin and reduces heat loss." Before she could develop her argument further, the other lady, who was from Yorkshire, cut in:

"Ooh, no! No, no, no, no! It was vasodilation, dilation not constriction, carrying more blood to the skin surface and therefore leading to great heat loss in the cold nights."

I leaned across and added: "As the drinker was no doubt unconscious at the time anyway, the death could have been caused by many factors, heat loss being probably only one of them."

They looked at me disapprovingly. "Oooh, I don't like that sort of thing," said the one from Yorkshire. They didn't ask me over. (JW)

The Swap

Brought up in near Victorian conditions in a tied farm cottage on a farm in Eastleach, he eventually landed a job in Kibuli, near Kampala. His father was a cowman and hadn't traveled much outside Wiltshire and Gloucestershire, except in the summer: ten days in Treorchy every year when the family visited his mother's parents. They had never owned a vehicle. They grew up with oil lamps and a bucket for a loo. It wasn't until he was twenty one, that the house was electrified and modernised. The farmer for whom his father worked was utterly amazed when he heard that his cowman would be flying out to Uganda to see his son. He was, in fact, completely incredulous. My friends parents, it has to be said, really did have a 19th Century view of Africa. In his mother's day, Africa was the "dark continent" where people disappeared or where others came at you with spears. In order to find the fare for their Uganda trip, his mother had secretly saved money from selling eggs to the locals and had hoarded the shillings over a two year period in a secret place, in case his father had demanded more Woodbine cigarettes! On their first day in Buganda my friend walked his parents through Kibuli village. A woman appeared from a hut carrying a one year old child. At that moment my friend was carrying his blonde one year old son. The lady rushed down her garden area screaming and shouting. It was a "Lets do a swap!" moment. It was all very good-natured and hilarious. The good lady held his son, his dear old mother took the little Ugandan baby and both were held aloft with much amusement by all around. After that, back in Gloucestershire, his mother could not stop talking about it. (JW)

The Cockroaches

I once bought a fridge in Africa. It was sturdy and strong. It was shaped like the ones we used to see in old American films. The gentleman who sold it to me swore that it was perfect. And so it seemed. I managed to get it into the house in Namilyango where I was living. I plugged it in in the kitchen. It came on. I carefully put inside it the cheese, the milk, the salad items and the fruit that I had bought that very same day. The following morning I bowled into the kitchen to take out my paw-paw. I opened the door and to my amazement saw an army of huge cockroaches. I looked down. They were on the floor. They were everywhere! I put it back in my boot and drove back to Kampala.

"No, no, no," the shopkeeper said in his second hand shop on Kampala Road. "You can't have your six hundred shillings back. It was perfectly all right when you bought it." He wouldn't budge.

In disgust, I drove back to Namilyango. I pulled back the silver foil that lined the back. It was a seething mass of the disgusting creatures. It resembled the inside of a seething beehive. I built a big fire in the garden and threw the offending object into the flames.

I don't know why but that experience often comes to mind when I try to remember my days in Buganda.

Hissing Cockroaches

We were sitting in the foyer of a hotel in Paris waiting for the receptionist to fumigate our rooms. We had both found cockroaches in our cupboards. "La bombe, the spray can," the manager had shouted at a harassed employee. We got talking about this and that but mainly the insects in question. He had told me he was a biologist and that he was from Mubende in Buganda. I told him my story about my cockroach-infested fridge. I called them giants. He said I should say 'huge', rather than 'giant', as the gigantic ones were on Madagascar, not in Uganda. The Madagascan ones, he said, are often called 'Giant', although the more common word was 'Whistling'. They are, he added, enormous and very slow moving.

"Whistling?" I repeated, astonished.

"Yes," he replied, "if you poke them with a stick, they hardly move, they just hiss. They can be as long as your thumb."

It's strange the things that can bring people together. (CM)

The Sack of Mangoes

There he was again, the man from Mubende, at breakfast.

"Wasuze otya nno? How was your night?" he asked.

'Bulungi. Fine," I replied.

"Wasuze otya nno?" I asked him.

"Bulungi" he replied.

"Do you think," I asked, "that the plague of insects referred to in the Bible could have been about cockroaches? Some scholars," I went on, "think that the Hebrew word 'arob' found in Exodus 8.21 and Psalms 78 and 105 refers to the *Blatta orientalis* or cockroach. He was not impressed.

"Cockroaches may be found," he replied, "in large numbers, but not out in the open. I think the biblical ones were locusts."

"So they don't swarm?" I asked.

"No, they don't swarm," he replied, "but sometimes occur in great numbers, such as in some long-drops, or at a food source. When I moved in to my second house in Soroti, a lovely old colonial-style building, where I was posted, it had been empty for a few months and someone had left a sack of mangoes on the kitchen floor. At night tens of thousands of cockroaches came out to feed on the rotting fruit. The only way to get rid of them was to boil up large sufriyes of water and chuck it over them. This took a few nights to complete."

"Forgive me," I said, "but what is a sufriye?"

"A sufriye is a cooking pot usually of aluminium and sold by weight and not diameter," he replied.

"And a long-drop?" I asked.

"A long-drop," he explained, "is a hole excavated deep enough so that no matter how much excreta or urine goes in, the bacteria etc. will be able to dispose of it at a sufficient rate that it will never reach the top.

"Ah!" I said, almost regurgitating my croissant. I wished I hadn't asked. (CM)

The Development Economist

I had a friend at Makerere who was doing a PhD in Development Economics. For his subject, he decided to investigate the plastic shoe industry in Buganda. He became restless. The topic was too pedestrian for him. His tutor pointed out the burgeoning hotel and bar business in Agrabah in the Sinai Peninsula, just to the north and east of Africa. It sounded exciting. He found it difficult to get hold of data. The people behind it, he was told, were nomads. He got into his Vauxhall Astra provided free of charge by the ODM and set off from Israel towards the mountains. Flagged down and bundled into a truck, he soon found himself in a room full of Eritreans. Puzzled, he settled down on the floor to interview his surprising companions. A tap was turned on, flooding the floor. His hosts then threw a switch to electrocute them all, just enough to take them to the edge of death. A mobile phone was thrust into his hand. He was told to ring home and ask for fifty thousand dollars in exchange for his release. His parents were out. He was told to leave a message. As he did so, melted plastic was dripped onto his back and onto the inside of his thighs. His ransom message consisted of blood curdling screams. Hours later, on coming round, he asked his fellow guests what on earth was happening. They explained that they were all fleeing from the fifteen year national service that was mandatory in Eritrea. They told him that the number of them trying to cross the desert ran into hundreds. Many had ended up in anonymous graves in Agrabah, their bodies having been found by passers-by at the sides of roads. The Agrabah morgue, no more than a big freezer, was stuffed with bodies. Each one's back was crisscrossed with scars from whips and electric probes.

"Are you all Eritreans?" asked the young economist. A woman came forward. She was from Uganda. A man called out from the corner. He was from Darfur. Others said they were from Somalia.

"But why did you come this way?" he asked.

"We were trying to get to Israel," they replied.

"What happens if my parents don't pay?" he asked.

"They will threaten to cut out your organs and sell them in Agrabah or even Cairo."

"These people traffickers," one added, "are becoming multi-millionaires through our suffering. The economy of Sinai is booming on our bodies. Our families in Eritrea have to go from mosque to mosque begging for funds to pay for our release. Our families are being bled dry. They say that once the money is in, we shall be released but we know that they will kill us. No one knows about our plight. If they do, no one cares."

I don't know what eventually happened to my friend. I don't know how he got out. I heard a rumour of a triple ransom and a helicopter rescue organised by the Embassy in Cairo but I don't know if it's true. He just won't tell me.

The Gash

We were jogging along a beach near St Andrews, talking about taxis. The cold wind from the North Sea made communication difficult. "*Matatus,*" he gasped, "were those taxis that zoomed about very fast all over the murram roads of East Africa, leaving a long plume of dust behind them." He went into the sea. I stayed on dry sand, running beside him, trying to avoid his spray.

"In our day," he went on, "they were usually Peugeots, 404s or 403s. They were notoriously dangerous. I passed one once on the Uganda part of the road to Nairobi. It had just been pulled out from under the back of one of those large army lorries. For a second it looked like an open top saloon with a red boot-lid and then I realised what had happened and drove on, a little slowly for a while." He increased his pace.

"It was one of those lorries," he continued, "full of soldiers, that introduced some extra airflow into my Opel Kadett one day. Dithering at a T-junction, one of these lorries reversed into me, creating a gash right along the bonnet. I couldn't escape because reverse was one of the gears that didn't work on my old car. A large guy got out of the lorry to come and see what had stopped him. He looked briefly at the damage, laughed heartily, and drove off. Needless to say, I learned to live with the gash."

"Was that gash in your bonnet," I shouted, "made in Uganda or Kenya?" The wind from the sea seemed now to be howling.

"It was done," he shouted, "in Kampala, but I carried it around until the old girl died, including on a trip to Serengeti where its clutch gave out in the North West of the park. I think the hole helped reduce overheating problems." He suddenly accelerated. He was still talking but I missed the rest. (DS)

The Clutch

I had wanted to ask my friend what he did when his clutch gave out in Serengeti on the way to Ngorongoro. I wanted to ask him if it was true, as it was rumoured, that he effected a repair by filling it with sand blown into the clutch housing through a handy plastic tube. I wanted to ask him if this worked so well that he started to drive the car enthusiastically, 'rallying it', to use the phrase that I was told he used later in Nairobi. I wanted to ask him if they got lost as they high-tailed it back towards the lake. I wanted to ask him if they had prepared for death by writing messages in the sand as they finished their last mint imperials before they were rescued by a park ranger. It was too late. He had disappeared into the distance. I had wanted to ask him if he was driven to sleeping in his car in the street in Nairobi because of the expense of repairs but he had disappeared into the spray. For a second I could have sworn that I heard a snatch of 'Chariots of Fire'. (DS, CM)

The Flight of the Phoenix

I don't know who he was. There are various theories about his identity. I did know a couple of characters who could have fitted the description. I have a feeling, though, that perhaps he flew away from Buganda before I had the chance to get to know him. He had bought an old Rolls Royce from an old colonial fellow out in 'the bush'. He was only interested in the engine and the chassis. He was scouring Kampala market for sheets of aluminium and lengths of wire. Out in the countryside, where he lived, he formed a sort of hanger inside a circle of banana trees by bending their fronds. Little by little the simple aircraft took shape. He came in and out of the city, scrounging pieces of metal from palm tree garages to fashion the wings. His plan, he said, was to fly to the Congo, where he felt he would be safe. He had been told that he couldn't leave the country until after his trial, following a terrible road accident in which someone had died. Nobody knows if he really did it, although a friend of friend of mine who was courting an Acholi lady on the old airstrip in Kololo swears he saw a glider-like aircraft with a motor take off from there one night in the dark. Some say he made it all up, after reading *The Flight of the Phoenix*, the 1964 novel by Elleston Trevor or after seeing the 1965 film based on the novel.

Porous Borders

I had a sceptical e-mail today about the young man in the bush who said he was building a plane to escape from Uganda. It read: "I've been thinking about the chap who was building a plane to escape from Uganda. I think you set this in the early 60s. Up until at least the end of 1967 there were a number of ways to drive out of Uganda undetected. I used at least three different routes between Uganda and Kenya, not because I wanted to avoid border posts, but because the routes were more interesting or shorter. One, and I think there were several others there, was east from the Tororo-Mbale road. Another was east from the Mbale-Moroto road and north of Mount Elgon. A further one was from Moroto towards Turkana. I managed all these in my Saab, although later, when I had a Land Rover, it was easier. I also accidentally crossed into South Sudan once, and it was possible to cross into Congo but not recommended. I am not sure about crossing into Tanzania, as I never tried. Therefore, why mess about trying to make a plane, unless you just wanted a good story? My theory is that he was trying to invent a failed money-making scheme, a form of begging."

"But he didn't have a car," I replied. (CM)

A Bad Day

I had a strange experience yesterday. I don't suffer from depression. I am lucky, I guess. However bad things get, I stay optimistic. It must be chemical. I can often feel that things are trying to suck me down but, somehow, I manage to swim back up to the rim of the whirlpool and backstroke lazily away. Many things in East Africa, in many ways a wonderful place, seemed to swirl chaotically around us, well, I suppose I mean around me. Things that are hard to list. The killings, the deaths. I heard yesterday that one of us was the first to go down with a terrible disease. I wasn't aware that anyone of us had.

We weren't aristocrats looking forward to the next party or lion shoot. We weren't missionaries adding scalps to our belts. We weren't middle class escapees, wallowing in the luxury of big houses with as many servants as we cared to employ. Did we fit in? Not really. Not then. The Professor of Spanish at St Andrews University announced in his first lecture that his job was to create square pegs for round holes. I suppose he was saying he wanted society to change and that we, or some of us, would be the agents of change. Our problem was that we were already square pegs in round holes. Perhaps he was just trying to make us feel at home. Then there was that other strange feeling in Africa caused by one word: Africanisation. We knew that it was right, in one way, but, in another, there was a feeling that it wasn't. It meant that we were stopgaps, *gastarbeiters*. We could not aspire to long term careers, not there, anyway. In one way, it could be said, we were being used. Success would eventually be rewarded by the termination of our contracts. We were a form of casualised labour. My vision, then, wrong as it turned out, of the future for myself, if I had stayed in the expat circle, was that of a corpse floating in Hong Kong harbour with a knife in its back.

Dave always made me think 'real'. There was, and is, something angst-making about his honesty. In a way, faced with the surreal collection of postcolonial characters, defrocked priests, religious fanatics, swaggering types in full colonial gear, all that we had to hang on to was our honesty. The solid middle-class called and call this 'integrity', a word which smacks of smug moral superiority. 'Honesty' feels a far cleaner word to me. Contact with Dave's honesty plunged me yesterday into a rare depression. It lasted less than a day. The daily challenges that I face now with equanimity suddenly became too much. The upper-class lady with dementia at my wife's table, who starts the conversation amiably and then moves quickly into deeply personal abuse, gets right under my skin. The brain damaged woman, who waits near the door for me and who is all over me like a rash as soon as I walk in to the home, immediately placing me in compromising situations, became unbearable. The Cockney with a speech defect who is desperate for my attention and whom I cannot understand and who calls me a bastard. The beautiful old lady, who cryptanalysed Japanese codes and intelligence at Bletchley Park, sitting there, unrecognised by any of the country's 'honours' givers, filled me with sadness. The old rocker lady, an Elvis Presley fan, who keeps crying "Help!" and to whom I say "I am here," to calm her down. The medical doctor with dementia who keeps falling down. The engineer who built oil installations in the Sudan, who tries to punch his West African nurse whenever she attempts to undress him. David Bowie's song "Where are we now?" playing again and again in the restaurant. My wife's dignity as she copes, unable to move, with her terminal illness.

Dave's undiplomatic honesty, "I am not into that stuff," when declining the invitation to join in saying Grace before that meal in Nairobi put on for him by the intensely religious Irish Catholic headmaster at the Aga Khan: all of these things, and others, combined to give me a bad day. (DS)

The Conundrum

We met by chance at Luton Airport. I was on my way to Madrid to launch a book. Dave was on his way to Andalusia to do some research on Maimonides. We got talking about this and that, particularly about acculturation in Buganda, our acculturation or second culture learning. We managed to get seats together and the plane took off.

"I secretly admired," I said, "that famous Economist who lived in a hut by the beach near Mombasa. I also secretly admired Peter Fogg from Hitchin for the way he got involved with indigenous culture and life. He even wrote, it appears, a Luganda grammar, which I haven't seen yet. He was not TEA. He got jobs at those rather unofficial schools that sprang up in the post-independence period, before new controls could be put in place. He married a Muganda. Later he went south (in Uganda) and became an authority on bees. He also became, curiously, secretary of a European club down there. Later he had a job at a 'grammar school' in the Luweero Triangle just before all hell broke loose in that area. Museveni launched his guerilla campaign against Obote 2 from in there. Many died. Patrick and his family were lucky to escape unscathed via Kigali."

Dave sat there thinking.

"I come now to the question. How is it, Dave, that I secretly admired and still do admire Peter Fogg and his struggle to achieve an authentic life, outside or free from the constraints, parameters and values of Western culture, as it was then? And how it is that I felt, deep down, uneasy about our presence in East Africa and almost even willing to accept the view that we were not wanted? Patrick stopped writing to me, when I asked him if he had ever heard a talking chicken. He didn't like my question at all."

The plane ran into some turbulence and we fell silent. We were over the Bay of Biscay.

"OK," I said, "it was more than a leg-pull. I can see now that he could have taken it that I was mocking his stance, his attempt to achieve authenticity. We, the TEAs, were a bit rough with each other. We still are. It's like water off a duck's back when we get ragged. Not so Peter. Do I admire his experiment? Yes … and no. Do I wish I had cultivated the Establishment people at the Kampala Club and Makerere? I am not sure. Sometimes I do, other times I don't. Mostly no, I suppose. Was I at ease with the TEA crowd? Answer: yes." Dave continued to sit there in silence. I could tell he was thinking.

"This all probably says more about me than anything. Can you help me untangle this conundrum, Dave?"

"It's the old anthropologist's dilemma," Dave suddenly said. He is from

Aberdeen and has a thick Doric or Aberdonian accent. He was originally from the East End of London. "When exploring and analysing a new culture, how much do you move out of your own culture? If you stay in your culture," he went on, sounding even more Scottish, "then you can become too judgmental about the one you are investigating. If you enter more wholeheartedly into the new culture and see how it works in itself, how it is consistent, etc., even if its morals and mores are different from your own, then the danger is that you abandon objective analysis. When religion gets involved, the objectivity flies out of the window, of course. In your position [he turned to look at me], when writing about Africa, I would try to be objective about all the different ways of life, although I would, I must admit, find it difficult not to show my detestation of the colonialists and their administration."

The plane went up and down as we passed over the mountains in the Basque Country.

"I knew some guys in Kampala," he continued, "and one in Tabora who had married local girls and who were, at the time, living happily, it seemed. They had abandoned their pasts and taken on local citizenship. I heard, much later, on a radio programme, about a guy who brought his African wife back here to live successfully. I was very keen to abandon 'Englishness' myself at one time and marry a Mugisu girl but it didn't work out. I know now that it would have been a disaster, as I was such an idiot. I wasn't mature enough," he added, "to go down such a difficult path. In the end I found a less difficult way of abandoning 'Englishness' by embracing 'Scottishness'."

The plane started to descend to Madrid. I felt we had been getting somewhere. The last thing I saw of Dave was his face in the aircraft window as I crossed the tarmac at Madrid-Barajas Airport. (DS)

The Anthropologist's Dilemma

I still feel a bit guilty about Dave. He didn't want to play rugby. He enjoyed the company, the beers in the club house, but he really didn't really want to play. He was tall and well built, ideal for the second row. He didn't stand a chance. The captain and I homed in on him. He had never learned the rules. He was in the second row and used to huff and puff around the field, trying to keep up with the scrums and line-outs, only to be regularly flattened. Whenever he picked up the ball, a rare event, a penalty was awarded. His best memory of the games, it turned out, was of some of the local African men who came to watch at Kololo. They could just not believe what the Wazungu, the Europeans, were doing to each other. Every time there was a collision and people were rolling about in a heap, the Africans would be rolling about laughing their heads off. The anthropologist's dilemma? (DS)

The Billiard Table

I find it difficult to write about the Kampala Club. I hardly ever went there. It was considered by many, rightly or wrongly, to have been a bastion of old colonialism. I played the odd game of tennis there. I learned today that it was taken over early on by Idi Amin for use as the Police Mess. They say it was used for other grisly purposes, I know not what, but I can imagine, while he was in power.

After Amin went there was a bit of a gap until after 1986, when moves were made to get it back by Club patrons: solicitors, civil servants and engineers, professional people. It took them three years to get the site back and to start the process of rehabilitation. In the event, it turned out to be an impressive achievement. In 1993 they were still removing the bindweed from the boundary fence and replacing its fabric. Inside the grounds an accommodation building was turned into a hotel called The Shanghai. It was managed by the same Taiwanese people who ran the Shanghai Restaurant. It had twelve rooms. The 'ng' of Shanghai was pronounced in Kampala like the 'ng' in the insult *ngombe wewe*, in English "You cow!" It is on Sezibwa Road just over from the Sheraton Hotel (which used to be called the Apolo, not after the Greek God but after the deposed President, Apolo Milton Obote). You know where I mean, on the corner of the road that goes up to the President's Lodge.

An extraordinary thing happened in the late 1990s. The billiard table just vanished. No one seemed to know where it went. A small light object disappearing, yes, that is believable, but how could a hulking great, full size, billiard table simply disappear? Were they after the slate?

The trusty Scrabble table, I am told, survives, having become one of the Club's notable features. The lights used to go out occasionally in the nineteen nineties but a friend tells me it may be better now. I am not so sure.

Explosions

I was sitting there in the City Bar, waiting for someone interesting to come in, pen at the ready, when up the steps came Clive. He had been posted to Moshi the year before. After the usual salutations, "Jambo" and all that, we settled down for a chat. He was very upbeat, not at all downcast, as he had been the last time I had seen him. He had, he said, got over his amoebic dysentery. There was a purposefulness now in his step the likes of which I hadn't seen before. He reminded me that he had been sent to Old Moshi Boys' School at the foot of Kilimanjaro in Tanzania. It was, he said, one of the best schools in Tanzania with bright and ambitious students. Even the President, Julius Nyerere, sent his son there. The town itself, Moshi, was very nice and quite wealthy. Its wealth came from coffee, sisal and wheat. There was the mountain to explore and the game parks and reserves. Amboseli, Tsavo, Lake Manyara, Ngorongoro Crater and Serengeti were an easy drive away. There was Olduvai Gorge. He is not sure why he was sent there. His subject was history but the school already had too many historians so he was asked to teach English. The place was very calm. The noisiest thing was the sound of rain on the roof and thunder, and the machine gun fire and deafening detonations from the training camp opposite, where Chinese instructors were training FRELIMO freedom fighters and guerillas before being sent to Mozambique to remove the Portuguese. (CL)

Realities

I had a friend in Africa who lives now in Ireland but was born in Malaya. In Africa he felt more real than he does in Europe. He lived in the countryside in Buganda, not far from Kampala. It felt similar, he says, to life on the rubber plantation of his childhood. I was born in England. I spent my first years listening to skylarks, walking through cool bluebell woods and contemplating harebells and cowslip bells. I am not really sure how I felt in Uganda. To me it often felt unreal. I began to back away from it and withdraw into the shadows. At times I felt on edge, as if I was stuck in the Princess of Wales conservatory at Kew Gardens amongst strange plants and flowers or trapped inside Whipsnade Zoo with the safety barriers down. When I retuned home, I began to open up again, unfurl to familiar reality, but not straightaway. It took me a while to shake off my mild agoraphobia. I remember feeling some panic when a herd of cows came rushing towards my wife and me, as we crossed a field in Mill Hill. Perhaps I haven't thrown it off entirely. There is nothing profound about this text. It's sometimes where you are born and spend your childhood years that dictates how you react to the world and where you feel at home.

The Pitcher Man

One of the strangest characters to walk up the steps of the City Bar was the Pitcher Man. He was an Acholi from Gulu. There was something radiant about his personality. His enthusiasm for his subject was infectious. I was sitting there in the shade on the terrace, trying to make sense of the events reported in the *Uganda Argos,* when he came in and sat down beside me. His name was Deogratias. He had just got back from a year in Madagascar. I asked him what he had been doing on that Indian Ocean island. He told me he was doing what he always did, research on pitcher plants. My ears pricked up. I wasn't sure why. Was it because Babu had allowed me to use my Austrian beer mug with a hinged lid which looked like a pitcher? Perhaps. I started reminiscing about the flowers of my childhood.

"One of my favourites," I began, "in our garden was the snapdragon. I liked it because I could open its jaws by nipping its head between my fingers. Seeing it open its mouth gave me a thrill."

He launched straight into the subject of his research. He told me that pitcher plants are carnivorous.

"They eat meat?" I asked, surprised.

"One of the largest," he said, "is *Nepenthes truncata*. Its pitchers can hold a pint and a half of fluid."

I contemplated my beer mug.

"Some say that pitcher plants can digest rats and mice," he added, watching me change colour. "People call them monkey cups from the fact that monkeys have been seen drinking from them." We paused to sip our beers.

"They sound a bit revolting," I commented, wishing straight away that I hadn't said it. He seemed not to notice.

"The biggest," he said, "such as *Nepenthes rajah* are found on Borneo. *Nepenthes lowii* can even eat tree shrew droppings.

'What?" I cried.

"Yes," he said, "that's right. *Nepenthes lowii* only occurs on a few mountains in Borneo. It is now known that they do not just digest insects etc. that fall in but also utilise animal urine and faeces, for nitrogen." He was beaming.

"Fish and chips?" I suggested, getting up from my chair and moving towards the City Bar restaurant, feeling a little queasy.

He nodded, delighted. (CM)

The Real

> Life's but a walking shadow, a poor player
> That struts and frets his hour upon the stage
> And then is heard no more. It is a tale
> Told by an idiot, full of sound and fury
> Signifying nothing.
>
> — *Macbeth* (Act 5, Scene 5, lines 17-28)

Is the world that this book describes real? In many ways it is. Some of the tales are constructed out of bits and pieces of personal and shared experience. Many reflect the reality that presented itself on a daily basis in the blinding sunlight on the City Bar steps, as character after character appeared from the plains, the mountains, the swamps, the game parks, the villages and towns, the schools and monasteries, the wars of Uganda and of the rest of Africa, north, east, south, west, Sudan, Congo, Rwanda, Kenya, Tanzania, Somalia, Rhodesia, as it then was, Mozambique, Burundi, Algeria. Were the stories they brought with them real? Well, most of the stories were told. Is the story any one tells us real? They seemed to be. Often I had no way of knowing. I took them on trust. I have to admit that at times some of the characters, like the Spitfire Pilot, seemed like actors in a play who had lost their way to the stage or who had popped out during performances for refreshment.

Fort St George

It was the beginning of summer. We were in the Fort St George pub on Midsummer Common in Cambridge. I don't know why but I was feeling reflective.

"I very nearly decided," I began, contemplating the froth on my beer, "to approach someone at Makerere with a view to doing a PhD on Francophone literature in Africa. What would have happened to my life, if I had done so? It's one of those 'What if?' questions which abound when we look back on our twenties. Who knows, I might have got caught up in the conflict in the Congo whilst interviewing a Congolese novelist!" I might have died of malaria." I took a sip of my beer. "In the event," I concluded, "I took the decision to apply to the University of London to do research on Spanish literature. It was a good decision, as it turned out. The problem is, or was, that one could never know, then, how a particular decision would turn out. Was going to Africa a mistake for me?" I mused. Friends had urged me to go to Latin America. That's where the real politics were, I was told. All I could see was wall-to-wall tin-pot dictators there. Africa was a tabula rasa. I probably got my lecturing job later in French, in London, on the strength of my African experience. The interviewing panel was made up of old Africa hands who had opened up colleges and departments in Kenya and the Sudan. Living, as I did, on Nakasero, among French speakers, from Rwanda, the Congo and France, really polished up the French that I had learned in Paris during my 'year abroad'. I taught French in Kampala. My PhD research author, Juan Larrea, wrote in French and Spanish. We used French together in Argentina." I looked up, expecting my friends to have nodded off. "Sorry," I added. Just feeling meditative this morning."

"I know the feeling!! " said Mike. "However," he went on, solidly, "I remember advice in the early '70s - that if one thinks that the wrong decision has been made and that things are just not working out, it is quite possible that if an alternative decision had been made things might have turned out even worse!! Sound advice in my view!!"

"A good philosophy, Mike," I murmured. There was a silence. Clive chipped in.

"At some time in the future I plan to list all the 'what ifs' in my life and see where different decisions would have taken me." He paused then went on: "After only a few 'what if' dichotomies you rapidly develop a web with literally dozens of final outcomes."

Brian, our host, sat there, in silence, staring into his glass. For some reason I found his silence the most interesting contribution. What was he thinking? Was he doing the maths? Did he regret any decision that he had taken? He had taken so many. Was he at ease with the way things had gone in his life? Did he think my question was stupid? Was his mind on another matter or was it simply jet lag after the flight from Dar? I felt like saying "A penny for your thoughts" but this was Cambridge. It had to be something else.

"Do you believe in the Jansenists' doctrine of Predestination?" I asked him, trying to get him to reveal his thoughts. "Or are you essentially Panglossian?" Why do I do that, I asked myself? Why do I go too far?

"What was that?" he asked, sitting up with a jolt. "My round, did you say?"
(CM, MT, BVA)

Brief Encounter

I bumped into her at the cash machine in the middle of Bury Park in Luton. You know the one I mean, the one near the two mosques. There is always a long queue that stretches right out into Dunstable Road, positioning itself, strangely, at a right angle to the wall, as if the customers are trying to avoid getting too close to the bank and being hit by falling tiles. She was behind me in the queue. She said she hailed from Buganda and that her husband's name was Lou. I don't know why but she told me he worked nights. I knew from the way she spoke that she had a heart of gold. I asked her if she knew the legend that a Celtic god called Lou or Lew may have presided over the five springs at Leagrave in Luton from which the River Lea flows. She said that she didn't and asked me to tell her more. I said Lugus, or Lug, or Lud, or Lyg, was the god of light and that the name of the local stream may possibly mean, the River of Light. The queue moved forward, just twelve more to go. She drew a little closer. She asked for more.

"Like Mukasa and Lake Victoria?" she asked

"Yes, sort of," I said, "Luton may be named after a Celtic God called Luw". I said that 'ton' meant 'big settlement' and that we were probably standing in the town on the river of Lugus, Lou-town.

"Go on!" she urged. "What was he like, this Lou?"

"Well, he may be related to the Welsh god Lley Llaw Gyffes," I explained.

"What does that mean?" she asked.

"The Bright One with the Strong Hand," I explained. "In Ireland they called him Long Hand."

"Oh!" she exclaimed, "anything else"?

"Well, Lugus was triplistic,"I replied.

"What's that?" she asked.

"A tricephalic god, which they think is Lugus, was discovered in Reims. You know, three heads.'"

"Oo-er!," she replied. The queue was moving faster now.

It was my turn at the machine. I haven't seen her since. I sometimes feel that she has been avoiding me.

The Last Straw

I eventually found them, the Luton Film Club group, underground, in a basement with a low vaulted ceiling, in The Hat Factory, a cultural centre in Luton. It reminded me of a cellar I knew so well in Spain. It was not at all what I had been expecting. I had imagined, when they rang me, that they wanted to make a film about me, about my poems and Luton. It was, in fact, a seminar about how to make a film. It was a complete misunderstanding. It happens all the time in Luton. I thought at first I should just get up and go but there were only three in the class, apart from me.

"Imagine a situation," the tutor began. "Call it 'The Last Straw that Broke the Camel's Back'." In a flash, my mind went back, to the Sudanese refugee camp, where I had done some voluntary work, briefly, in Uganda. I saw myself approaching a mud hut that was no more than a small dot at first, in the distance. I reached it and went in. I could just make out in the darkness, fifty young men sitting cross-legged on a smooth bare earth floor, barefoot, silent, no shirts, just shorts. I felt their eyes alight on my flip-flops. Sweat was running down between my toes. All I could hear was the sound of a cricket outside. Then, to the right, from inside a thicket, came the sarcastic laugh of a hornbill that looked like the toucan I used to contemplate, years before, on a hoarding at the station in Luton, with a bubble emerging from its beak containing the words "My Goodness, my Guinness!" I could have murdered one at that moment.

"Je suis Bob" I said, pointing to myself and looking around, in vain, for a piece of chalk and a blackboard. "Je suis de Luton". There was nothing: no light, no window, no table, no chair, no cupboard, no pictures, just the dark hut and the boys, and a doorframe filled with dazzling light.

"Je suis Ben Agwang," one replied. "Je suis de Juba". The sound of an approaching lorry could be heard.

The 'headmaster' was a Sikh. He wore a UN uniform. He was a kindly-looking man. He had a turban and a well-groomed moustache. He sported a beard that looked as if it had spent the night in a lady's hairnet. I thought of Dalí's pointed whiskers and how he kept them in place with a hairnet, in his home in Port Lligat in Catalonia. The head called me outside.

"I have some more for you," he whispered. Another fifty boys were coming towards us. I saw a red flash on the shoulder of the soldier who was driving the truck. Ugandan army. The boys tried to squeeze into the hut but it was impossible. There was no room. I stood in the doorway and asked them to sit outside, in a circle. There were now two circles, one inside, one outside. "Je suis Monsieur Gurney". The introductions started again. I was moving from circle to circle.

We heard the sound of another engine approaching down the dirt road. Stepping out into the sunlight was like opening an oven door.

"There must be a mistake," I protested, squinting at the new arrivals.

An official pointed to a sausage tree with a rotting trunk groaning with fruit: "That's your new classroom!" It was like a scene from the Bible, with me standing like an Old Testament prophet in the middle of a crowd that was waiting to receive the glory of French civilization. There was a cough in the basement.

"Is this true?" I was asked rather rudely by a member of the group. He is from Bangladesh and is famous in the town for his songs about love.

"It depends on what you mean by true," I replied. The bubble had burst. The moment had passed. In my mind's eye I saw myself, the children, the hut and the tree, all disappearing, like dots, into the distance, as if viewed from the open door of a departing helicopter.

The Heart of Africa

People from all over Africa would arrive at the City Bar. There was the friendly miner from Kigezi, 'the Tungsten Man' we called him, who was praying for World War Three, and for the mountain of wolfram he was sitting on to go up in value. There was the famous princess from Toro, the most beautiful woman, some said, in Kampala, who worked as a model in London, and to whom Melvyn, the ex-busker on the Paris Metro had taken a shine. There were the intense young journalists from *The Times* and *The Observer* who kept asking us again and again what on earth was happening. There was the Battle of Britain pilot, reduced to working as a mercenary, who, in his Spitfire, appeared to have been strafing Che Guevara in the Congo. There was poet we called Pipitek Okot, whose real name, we learned later, was Okot p'bitek, who read us a long poem that he had just translated from the Acholi called *The Song of Lawino* about the threat to the tribal way of life from Westernisation. There was the gleeful painter called Saul Olek who came from Gulu and who seems to have just disappeared. There was Harry Harbottle, in charge of the city's water, who was always there, wide-eyed and welcoming, an elbow on the bar. There was the Irishman who ran a brewery by Lake Victoria who hinted at having hidden depths that no one ever glimpsed and who promised to reveal to us his brewing secrets but never did. There was the Frenchman from Algeria, the torturer with a shady past in a colonial war who fancied himself as Kampala's ladies' man and who seemed to be on permanent 'R&R'. There was the pretty young Englishwoman with the beautiful knees, with whom it is was impossible not to fall in love, who was doing a doctorate on ears on certain insects' legs. There was the exhausted botanist who had spent years combing the jungle for a cure for cancer that he never found. There was the young cultural attaché from the French Embassy, who was legally avoiding doing military service, and who managed to get us crates of cognac and casks of tax-free Chianti for our parties. There was the linguist who kept talking about recording the rich oral traditions of Uganda before they disappeared but who never left the bar. There were beautiful young English girls who had hitch-hiked down the Nile, crossing Egypt and the Sudan, for whose fair hands there was great competition and much offering of spare beds by Kampala's bachelors. There was Brian, whose dad was from Ceylon, who grew up in Kentish Town and went to school in Soho and edited Obote's Second Five Year Plan. And then there was Babu, the bar owner, always there with a sympathetic ear, who hailed from Gujarat and was always willing to cash a cheque for the dusty traveller.

The Gallery

If only I could remember the name of that place. It was at the foot of Kololo Hill in Kampala. An image keeps coming back to me, of a barman, a 'Geordie' perhaps, on his last legs who lived on brandy and milk. Around the walls was a gallery of photographs of his customers. There must have been thirty or more. They looked quite young. Nearly all of them were British. We got talking to the barman about them, what they did for a living: railways and airports, copper and cotton, coffee and tea, swamp drainage and drains, hydro-electricity, plastic shoes. They sounded interesting. I asked him which days of the week they came in. His chest seemed to swell with pride, as he announced that they were all dead. He was still here, was the implication. He was a survivor. Would I like my picture taken, he asked? He nodded towards a studio he had out the back. I thanked him profusely but declined his offer. For a second I almost understood why the Karamajong threw their spears at me when I tried to take their picture. "They think you are stealing their souls," my driver had said. I can still see those faces in the photographs but not the bar's name. None of my friends can remember it, apart from one who says he can just remember the 'International Bar', nestling amongst a small group of shops on one of the hills. It was, he says, used by high-ranking Ugandans, like Felix Onama, a former Foreign Minister, who was shot outside.

The Dead Man

I don't know why I did it. I hadn't met him before. Was it out of boredom, the need for a change, pity, the scent of a good story, the parable of the Good Samaritan?

"I shall be dead by the end of theday," he said, "unless you get me to Bujumbura". What do you do when a stranger comes up to you in a bar in Kampala and says that he is about to die, unless you do something? He said he was the head master of a school in the bush in the north of Buganda. He had, he said, built it with his own hands. He said that he had spent much of his life building schools in Africa, one after the other, making the bricks with his own fingers out of the red mud and now they wanted to kill him.

"Who wants to kill you?" I asked.

"Kabaka Yekka and they will, unless I can get to Burundi now," he pleaded. He explained that he had fallen in love with a girl of eighteen, the daughter of a chief and that she was one of his pupils.

"Will you take me there?" he pleaded. He had the eyes of a dying man. I thought of nights spent alone, in the jungle. I thought of Graham Greene. He nodded towards a white Mercedes parked outside the City Bar. I felt I had no choice. We drove to my flat, picked up my passport and we were off. The road south was straight, empty, new. I drove flat out across the Ankole plains. Swifts thudded against the windscreen. As we approached the border, I saw that his face had become like that of the man in the poster who was about to be killed, a revolver held against his temple, in Vietnam. There was nobody. No youth wingers. A hand waved us through. We took a roundabout route down to Burundi, like tourists, past lakes, hills and volcanoes. We saw nobody. The Congo was not far away, on the other side of the lake. Bujumbura was empty.

"Que se passe-t-il?" I asked the hotel owner.

"C'est la révolution," he replied.

My new friend waved goodbye, as he climbed the steps and entered the jet that would take him to JFK. That was the last time I saw him. I opened an envelope that contained the address of a lady to whom he wanted me to give the keys. I drove down a track in Buganda between coffee bushes and banana trees and saw the tin roof of a hut made with red bricks, where I handed over the keys. She was a regular at the New Life Club, near the protestant cathedral.

The Complainer

No one can remember now the name of the complainer. He was full of hard luck stories: his passport had expired, his long johns had been stolen, his mosquito net didn't work, he had an ingrown toe nail, he couldn't sleep because of the cries of the muezzins calling the faithful to prayer and the dogs that barked at each other all night long. The Pied Kingfishers' calls gave him a headache, he had a bad stomach from eating fried snake cooked at the side of the road near Makerere. He hated being called a *mzungu* wherever he went. He had developed a cough from the black smoke belched out by cars and from the charcoal burnt in a million stoves. He moaned about everything, not just about the food in the halls of residence, the bilharzia in Lake Victoria, the jiggers that got under his toenails because he wore flip-flops on the university lawns, the mosquitoes that seemed to squeeze in through the fine metal mesh that covered his windows and the heat and the humidity just before the storm broke each day at three in the afternoon. No, he moaned, too, about the bats on the washroom floors, the geckos on the walls, the snakes in the drains, the pythons at the dump, the weaverbirds that messed up the grass in the hotel garden in Entebbe, the hornbills that woke him each morning with their horrible laughter, the packs of wild dogs that roamed the university campus at night, abandoned by their owners, who had gone back to Kent and Kentucky, the lion that came to investigate him while he was having a pee on the border with Kenya, the nsenene (bush crickets) that fell to the ground around the street lights upon which people feasted, the termite hills on the football pitches that provided so many with additional protein, the droppings of the bats that rose up in a cloud each evening down Kampala Road on their way to the Mabira Forest and the Ssese Islands. Yes, all he did was complain.

The Stone Thrower 1

I had a friend in Africa who taught at a school in Kianyaga, a small village on the southern slopes of Mount Kenya, not too far from Embu. It was about a year after he had arrived and he was occupying a house in the school grounds. Late one afternoon he was sitting in the living room when there was a great crash from the back bedroom. He rushed along and found a broken window and a rock on the floor. It was rather shocking as there had been no ill feeling as far as he was aware and he was unsure what to do for a moment. While he was pondering the situation, there was another crash from the other bedroom and he was in there in a flash and saw a young chap outside. He lost his cool a bit as he then rushed outside and yelled at him. The culprit took off into a stand of maize and my friend took off after him. Luckily, a couple of schoolboys were coming up the lane and saw what had happened. They decided to chase this chap through the maize while my friend decided quickly that the stone-thrower almost certainly was going to have to come out onto the road about fifty yards away. So he ran around the outside of the patch of maize and, sure enough, a couple of seconds later, this chap came running out straight into his arms. It was at this point he realized that the guy was pretty much blotto. Luckily he was quite small and my friend was quickly able to put an arm lock on him and the schoolboys, by then half a dozen or more attracted by the commotion, frog marched him back to the school.

After a bit of debate it was decided to take him down to the police station about a mile away and they decided he should be tied up. The only rope they could come up with was a 150 ft climbing rope which my friend had in his possession and the culprit was trussed up to look pretty much like the Michelin Man or a giant hot dog with his head and feet poking out. The boys were really angry with him and carried him like that down to the police station. There he was duly arrested and charged with attempted breaking and entering.

A couple of months later my friend received a subpoena to appear at the courthouse about twenty miles away and he had to beg a day off work and drive there, with one of the student witnesses, for a two pm hearing. The judge was a very pleasant Indian chap and it was a pretty informal affair. He asked what had happened and they gave their side of the story. He spoke to the defendant (now completely sober) who said that he really didn't know anything about the event as he had been drinking. The judge pondered a little while and pointed out, more to himself than anyone else, that the culprit had been in custody for a couple of months and had really only broken a couple of windows. He then looked at my friend and said, "Could you swear that the man whom you caught coming out of the maize patch was the same chap that you saw going in?" My friend thought for a while about it and the fact that he never really saw his face, and that common sense certainly would say that it had to be the same person. However, he replied, "No, I couldn't swear to it". The judge's response was, "OK, case dismissed".

You might think that would have been the end of the little saga but there's more. My friend walked out of the court and went to open his car door. Then he saw the defendant being released from the side of the court house. He walked slowly towards my friend and his student and said something in Kikuyu which his student translated for him as "He is asking for a lift back to Kianyaga please, as he has no transport". He thought 'what the hell' and so they gave him a lift back home and he thanked them politely and vanished down a track by the side of the road. (CT)

The Stone Thrower 2

He wanted to tell them that he didn't know why he did it, that he just picked up a rock and threw it at my friend's back bedroom window, that he picked up another one and threw it hard at the second bedroom window. He wanted to say that he had been drunk and that it just came over him. He didn't say that Mount Kenya was a sacred place. He didn't say that deep down he felt it was wrong to build anything foreign, even a school, on the slopes of God's throne on Earth, where Gikuyu, the first man of his people, had ascended and spoken to Ngai. He didn't tell the judge that he resented the way that the school turned its back on the mountain and that his people, as a sign of respect, built their houses with their doors facing the summit. He didn't mention the fact that he had heard that some of the teachers had said that that was all rubbish. Nor did he tell the court that he felt that he was beginning to feel like an outsider amongst his peers. He didn't say that his parents had been too poor to send him to that school, even though he had been one of the brightest boys in the village. He didn't tell the court that he felt that an elite was being formed that excluded him, one that was being brainwashed. He felt like telling them that but perhaps he only half-believed it. It was one of the ideas that those who had not got in to the school used as a form of comfort. He didn't tell them the worst, that his grandfather had once owned the land on which the school was built, there, in Kianyaga, snow mountain village, the ostrich's resting place. Neither did he tell them that his family lived in a mud hut that didn't have any windows. He didn't say to the court that he knew the teacher did not own the house and that he, the teacher, would not have to pay for the repairs. He knew that it would have been no good telling the judge, a very nice Indian, any of this. He just said that he had been drunk, which was not a lie. Perhaps the judge sensed his reasons for the violent gesture. Perhaps there was something else behind his decision. The stone thrower doesn't know why but he was let off. Looking back now, he is not sure why he did it. He was no longer sure that he believed in Ngai nor, for that matter, in the God of the Europeans. He was no longer sure that Gikuyu or Adam existed. He was no longer sure, in fact, that his door ought to face Mount Kenya. (CT)

Guy Fawkes and the Kikuyu

I can understand how it happened. There seemed to be a need to keep a tight lid on things back then. Iron discipline was required in that school in the heart of the Kikuyu tribal area. After all, it wasn't that long after the end of the Mau Mau rebellion. Now, for readers in Africa to make sense of all this some background is in order. The British, rather curiously, celebrate a certain date. They don't think deeply about it. They just do it. To me the whole thing feels surreal but children love it. It takes place to commemorate the foiling of 'The Gunpowder Plot' in which a group of plotters planned to blow up King James I and restore a Catholic monarch to the throne. One of them, called Guy Fawkes, was apprehended in the early hours of November the fifth,1605, sitting on twenty barrels of powder under the House of Lords. We burn his effigy on bonfires on that date. In Lewes, I have heard, they parade effigies of him and Pope Paul V who became Head of the Catholic Church in the same year,1605. Lewes boys, they say, chant 'Burn the Pope' as they let off their bangers. It all smacks of political incorrectness. It feels mad. Others feel, though, that it is a pro-democracy festival but that hardly stands up to scrutiny. I can't stand it now because it frightens the birds in their sanctuary out of their wits in Verulamium Park here in St Albans.

Enough of that. An incident took place at a school, in the heart of the area lived in by the Kikuyu. A group of young teachers decided one Guy Fawkes' Night to let off some fireworks, unannounced. They waited until dark, when the students were busy doing their homework, and then released the salvo of rockets and firecrackers. The effect was devastating. Many of the boys had had recent experience of armed assaults on their homes and villages. On hearing the explosions, they panicked. They poured out of the doors and through the classroom windows, running wildly in all directions. Some disappeared completely for several days, and could only be persuaded that it was safe to return with the greatest difficulty. The matter came to the attention of the local police. In due course, each teacher was summoned, individually, to the headmaster's office, where a police superintendent gave them a caution. Looking back, they were lucky, not to have been deported. Instead, each one was given a rocket. (AC)

The Lock

People reacted in different ways to the waves of school strikes in the nineteen sixties. I know of one headmaster who hid in a bed in the girls' quarters and eventually escaped through a back window in their dormitory and made for the Congo border. Not to be left out, there was even a riot at Namilyango. The students started breaking the windows. Don't ask me why. It was complicated. I wrote a dissertation on it, *Twenty Reasons,* fifty years ago. A friend of mine, who now lives near Cork, was one of the few teachers left on the campus. The others had gone somewhere for some reason, on a spiritual retreat, perhaps. He rushed to the headmaster's house. The head was an old Dutch priest called Father Kuipers.

"They are breaking the windows!" my friend gasped. The priest was in the middle of trying to mend the lock on his door.

"Don't bother me now," he said, exasperated. "Can't you see that I am busy."

My friend said "Fine" and drove away, retreating to the safety of the City Bar in Kampala fifteen miles away. (NH)

The Bullet Car

Phil was a bit of a character. He came from a village near Bedford. His father was a top consultant in the School of Hygiene and Tropical Medicine in London. Phil had opted out young. He had passed his A levels at an early age but was told by Bristol University that he was too young to join them. He found middle-class England too ordered. He tried to find what he called a primitive life-style in the Middle East and North Africa. Both ventures had proved to be disasters. He became highly unconventional.

Jean-Pierre Bosco, whose parents were from that area around Kisenyi and Goma that straddles the Rwanda-Congo border, taught French at the same school. It was called The Life of Jesus Grammar School and was situated inside the Luweero Triangle where the war against Amin would eventually to be launched. Jean-Pierre also prided himself on being unconventional but he envied what he saw as Phil's more extreme unconventionality. "If only I could be more like Phil!" he would sigh.

Phil had bought the King of Rwanda's car. He had beaten it into the shape of a bullet. He christened it 'The Bullet Car'. Jean dreamt of driving it around Kampala. It became an obsession. Oh, how he envied Phil!

When Phil first heard about the car, he knew that he had to buy it. He had envied his father's Jaguar. The thought of his dad cruising down the M1 motorway in it each day, from his mansion near Silsoe down to Malet Street in London, even now stuck in Phil's craw.

A friend rang to say that had seen a beautiful old car on a piece of wasteland next to a palm tree garage-cum-dump on the outskirts of Kampala. It took a long time for Phil to locate the owner but eventually he found him. He was a diplomat, somewhere between forty and fifty, rather overweight and with an unhealthily pale complexion. He told Phil that he and some fellow Belgians had escaped from Rwanda in the vehicle and that it had been one of the former King of Rwanda's fleet of state cars. It was a grey Jaguar Mk 5 coupé, 4.2 litres, with a podium behind the front seat for the king to stand on whenever he wanted to wave at his subjects.

Jean-Pierre envied Phil but he never showed it. He always managed to conceal his envy from Phil who, he felt, had had a better start in life. Above all, he envied Phil's car. One day, Phil had to go back to England for a few days for a family funeral. Jean-Pierre saw his opportunity. At last he could fulfil his dream of driving the King of Rwanda's car around Kampala.

The car had no papers. Phil had used it for a year with false number plates and a forged window sticker. The new government had started enforcing 'The Dangerous Mechanical Condition' law. If Phil had been caught, he would have lost his licence and the car. These would only be returned after an inspection. Jean-Pierre didn't know any of this. He didn't even have a licence. The steering was dangerously worn. There was about three quarters of a turn of slack on the steering wheel and it had no insurance. There would have been serious consequences, if the police had stopped Jean-Pierre.

All of this coincided with a visit to Uganda by a member of the British royal family.

Jean-Pierre drove down the murram road away from the school. He felt that the banana trees were waving ecstatically at him as he sped past.

In Kampala he saw a friend, Henry Lubanga. They started to drive around the city but found that many of the streets had been closed off so that the visiting royal party could be driven straight to the former Governor's house on Nakasero. While they were driving around, trying to get somewhere, a police roadblock mistook the car for the royal conveyance and waved them onto the royal route! So Jean-Pierre drove along the crowd-lined route, wrestling with the wheel, while thousands of people cheered and waved flags. His friend Lubanga climbed up onto the podium in the back. As they approached Makerere University College, Lubanga, bare-chested, waved at the awe-struck crowds who waved back confused. They were expecting Princess Margaret.

Feeling ecstatic, Jean-Pierre decided that it was time to head back. Henry Lubanga got out. Jean-Pierre looked for a back road that would take him back to Luweero. He did not know that there was a problem with one of the carburettors (the car had three).The faulty one started spraying gallons of petrol on to the side of the engine and all around under the bonnet. The engine became slightly sluggish. He could hear the fuel pump on the petrol tank ticking fast. He didn't know that, normally, Phil would stop the car and tap the carburettor in a particular way in order to fix it.

As it careered back down the red murram road, with a surface ridged like corrugated iron that felt like it had been strewn with ball bearings, the car's engine burst into flames, scorching the banana trees on either side of the road. The car carried on hurtling along in a ball of flames, filling the air with thick black smoke until, finally, it crashed into a tree.

Jean-Pierre was already dead when the villagers arrived at the scene. It was said that he would have been blinded, immediately, before dying.

Seigneur Hugh de Gournai

I had just arrived in Kampala. The journey from Mombasa to Kampala by train had been long and eventful. My grant to cover my needs as a student at Makerere would be arriving at the end of the month. This was awkward because I had spent all I had on the Rhodesia Castle, the ship that had brought us from London Docks to Mombasa. The lobster had been free and we had had it every day but the bar bills had mounted up. I am not proud of this fact now, nor was I then and I knew that the manager of Barclays Bank would certainly not accept it readily as an excuse.

Needs must. I plucked up courage and went into the bank. Barclays Bank is an imposing edifice on the corner of Kampala Road and Entebbe Road. It was possibly the most beautiful bank in the street: perfect symmetry, cool white walls, a flattish almost Greco-Roman style roof, a majestic balcony fit for a Latin American president to deliver speeches from, three central archways, the central one of which was the main entrance. I suppose you could call the style 'colonial'. It always reminds me a little of the American campus-inspired university building of Deusto in Bilbao.

It was impressive. It was meant to be. It was saying, "We shall be here for a very long time, possibly a thousand years". It impressed me as I made my way up its steps into its dark interior. Today there is a large notice that tells you, reassuringly: 'This is a weapon-free area. Please hand your weapon to the guard at the entrance'. Back then, in September 1964, it was an oasis of peace.

Putting on a brave face, I went up to the counter. An aloof-looking clerk saw me waiting and made me wait even longer. He eventually strolled nonchalantly over and said, rather curtly: "Ye-e-e s?" He sounded bored.

"Can you lend me some money?" I blurted out.

"I beg your pardon?" he asked incredulously.

"Can you lend me some money?" I repeated, emphasising the final word but trying not to sound too impatient.

He looked me up and down, as if examining something the dog had just brought in. In a way not untypical of the young – in those days my diplomatic skills were a little unpolished - I said, rather aggressively: "Can you lend me some money? You are a bank, aren't you?" My reply clearly horrified him. He took a step backwards.

"I need one thousand shillings". He was speechless.

"One thousand shillings! What's your name?" he asked with a sneer. I felt that he was reaching for something to write on. This is going from bad to worse, I reflected.

"Gurney," I called out loudly. I heard my voice echoing around the hall. Well, I wasn't ashamed of it. People have often looked surprised when I give it. It sounds slightly amusing in English. "You mean like the gurney they put you on in hospitals in America?" is the usual question, among others.

He took another step backwards. He looked totally horrified now. I noticed that beads of sweat were forming on his forehead. I put it down to the emotion of horror that he was experiencing but then I noticed a change in his demeanour. It didn't happen immediately. The drops of perspiration began to slither down his face. I noticed a flicker of what looked like a nervous but friendly smile around one corner of his mouth. He took one step towards me, then another.

"Not one of THE Gurneys?" he whispered. I swear I saw his hand go involuntarily towards his wallet.

I had to think quickly. What on earth was he talking about, THE Gurneys? My response was immediate. I have always been able to spot a good thing when I see it. I felt that I was on to something. Call it the survival instinct, if you wish. Biologists call it 'opportunism', a term used, by them, in a non-judgemental way.

"Of course," I responded confidently.

His hand began to shake. I could see that he was reaching out to me as if to shake my hand but the glass was in the way.

"How-how, how much did you say you want?" he asked meekly, attempting a forced smile, displaying his neat teeth.

"What's your name?" I asked, getting the hang of things a little, going along with a situation I didn't fully understand. I moved my hand to an inside pocket, reaching for a small black diary I kept there. The tables were turned.

"B-B Bellamy," he stammered. I pretended to write his name down.

"That will be one thousand shillings, then," I repeated imperiously.

For a moment I thought that he was going to take the notes out of his own wallet. He reached into a drawer.

"One hundred, two hundred … ." He carried on until he reached one thousand.

"Thank you, Bellamy," I said curtly. I was tempted to add "my man" but I didn't. I turned and left the bank in a dignified manner and with a new spring in my step.

Outside a feeling of total bewilderment came over me. What on earth had all that been about? It so happened that I was due to go training down at Kampala Rugby Club that afternoon. As soon as I entered the bar, I saw Fred who worked as a clerk in what was called then National and Grindlays Bank.

"FRED," I shouted, "I have just had the strangest experience!" I related the whole sequence of events: the scorn, the metamorphosis, the servility, the beads of sweat, the effect the word 'Gurney' had had, working like the 'Open Sesame', the 'iftah ya simsim' magical phrase in the tale of Ali Baba, which opens the mouth of the cave in which forty thieves had hidden their stolen treasure.

"My God, don't you know?" he spluttered in amazement.

"Know what?" I asked completely baffled. The following words came like a bombshell.

"The Gurneys founded Barclays Bank and I think, I need to check, that the words 'Gurney's Bank' appeared at one point on Bank of America cheques or notes". You could have knocked me down with a feather. I felt faint.

"You look as if you need a drink', he said, always willing to undermine my efforts to keep fit. He didn't play rugby. He was only there for the beer and the company.

"Oh, go on then," I said, without a protest. I needed something to settle my nerves.

He went on to tell me the most strange things. There was, he said, a Norman knight called Hugh de Gournai who fought well at the Battle of Hastings in 1066 and was given Norfolk as a reward by William the Conqueror.

"What! Norfolk?" I gasped.

"Yes," he confirmed, "and some say – I don't know if it is true - that William threw in South Bedfordshire as a bonus. With the rich Norfolk soil and more than one harvest a year they, the Gurneys, became wealthy farmers who amassed capital but didn't know what do with it. Christianity forbade usury. Lending money and charging interest was a sin. Eventually they, the Gurneys, the Barclays and some others, the Lloyds perhaps, met in a pub in Norwich and decided to break the taboo surrounding lending. By the way," he added, "that's one theory about how capitalism started, the Normans and their law of primogeniture, which meant that all the money ended up in the hands of the eldest son. Pockets of capital accumulated all over the place. The bank, by the way, had started in a basement. The money was kept in a large chest guarded by a man with a shot gun and a dog. Er, not sure about the dog." He went on and on. It was all incredibly interesting but I had already got the picture. The next day saw me striding swiftly back up the majestic steps of the bank. I made a bee-line for Bellamy.

"Bellamy," I called out, "another thousand shillings!" I nearly clicked my fingers but I thought that that would be taking things a bit too far.

He stared at me with a look of total disgust, turned on his heel and walked away. He had obviously made a phone call!

From that moment on I cashed my cheques with Babu, at The City Bar.

Later I heard that Idi Amin had gone into a bank with a bar of gold marked 'Gouvernement du Congo' and that a clerk had given him far more than a thousand shillings for it in exchange. Well, Amin had more clout than me. I am not sure if the clerk was my friend Bellamy but I like to think it was he.

Henry

Henry was a cheerful sort of bloke. He always served you your beer with a smile and a joke. He was the club barman of Mbarara Rugby Club in the nineteen-sixties. Henry didn't played rugby. He was always there, though, behind the bar at the end of training with his reassuring presence, getting the glasses ready, changing the barrels. Later Henry tried his hand at playing, very unsuccessfully. He was not the greatest physical specimen, very uncoordinated, not at all sporty. He committed the fatal mistake, when he was on leave in the UK, of charming a girl with his hogwash about his alpha male life in Uganda. He told her he was the powerhouse in the best rugby scrum in Uganda. He told her he was unstoppable when he had the ball. He said that he could fell the fastest three quarter. He said that he was the lynchpin of the team, lock, number eight. With his incredible strength and muscle Mbarara won every ruck. His girl-friend was deeply impressed. Henry, in her eyes, was the perfect man to father her children. They got engaged.

Henry returned to Uganda ahead of his fiancée and then, realising what he had done, desperately tried to get fit and learn the rules of the game. He picked her up at Entebbe airport on the very day of a crunch match against Jinja. Jinja had started recruiting massive soldiers from the barracks in the town. One was called Idi Amin. Henry had told Jill that Amin came down like a sack of potatoes as a result of his perfect tackles. Sadly, Henry was seen to be hopeless and had to admit to his deceit on the very day that she arrived. She actually saw his body being trodden into the mud, as if he had been trampled by a herd of stampeding hippos. It was not really the best way to start a marriage. (DAS)

The Lazy Man

I may have given you the wrong impression about my social life in Uganda. I may have led you to believe that I spent all my time in a bar.

Let me explain. There were several choices. There was the Kampala Club which was fiendishly expensive. There was Okello's Bar which was a bit of a spit and sawdust place. There was the Rugby Club which was often empty during much of the day. There was the Makerere University Club which could be rather cliquey. And there was the City Bar. Now, it was, in some ways, more of a club but without a joining fee. You could play billiards, for example, and have a good meal. For me it was the easiest option.

I have never had a curry since that was better than that served by Babu in the City Bar Restaurant. The side dishes, for a start, were out of this world, a meal in themselves: pineapple, coconut, tomatoes, cucumber, relish, banana, sultanas, paw-paw, peppers, the list went on and on. I understand that the cuisine was basically Gujarati and had evolved into something more local. I didn't need to go any further.

That wasn't the best. It was the place which really interesting people made for when they arrived in the city. It was fascinating just to sit there, without stirring, in the city centre, lie back and bask in the stories that flooded in. There was no need to go outside the municipal boundary. The world came to you. It suited my lazy personality down to the ground. The sun shone down, flooding my lazy body with its heat.

Colin came in, covered in dust. He dusted himself down and ordered an ice-cold Bell, the local lager.

"I have a friend," he began, "quite a bit older than me, who owns a cattle ranch north-west of Nanyuki in Kenya. It's the second last farm before it becomes scrub and the road ends." He took a deep sip of his lager.

"It's practically desert," he went on, "and they reckon on ten to fifteen acres per cow. I believe this farm is 5000 acres." He ordered another beer.

"He has a couple of hundred cows," he said with an "Ah!" wiping his top lip with the sleeve of his safari jacket, "and goats and a couple of camels to fetch water from the river nearby. His wife is a charming local lady and he has five gorgeous copper-coloured daughters in their teens. He's an Australian who has been all over the world. He even worked for a year or two on the Alaska Highway in the 1940s. There are bomas made of thorn bushes dotted around the farm so that they can corral the cattle overnight to keep them safe from the lions of which there are a lot in the area."

This is the life, I thought. I can stay here for ever listening to these tales, without moving a muscle. I stretched my legs out.

"Whenever the farm workers report lions in the area," he continued, "he takes his rifle and goes and sleeps out at the boma. It seems to me that this is more often than not and when I visit, I sleep somewhat nervously in a tent next to his battered old Land Rover hearing grunts and roars that sound a bit close for comfort."

I snuggled deeper into my chair, the one from which I would watch the world going by without raising a finger. I was enjoying the story.

"One morning the workers," he went on, "reported that some thieves had stolen a dozen goats. One of his workers is an incredible tracker and we grabbed him and a few other workers, the guns and the Land Rover and the tracker had no trouble finding their tracks. We started around eight in the morning and with all of us crammed into the Land Rover, we followed the tracker who was going at a steady jog, except for an occasional pause, as he cast around when the track got confused - never more than a couple of minutes - and off we set again."

This is the life, I felt. I can let others do my living. All I have to do is sit here and listen.

"A lot of the ground was very rocky and there were no hoof prints but it never seemed to cause him any problem - he would see a bit of bent grass or a leaf torn off a bush and off we would go again."

He paused. I ordered my new friend a third Bell and a cappuccino for myself. The heat was making me sleepy.

"It took us about five hours," he continued, "but we caught up with them. As soon as they saw us, they ran off into the bush, leaving the goats behind. For good measure he fired a couple of shots over their heads, handed the gun to me and told me to have a go. It was the first time I had ever fired a rifle, in fact, and I had a bit of a bruise afterwards to prove it."

I felt myself suppressing a yawn. I wasn't bored. It was the midday sun. I felt exhausted just imagining the scene.

"We rounded up the goats," he said, "had a makeshift lunch and returned home, leaving the workers to bring back the livestock. All in a day's work for him but an adventure for me," he concluded.

I felt I had just watched a film with a script by Rider Haggard. I felt I was in one of the best seats, the most comfortable one. No need, I thought, to venture out far. There's too much going on out there. He excused himself and went to the 'bathroom'. The next thing I knew, Babu, the bar owner, was tugging at my sleeve.

"Sir, sir, do you want supper?" My friend had gone. It was bed-time.

Charlie

It's strange how our paths can cross in life. Charlie Barton and I were good friends forty years ago in Kampala. We played rugby together. We then went our different ways. I ended up lecturing in London, he ended up farming in Australia. Walking up the narrow road that winds its way up through the village of Port Eynon in Wales I saw a tall figure come striding towards me.

"Charlie? I called out.

"Bob?" he replied.

He told me to my amazement that he had grown up in the very village where my wife and I were living. Years later I saw his name on the internet and decided to get in touch. He told me he had bought a 'toy' farm of two hundred and thirty three acres outside Canberra where he grows weeds and wombats. And today he told me that he had just been back to Nakuru to the school where he once taught. He told me that they keep a herd of cows on the playing fields and convert the cowpats into biogas for cooking in the kitchens. He never seems to change. His sense of humour is still the same. None of us has grown up yet, he says, but there is still time. (CB)

Kay

I had a soft spot for Kay. I don't know why. There was something appealing about her seriousness, her earnestness. She was one of the young women on the boat out. She could be terribly intense, off-puttingly so, at times. The last time I recall having seen her was when we bumped into each other was in the street in Kampala. Red-faced and agitated, she was groaning, "Expired, expired!" She seemed to be involved in a dramatic monologue and was waving an object in the air. The unselfconscious performance was reminiscent of the best of Shakespeare, Harold Pinter or Eugen Ionescu.

"Who has expired?" I asked.
"Not who, what," she gasped, as if struggling to breathe. "My passport has expired."

I have often wondered what happened to Kay. I had expected at any moment to hear that she had flown back to England. She was a bit like many of us, a fish out of water. Was it that that drew me to her? There was something attractive about her, something sensual. Her facial bone structure was eye-catching, if only she hadn't worn those off-putting horn-rimmed glasses. I suppose they were a form of defence. I often asked myself why I didn't become a close friend. I felt she wouldn't have said no. She seemed quite lonely. She had more substance than the women I was drawn to then. She disappeared into the outback of East Africa and no one ever saw her again. I have often wondered if she got married.

The Spider Man

I was telling some friends, who come from West Africa, about an experience I had late one night in Gulu, in the north of Uganda. I had misjudged the distance, I didn't get there till late. It was dark, I was shattered from the driving. I arrived at his house which was in the middle of nowhere. I was too exhausted to eat, too tired for a pint. He showed me to my room. When he opened the door, I felt it had not been used. The air was warm and stale. He pointed to my bed and wished me a goodnight's rest. I approached the bed, which looked well made up, only to be greeted by an astonishing sight. As I sat on the edge to remove my shoes and socks, I found myself surrounded by an incredible performance. The room was the home of an extended family of large jumping spiders. Up and down they went, as if on strings, reaching four or five feet. It was like a ballet. From where I was sitting, on the edge of the bed, some seemed to rise even higher. I began to have the feeling that they were protesting at being disturbed. Or was it that they were just pleased to see someone from Kampala? I was too tired to bother about them, fell back on the bed and went out like a light.

"Did it happen to you, in real life, or did you see it on TV?" asked Lewis from Ghana who likes Robert Mugabe. He's a very nice chap but he can be slightly annoying.

The Greedy Academic

I first met Jones on the ship that was taking us out to East Africa, the Rhodesia Castle. He had put a notice on his door: "Dr Lawrence Jones, professor of English, Makerere University College, Kampala'. He was neither a PhD nor a professor. He had done it, he told me, to ensure a) that he had a cabin to himself and b) that he received good room service. He gradually became an authority on the literature of Francophone Africa. He had slipped out of Uganda in 1971 when Amin rose to power. I heard that he was writing a book about Lord Lucan in West Africa.

He had had a deprived upbringing. His father, a miner, had even taught him how to straighten bent nails rather than throw them away. This deprivation had led, in him, to a curious form of greed. This greed expressed itself in a strange way. Whenever he spotted a potentially rich seam of academic research, he was drawn to it like a glutton to a Big Mac. Nothing gave him greater satisfaction than seeing rows of offprints of his articles on his shelf. Row after row of them met his eyes whenever he entered his office. His mouth would fill with saliva at the sight. Words cannot describe the ecstasy he felt when he spotted a mouth-watering banquet: the literature of Equatorial Guinea.

His intellectual greed had a distorting effect on his whole demeanour. It so consumed him that he lost the ability to see himself clearly. He had become unable to see how others saw him. Greed was turning him into a grotesque. He was not English but over the years he had ironed out his Welsh accent and become, in his eyes, an English gentleman, but, in the eyes of others, 'a cocky bastard'. This was the general view of him in London.

Prior to the interview he had circulated, throughout the Waterford campus, a list of his most important publications:

Articles

"María Nsue Angüe's *Ekomo*, a Critique of the Patriarchal World of Postcolonial Africa"

"Suffering and Silence in Ciriako Bokesa's 'poemario' *Foam Voices*"

"Juan Balbao Boneke and Suffering in his anthology of poems *Dreams in my Jungle*"

"Donato Ndongo-Bidyogo's Ironic Vision in *Shadows of Your Black Memory*"

"Raquel del Pozo Epita and The Search for Identity in *Ceiba*, 1966-1978"

"Narratives of Exile in the work of Donato Ndongo-Bidyongo and Francisco Zamora Loboch"

"The Violence of Spatial and Spiritual Displacement in Francisco Zamora Loboch's *Bea*"

"Homesickness in Juan Balbao Boneke's poem 'Where are you Guinea'?"

"Bubí Customs in Daniel Jones Mathama's novel *A Spear for the Baobi* (Barcelona, 1962)"

"Post-Colonial Poetry in the Fang-Ntumu, Fang-Okah and Spanish Languages in Guinea Ecuatorial"

Books

Unknown Spanish Writers of Sub-Saharan Africa

Equatoguinean Writers, An Anthology (in press)

He got the Waterford job. Many thought that he wouldn't. He presented as such an arrogant person that they thought the Irish might baulk at appointing him. He came across as a caricature of an Englishman, an increasingly rare type these days, thank goodness. The Vice-Chancellor had been a missionary in the very country that he, Jones, was researching. That was the clincher. The VC was dazzled by the list and just ignored the dreadful persona.

Some years later I bumped into Lawrence Jones in Malet Street in London. He looked down in the dumps, crest-fallen, in fact. "How did it go?" I asked. I knew that within five minutes his strutting cockiness would have proved his undoing. He told me that it had been a disaster. 'English get out' threats were slipped under the door of his office. He had sent his wife and children back to England while he soldiered on for a while. Eventually he realised that the time was approaching when he had to throw in the towel. He put in his resignation. They just didn't like him. Even the Vice-Chancellor had turned against him.

"What now?" I asked. His eyes lit up. A bead of saliva appeared in the corner of his mouth.

"I am off to Melilla and Ceuta," he announced, his old swagger returning. He had, he told me, landed a huge grant from a wealthy Gulf state to study the literature of Islamic commitment in Spanish enclaves in North Africa.

The Praying Mantis

We were in an art gallery in London, standing in front of M. C. Escher's 'Dream', staring at the praying mantis.

"In Uganda I always found them creepy," I commented. My friend wanted to talk.

"I had several praying mantises in Uganda and Hong Kong," he began. "With huge eyes situated on its triangular head, the mantis has superb vision. To add to your impression of 'creepiness', if you first gained their attention with a finger moved across their vision, the head would gradually turn and follow the movement of your finger. One could almost believe, at that point, that there was a reasoning being behind that mechanical exterior. Each eye is composed of several thousand individual facets, each acting as a separate eye, so that the vision comprises myriad images, each slightly different from each other and giving depth. Their absolute immobility when stalking prey gives a mantis camouflage whilst the moving prey drifting across their vision is highlighted as a progressive three-dimensional image so that the final lunge is unerring, trapping the victim in those huge spiny front limbs. If the prey has any feelings whatsoever, spare a thought as the mantis mechanically and unemotionally chomps into its body, held totally immobile. I loved to watch them feed on locusts in the Kibuli laboratory." He paused then went on.

"One alarming fact is that the male mantis approaches the female - normally twice or more in size - with great care and caution. And well he might as, in a final gesture, the female eventually allows copulation and then promptly devours him. A perfect analogy to humans, from my experience."

"Yes, I am sorry about that," I replied. He looked sad. I knew who he was thinking about. I didn't like to ask him about her. I had always wanted to ask him about the Lebanon he knew where he had met her but it was a no-go area.

"Let's look at this picture here," I added, trying to change the subject. "It shows a bishop or an abbot wearing a mitre, stretched out on a catafalque. Is he dead? Is he praying? One only lies on a catafalque during, before or after a funeral. His hands are folded like those of a corpse. His eyes are closed. He could be sleeping. The drawing in black and white gives him an ashen, lifeless pallor."

My friend drew nearer to the picture.

"The buildings around the body and the mantis," I went on, "seem to be coming apart. The bishop's world and his power are disappearing. The mystery of the dark universe beyond the bishop's palace that seems to be floating in space is beckoning."

My friend was now peering closely at the details.

"What is it about the praying mantises?" I continued. "Why have they always fascinated me? "I sometimes thought it was the name itself that intrigued me. Is it spelt 'praying' with an a or 'preying', with an e? Why juxtapose a bishop with an insect? Is the insect about to make love? Escher certainly seems to be playing with the pun 'praying and preying'. Its claws are raised in prayer. They also seem to be on the point of devouring the body on which it is kneeling."

"Are preying and praying a pun in Dutch?" he asked?

"I don't know," I replied."I don't think so."

"The details are very precise," my friend whispered. There was no one else left in the gallery.

"Is he saying," I asked, "that bishops who prey on the souls of the faithful are on the way out, no longer relevant? Is the drawing anti-clerical? That thought too makes me uneasy."

"The creature's taxonomic name, *Mantis religiosa*, means 'religious mantis'," my friend volunteered.

"Ah," I added, "Escher is linking the two, the bishop and the insect, via a pun. *Catafalco* in Italian means scaffolding as well as catafalque. The scaffolding that supports the cleric is disintegrating. I'm beginning to get it."

"In Spanish *catafalco*," my friend said, "can mean a cenotaph."

How did he know that? I remembered he had once lived in Mallorca.

"How can the mantis eat a man of stone?" I asked. There was no reply.

Digging deeper, he replied, "Mantids belong to the insect order Mantodea and Mantodea comes from the Greek word μάντις (pronounced mantis) meaning prophet. Escher's mantis is not dead but the bishop looks it. The insect's look is triumphal. It has won."

"Good point," I agreed. The end of religious prophecies about the future?

"Could be," he nodded.

Then I said, as if having a revelation, "But it's called 'The Dream'! The picture isn't real. The death isn't real. The mantis is only alive in a dream. What does the dream mean? Are the various levels of meaning we have detected its overall meaning?"

"It isn't a dream," he replied. "It's just called that. Dream is used here as a device to explore some ideas."

"Is Escher depicting a dream he had or is he asking us to ask if the bishop is dreaming about the mantis?" I asked. We were tying ourselves in knots. Perhaps that was Escher's intention.

"The mantis looks triumphant," I observed. "Is this picture a reference to destructive sexuality?"

"When was it done?" my friend asked.

"It says 1935," I replied.

"A troubled time," he reflected. The insect looks like a giant alien from the black outer space in the background of the picture. Hitler and Stalin were on the move destroying old certainties. Holland, the artist's country, would soon be invaded.

"The church used to use insects in exorcisms in the Middle Ages," I said. "In Bushman mythology, the mantis is an important god of creation, Kaggen". I was casting around for something to get hold of.

His final comments astonished me. "I think,' he said, "that you have to go to the work of Chuang Tzu. He dreamt he was a butterfly flying freely in the air. In the dream he has no idea that he is Chuang Tzu. Did the butterfly ask existential questions? Just by asking such questions in this way Chuang Tzu experienced spiritual freedom."

"How did you know that?" I asked, trying not to sound surprised.

"I found a book on Chaung Tzu in a second hand bookshop in Hong Kong," he replied.

Night was falling as we made our way to the underground station. Stars were beginning to appear in the sky. (JW)

(http://www.wikipaintings.org/en/m-c-escher/dream)

The Green-Eyed Monster

> Iago: O, beware, my lord, of jealousy;
> It is the green-ey'd monster, which doth mock
> The meat it feeds on. That cuckold lives in bliss,
> Who, certain of his fate, loves not his wronger:
> But O, what damnèd minutes tells he o'er
> Who dotes, yet doubts, suspects, yet strongly loves!
> Othello: O misery!
>
> (*Othello Act 3, scene 3, 165–171*)

Mukasa and Okot were the greatest of friends. They and their band of fellow Makerere academics went everywhere together. When they were students you would often see them together with pretty girls on their arms in the New Life Club. They practically had their own special seats in the City Bar. The barman in the Gardenia even kept special beer mugs for them inscribed with their names. If you couldn't find Mukasa and Okot in one of those three places, you would definitely find them in Okello's Bar, or in the International Bar or Susanna.

And that's how it was, until one day Mukasa had to go to England to do some qualification or other. While he was away Okot applied for and got a job in the English Department at Makerere. English was on the up. Students could see that it was the key to a prosperous future. It was English with everything: English with Economics, English with Business Studies, English with Politics, etc.

Everything was going smoothly. Okot was building up a team. He needed someone to co-ordinate a new idea of his, French for Business. Uganda had French-speaking neighbours to the south, west and north, Burundi, Rwanda, Zaire, Chad and so on. The trade possibilities were enormous. Margaret turned up. She was from the Central African Republic. She was a 'stunner' but, somehow, Okot didn't fancy her. She seemed to him to be a bit too free and easy with her favours. Anyway, he was married, although, if the truth were known, things weren't going too well for him on that front. His marriage was rocky. His wife seemed to be getting on a bit too well with too many ministers. The one in Fisheries worried Okot in particular.

To cut a long story short, Margaret and Okot shared an office on the Kampala campus. A sign saying 'Languages for Business' adorned their door. He liked the arrangement because he could practise his French with her and she liked it because she could work on her English. She found Okot attractive into the bargain. They alternated between English and French. Okot's English was cut-glass perfect. A product of Budo school, he spoke English better than the average Englishman. He wasn't too keen, to put it mildly, on Margaret's sexual arrangements, as has already been said, but, then, who was he to talk? "Let he who is without sin cast the first stone," he used to say to himself, whenever he saw her dropping off a student in the city.

Mukasa came back after a stint at Goldsmiths. It was clear to Okot that his friend was at a loose end. He kept applying for jobs in the world of Uganda's media but there still weren't many of those going. He was hopeful of getting into Uganda Educational TV or on to the *Uganda Argos* but nothing was happening. *Munno* wrote saying they were interested in his CV but he hadn't told them he was an Anglican and he was nervous they would find out.

"He needs some female company," Okot decided. He introduced Mukasa to Margaret. That's when it all began. Things went well to start with but then Mukasa had to go back to London for a viva voce exam. He seemed to be away for quite a long time. The message came back that he had had to rewrite part of his thesis on documentaries and that he would be delayed.

Okot felt sorry for Margaret. He could see she was missing Mukasa's company. He knew, too, she was homesick for her country. He began to ask her out, not on a one-to-one basis, but with the rest of the Makerere group. He was not really aware of it but it seems that Margaret was beginning to fix him in her cross hairs. Nothing happened but in her imagination she had rehearsed things so well that she began to imagine that something really had happened.

Mukasa came back from London. The date of the wedding was fixed. Okot, it has to be said, was, in one way, horrified. He had never planned or expected Mukasa and Margaret's relationship to go this far. He had only been trying to help a friend with some 'R and R', to provide him with a bit of fun, in his hour of need. It hadn't dawned on him that Mukasa might fall head over heels in love with Margaret.

The wedding took place in Bangui, in the Central African Republic. Okot was not invited, which he felt was odd but he was so busy at the time with marking that he didn't make a fuss. The CAR felt like a bit of a trek. He was also slightly relieved because he felt guilty at what he had done, bringing this unlikely pair together. He calmed any other fears he might have had by noting that no one else he knew had been invited either. If they had, he was not aware of it.

He then began to suspect that Mukasa was ignoring him. Worse than that, it felt that he was giving him the cold shoulder. The feeling became a conviction that Mukasa was actually sending him to Coventry. He wondered what he had done to offend them. He realised he had not sent a present but, then, he hadn't been invited and Mukasa had often said he wasn't into 'bourgeois' things. All communications ceased. In one way Okot couldn't be bothered. The rift was partly obscured by the fact that he himself was heading for a divorce. His mind was elsewhere. His Acholi wife, Helen, was beginning to attend international conferences in her new job in the Tourism Department. There were rumours that she was seeing too much of her head of department. This didn't worry Okot overmuch because he was also absorbed with another woman whom he was soon to marry.

One day it became blindingly obvious that something was really wrong between him and Mukasa. It was totally out of character for Mukasa to stay silent for so long. Mukasa could not, by any stretch of the imagination, have been described as a shrinking violet. Far from it. Okot began to get annoyed. Why hadn't Mukasa told him what was wrong between them? Annoyance started to morph into a simmering resentment. Slowly, he felt the hot magma of anger rising within him. It lay there bubbling in his stomach. He managed, though, to repress it. He was an academic, he said to himself. Academics have to control violent emotion. They have to be calm role models for their students.

Some years later, he and his new wife Cécile, from Zaire, were playing with their two boys on Kololo Airstrip with the remote controlled Beach Buggies they had bought their sons for Christmas. The children were ecstatic as they raced their cars round and round on the tarmac.

Okot suddenly saw Margaret walking purposefully towards them. His heart sank. To his surprise, she said she had come to say sorry for what she had done. I say 'surprise' but somehow Okot had been half-expecting this moment. After all, he and Margaret had been close colleagues. She had been one of the 'gang'. They had confided in each other, a thing which Okot had found slightly embarrassing when Margaret had got on to certain topics. In a strange sort of way their past friendship, and the intimacy induced by sharing an office, had acquired some of the characteristics of love. He knew, deep within him, as did she, that it could easily have tipped over into something physical. Hadn't he, after all, appointed her for her looks? He had resisted temptation out of loyalty to his friend Mukasa but he had had to admit to himself that, on the odd occasion, that noble sentiment had been in danger of evaporating, especially during Mukasa's long absence in south-east London.

"What have you done?" he asked, pretending to be puzzled. Deep down he knew vaguely what it was about, even though he had never really allowed the thought to rise completely to the surface and he didn't know how far she had gone.

"Something terrible, she replied. "something really, really terrible."

"I am sure we all have," said Okot, trying to defuse the situation. There was an awkward silence.

"Well, what is it? Spit it out!" Okot said quietly, trying to smile. He felt, briefly, like her boss again. He was hoping for some sort of explanation of why his friend Mukasa was blanking him, even though he knew why, without being able to put words to it.

"I can't tell you," she said. "I can't tell you but I am really, really sorry."

"About what?" he repeated, trying to sound mystified.

"I just can't tell you," she replied.

"Is it about a lie you have told?" he asked. She didn't answer. He knew that it was. She didn't have to tell him.

"Come and have a cup of coffee," said Okot's wife Jenny in a kind, motherly voice, gathering the children protectively into her flowing dress. "We are just over there." She pointed at their house.

"I know," said Margaret. "I have often driven past, trying to summon up the courage to drop in and apologise but no, no, I can't. I just can't. I can't come in. I have to go," she said and she walked away. Okot looked at his wife and shrugged his shoulders. It was time to feed the children. It was getting late. There was a growing chill in the air. Cécile didn't badger him for an explanation. She knew. She even felt almost charitable towards Margaret. Margaret had done her a favour. She had never really met Mukasa properly but from what she had seen of him and heard, he could be overbearing. She was secretly glad her husband was no longer friends with Mukasa.

A little while later Okot realised that something strange was happening. One by one his friends stopped ringing. Nobody called in any more at the campus office. He decided to take the bull by the horns and ask Kiwanuka, with whom he was still in touch, what it was about. Only Kiwanuka, he perceived, had stayed faithful to him. Kiwanuka spilled the beans.

"She told her husband that you forced yourself on her while he was in London," he blurted out.

"What? *Forced* myself?" Okot shouted. It was not clear to Kiwanuka what Okot meant by repeating the phrase in that way but he had a shrewd idea.

"You know, that you pulled rank to, you know, to have your way with her," Kiwanuka whispered.

Okot burst out laughing. Kiwanuka did too. They both knew why they were laughing.

"You are *joking*, aren't you?" Okot said.

"I know, I know, it's ridiculous," laughed Kiwanuka nervously. "You wouldn't have touched her with a barge pole. I remember you saying that, after a few glasses, at one of the Vice-Chancellor's parties. Okot didn't like being reminded of that comment. He stayed silent.

"Why did she *say* that?" he asked Kiwanuka with a tone of affected disbelief. "It seems, from what I have heard, that she was jealous of your friendship with her husband," Kiwanuka explained, "She wanted to drive a wedge between the two of you. It happens, you know. Didn't you notice?"

"Mm, well, she did stub out her cigarette once on the back of my hand," Okot answered, with a wry smile. He looked at the back of his hand for the scar. He felt strangely fond of it.

"Ah!" sighed Kiwanuka, with a sigh and a tight grin. "Yes, I remember that. It was done with a sort of a 'What are *you* doing here?' sort of look."

"Yes, I suppose so," Okot replied, feigning weariness. He could feel something stirring within him.

Kiwanuka decided to beat a retreat. He could read the signs. He could see that something was beginning to bubble up within his friend.

Later that day, what Kiwanuka had told him really began to hit home. The smouldering coals within him began to ignite. He began to see at long last the magnitude of what had been done to him, the sheer injustice of it all.

Over the next few days, his rage began to grow incrementally. It began to possess him like an evil spirit. At first it didn't seem to have a target. He could not work out if he was angrier with his friend or with his friend's wife. Slowly he began to realise that he was angry with them both. And it was he who had introduced them, he kept repeating to himself! His anger began to shift, away from Margaret, towards Mukasa. For some reason, he couldn't stay angry with her for long.

Meanwhile, at Uganda TV, where Mukasa was now working as a continuity assistant under Bob Astles, a process similar to sympathetic magic, or telepathy, began to take place. A similar emotion to that of his former friend was beginning to well up in Mukasa. Mukasa and Okot had often said, in the past, that they knew what the other was thinking, even from miles away.

Margaret had never actually told her husband that she had slept with his best friend. All she had really said was that Okot had 'tried it on once or twice'. It was not specific but she said it in a rather heavy, mysterious way, full of innuendo, that made Mukasa suspect that there was more to it than met the eye. It was more than a 'No smoke without fire' sort of feeling. He became convinced, within himself, and without mentioning it to Margaret, that his friend had done the dirty on him while he was away in London. He realised that he had not been a paragon of virtue himself while at Goldsmith's and had even had a brief fling with an Art and Design post-graduate English student but, somehow, in his mind, that didn't count.

Each one of the former friends began, at the same time, to plot his revenge.

Okot was enraged that his best friend could believe that he could do such a thing. Perhaps it might have been possible to do that with the wife of somebody who was not his best friend, an acquaintance who was estranged from his wife, for example, but with his best friend's wife, how could Mukasa entertain such an idea after all the confidences they had exchanged in the past?

Mukasa, on the other hand, began to feel more and more like Othello after Iago had poisoned his mind against his wife, Desdemona, except that in this case it was the wife herself who had aroused the green-eyed monster inside his head. She, for her part, perversely, experienced something akin to joy at the way she could fan the magma rising up her husband's gullet. It gave her a feeling of intoxicating power over him. He had always been too bossy with her anyway, always wanting to have the last word. Life with Mukasa had begun to feel like one long put-down. She had, at last, found a way of subverting and undermining his bossiness.

For Mukasa, it was as if the monster's tentacles were reaching down through his very nostrils and thrashing around on his face, like those of the live baby octopus he had been obliged to swallow whole, as an aphrodisiac, during a fateful meal with Chinese TV executives in Beijing. He felt the creature's imaginary arms were stopping him breathing. Honour had to be satisfied, he said to himself, but how? Jealousy was choking him. He felt its hands tightening around his windpipe.

Kondos, gangsters, were approached by one of Mukasa's friends at the White Nile Club, on the Entebbe Road. There were plenty of them around then. Various political parties' youth wings had been disbanded during the seismic shifts that had affected the country after the Nakulabye Incident of 1964 and The Buganda Crisis of 1966 when Obote unseated the Kabaka. The country was awash with arms. It was the year before Amin came to power and swept them all, in one fell and strangely well-informed swoop, into Lake Victoria. At that moment, in 1970, *kondos* were two a penny.

In the meantime, Okot was planning his revenge for the assassination attempt on his character. He was convinced Mukasa must have known that his wife had been lying and had decided to do nothing about it. She had a strange power over her husband, he thought. She was capable of causing him the greatest embarrassment. On one occasion she had thrown her plate, heaped with food, against the wall in the Imperial Hotel restaurant to underline her displeasure at one of his supercilious remarks. Secretly, for all his bravado, Mukasa was terrified of upsetting her. He couldn't bear the scenes, especially those that took place in public.

A friend of Okot, not Kiwanuka, who had sensed that something bad was about to happen and was lying low, approached an unsavoury character, a European, who worked in the Speke Hotel. Kondos were contacted, via a third party, at the Crested Crane. A contract was taken out on Mukasa.

Each group of gangsters had its precise instructions.

A week later a body was fished out of the water at Bugali Falls, down by the Owen Falls Dam at Jinja, by the prophet Jaja Bujabald. It had tape round its mouth. Its hands and feet were tied. It was Mukasa.

In the same week Okot's burnt out Toyota was found next to Rubaga Cathedral.

There was no sign of a body. To this day nobody has been able to find out what happened. Cécile, Okot's wife, noticed a big dent in their online current account that week.

What happened to the wives, you ask? Well, Margaret went back to Bangui. It is rumoured that she is well in with a big noise in the Ministry of Education and is in charge of English teaching in the capital city.

As for Cécile, the innocent party in this sorry tale, rumour has it that she is living in the capital of another African country in West Africa and that her sons are doing well at school. It is rumoured that Okot is with her, although nobody has been able to confirm this. It is said that he is working as an *assistant de langue anglaise* in a lycée in that city. Life is not easy for them but they are gradually getting things together.

Kabs

They say that the Kabalaga district in Kampala never sleeps now. I rarely go to the City Bar in the centre of the city. The traffic in the city centre is just too bad. My conversation in Punchline, near the Uchumi supermarket - the bar in 'Kabs' that I prefer to De Posh and Capital Pub because of its friendly beer prices - was proving soporific to my friends.

I was trying to work out if we had been 'trapped' in Uganda for the duration of our contracts, owing to the prohibitively high cost of flying. I just couldn't find out, I told them, how much a return ticket to London was in 1964. Not a single one of my colleagues could remember. You could almost hear them wracking their brains. They were tired, it is true. The flight out to Uganda from London for the reunion had left us all jet-lagged.

"It was in the days," I droned on, stating the obvious, "just before cheaper mass air transport came in. We had gone out by ship. It took us ages to get to Africa owing to the accidents the ship had en route. I am beginning to despair," I went on, "of ever finding out how much a flight was in the sixties. Not even the local travel agents are of any help. I have rung them," I added.

The data, I was beginning to conclude, were lost in history when, out of the blue came the answer, like a flash of lightening on a clear day. It was, admittedly, about the year 1966, but it solved the problem.

"I can tell you precisely," Brian said, "what a one way ticket from Entebbe to the UK cost in 1966. It was £159." I was flabbergasted.

"How on earth did you remember that?" I gasped.

"Therein lies a long tale," he replied. "When I was in government and living in Entebbe I did not frequent the club (probably because of some silly residual radicalism) but took my evening drink at the Lake Vic hotel with a delightful group of young Ugandans who were being inducted into the diplomatic service. One particularly nice member of that group was an Iteso lawyer, Stephan Ariko. Well, one evening he was bemoaning his fate. He was bored with the diplomatic service and wished to return to Cambridge to do a postgraduate degree but could not find funding for a ticket. I was a bit drunk and wrote a cheque for his fare (£159), telling him to pay it back when he could. Of course, the next morning I thought what a bloody fool I had been and that I would never see that money again. He went, got his degree, lived in Kampala, and was appointed by Amin, I believe, to be a member of the EA Legislature. Later he made the mistake of becoming Minister of Justice (or Attorney General) under Obote! However, he was a thoroughly decent guy who should never have got embroiled in the murky world of Ugandan politics. Anyway, some time in the 1970s I received a cheque for £159 from a cousin of his who was a sailor and who was able to access foreign exchange while traveling. Sadly, Stephan died in the 1980s. Of that group who met at the Lake Vic, I do not know any who have survived."

No one said a thing. We just stared into the disappearing foam of our lagers.

"About £300, then, for a return ticket. More than a quarter of a year's salary. We were stuck there then," I concluded glumly. (BVA)

What do you write about Africa?

What do you write about Africa? What do you put in and what do you leave out? Do you write about the heroes who saved so many people during the recent attack at the Westgate shopping mall in Nairobi? Or do you write about the girl who is lying in a pit among rotting corpses and is raped each day, they say, by soldiers in the Congo? Do you write about child sacrifice and the mutilation of children, of organ harvesting? Do you write about Paul Theroux's frosty stare at the university bar? Do you write about the army officer, an habitué of the Makerere Staff Club, who rushed out into the city during one of Amin's curfews to get fresh supplies of beer and who then, when he returned with the crates, crashed into the car of one of the club's members? Do you write about how the club raised a collection to pay for the damage to be repaired because all knew that no insurance company would believe his story? What do you write about? I don't know. (MT, CM)

Warmth

I came out of the Chinese restaurant in Bute Street, Luton, the 'Sun Doo', where I hadn't been for forty years or more: sweet and sour pork, bamboo shoots and mushrooms, fried egg rice - delicious, still the same.

The Town Hall Clock struck a quarter to eight. Its sound enveloped me like warm water. Its chimes seemed to penetrate every corner of the town centre and my body.

Familiar windows at the back of decaying buildings in Cheap Side lit up, catching the light of the evening sun.

I went into the shop opposite. It was run by a Russian who told me in broken English that he hadn't heard of a newspaper called *Luton on Sunday*. I came out clutching *The Zimbabwean* instead.

And there he was. He was going up to people who were just ignoring him. He came up to me. He said his name was Ricardo. He said he was from Asturias.

His Spanish was as clear as a bell. He had fifteen pence in his hand and said he needed fifty. He didn't look too good. I gave him fifty, wishing him good luck in Spanish and apologising for my 'acento lutonense'. Neither he nor I could really accept what was happening. He said, I don't know why, that there were more English people in Benidorm than Spaniards.

"Hasta luego (See you later)," he said.

"Sta logo (See yer)," I said, in a northern Spanish accent, as a friendly joke. He smiled.

I could feel the warmth of the sound of the clock and the bamboo shoots still stirring in my veins as I drove off up New Bedford Road.

Baring the Load

I had a strange email from an American friend today. It contained a photo of an old-fashioned chair the straw seat of which seemed to have been strengthened with the lid of a Baring biscuit tin. I asked the sender if it was 'load-Baring'. He replied that Baring biscuits were a staple of his at Kagumo School in Kiganjo. He said that he had acquired the habit from his English friends there.

Another email arrived in which another friend, also American, revealed that he had 'cracked' the mystery of the popularity of Baring biscuits. He said he had once met an English expert who worked for a Swiss friend in the Food Technology Department at Nairobi University. They were rained in for a couple of days in a small tent on Mount Nyiru. They had got round to discussing the Englishman's PhD topic: 'The Breaking Strength of Tea Biscuits'. The central device for measuring this was a finely calibrated jack linked to a sturdy pair of dentures to get the load bearing right. The thesis concluded that the crunch of a tea biscuit, at first bite, is as crucial to sales as the sound of a closing door is to the sale of a Volkswagen Golf.

I hadn't heard of Baring biscuits before. They weren't widely known in the circles in which I moved in Uganda. I looked at Douglas Collins's book *Tales from Africa*. He describes how he located these special items in a small grocery store on the shores of Lake Nagubabu a few miles from Masaka. I learned that they had been named after Sir Evelyn Baring, a Governor of Kenya, who had officially opened the factory.

The emails started pouring in thick and fast.

One said, "Not only is the 'crunch' essential, but whether or not the biscuit becomes two pieces on breaking, or a number of smaller crumbs, or, worse still, if dust-like particles are produced. This is particularly important if you eat them in bed. Tea biscuits can be made almost perfect with these characteristics in view and were, of course, essential in maintaining the Empire, unlike 'crackers' which 'Brits' were very hit or miss at creating. The often poorly constructed crackers may have led to our downfall."

"Imports of tea biscuits into the UK," yet another email said, "have done poorly due to some foreign efforts sagging when placed between jaws and released by the hand, or, being fibrous, requiring twisting movements, or, worst of all, dissolving into a pile of mush when dipped into a cup of tea." (BG, MR, CM)

Dalí and Josefu

"It says here," the barmaid said, "that Salvador Dalí sold a blade of grass to Yoko Ono for thousands of dollars. She had asked him for a hair from his moustache." Fearing she was a witch, the barmaid explained, Dalí had balked at giving her a whisker but had sent her instead a blade of grass from his garden. "It's in Samantha Lear's new book," she added. I remembered Josefu, the cook in Namilyango, who told me one day that a young lady called Maria had put a curse on him. He begged me to send her away. I told him not to be silly and not to mention it again. He began to get sick. He seemed very relieved when Maria left to live in Kampala. But it didn't end there. He continued to complain about another woman who, in his mind, was also a witch and who had also bewitched him. Every effort was made by a friend of mine from Galway to get him better. They went to the best doctors, as well as to the very best *ngangas* - medicine men and women. No one could find out what was wrong. He eventually went back to his wife and children in Toro and just faded away. Mind over matter, you could say. The barmaid finished reading the article on Dalí: "Apparently," she said, "he couldn't resist the lure of a cheque, however he got it".

Ostriches

To Chinua Achebe (1930-2013)

Nobody that I know actually thinks that ostriches bury their heads in the sand. Some say that they put their heads to the ground when they sense a distant danger. Are they listening for an approaching predator's footsteps? When they do that, they look like mounds of earth or large anthills of the savannah. They say that it is possible to get so close that you can almost bump into them. I never really believed that they buried their heads. The ground in Africa nearly always felt too hard for that. I may have had the thought that they had strong feet for digging. Why I am so concerned? It's just that I have been wondering about all this recently as I read more and more references to the Prime Minister, David Cameron and his Chancellor, George Osborne both of whom are accused of burying their heads in the sand. Is it a foolish thing to do? Do ostriches really save their skin that way? Surely a lion wouldn't be fooled? They have a keen sense of smell. Pliny the Elder wrote that ostriches "imagine, when they have thrust their head and neck into a bush, that the whole of their body is hidden." Some say that the myth arose from the fact that they stick their beaks into the ground when they swallow sand and pebbles which they need for grinding up their food in their crops. A friend of mine says that children, at an early stage, probably think that they cannot be seen if they hide their heads in their hands. Similarly, if they can't see you, they think you don't exist. The National Geographic says that it is a form of defensive behaviour and that the birds are just lying low, appearing, from a distance, to have buried their heads. Some say that some of Uganda's intellectuals survived Amin's purges of the intelligentsia in the seventies by becoming teachers, by lying low. (CM)

Brief Encounter 2

We had agreed to meet in The Museum Tavern. We hadn't seen each for over fifty years.

"Karl Marx probably drank here, when he was writing his books over there," I said, nodding towards the British Museum over the road.

"No, it was somewhere off the Tottenham Court Road," Brian replied, "I have been there." Things had started badly. It was going to be one of those reunions. The group stared into its beers.

"Bureaucracy!" said Clive, coming to my rescue. "I can't believe the red tape in Britain." Brooks nodded and said it was the same in America. Eyes remained turned down, contemplating the vanishing froth.

"In Uganda, I said, "I found it worked well." The group looked up, surprised. "Yes," I said, "I needed a driving licence urgently because I was living with Niall at Namilyango, fifteen miles from Kampala, and couldn't get into work at Kitante. I went to the Ministry and asked for one. What was his name, Da Souza? He gave me one out of the drawer, saying I had better take some lessons. I had had some help from friends but I took a couple of official ones which didn't include reverse parking, at which I am still hopeless." The group lifted their glasses and took a deep swig.

"Ah, I had to pass a bribe in Uganda," said Clive, "through Saira's Driving School in Soroti in order to get my licence. The inspector, grossly overweight, was eventually given fourteen years for corruption. If you didn't pass him a bribe, he would do things like getting you to park on a hill and putting a matchbox behind a rear wheel and telling you to move off. If you rolled back even a couple of millimetres, it was sufficient to crush the box and you failed. A friend of mine, Roger, refused to give a bribe at first but having failed three times, he eventually succumbed." He paused for a sip of his ESB.

"When I took the test," he continued, "there were four of us in the car: the examiner, two Asian lads and me. Each drove for about three minutes. One lad couldn't work three pedals and the other didn't get out of second gear. We all passed. When I wanted to get an International Driving Permit on leaving Uganda, I took all the paper work plus two photos to the appropriate office. I was asked if they were passport photos. When I replied 'Yes', the guy said they were not suitable because the form said: 'Passport type photos'." He took another sip.

"I went off to the City Bar for a couple of beers, returned an hour later and found, as I expected, that the guy had gone off duty and there was someone else. I presented the same documents and photos again. On being asked what sort of photos they were, I said 'passport type'. 'Fine', he said, and I got my licence. Getting a UK licence is another story, and my final test was in Hemel Hempstead where there is that amazingly complicated roundabout."

"The Magic Roundabout," I said.

"That's the one," he said. By now the beer in the group's glasses was approaching the Plimsoll Line. Brian joined in.

"I gave up driving some twenty years ago, in the public interest. I got a licence in Uganda after failing two tests. Reverse parking was my downfall, then, and subsequently. I more or less did it by ear. In the end Professor Clark wrote a letter saying it was in the public interest to give me a licence, which worked.

I did take lessons from a hopeless Eastern European who had a driving school in Kampala and was waiting to emigrate to the US. I forget where he came from. Did any of you come across him?" The group looked blank. I went to buy another round.

"Great stuff!" Mike interjected, responding to Brian. "Raises the question of public interest! Debatable, of course. I didn't come across the driving instructor in question but I have given a few driving lessons myself over the years. Thoughts such as 'steer clear of this one …' come to mind. My father learnt to drive in a three ton truck, graduating from a motor bike, when he was in the army in the 1930s. Then, when he bought a Hillman Minx, when we were in Wilhelmshaven in the 1950s, I went with him to Bremen to collect it. We went off to the docks with the dealer to get it. Once there he gave my father the keys and said that he should follow him. Twenty years after learning to drive a heavy goods vehicle! He made it!" The group slowly emptied their glasses.

"Another one?" said Dave, moving towards the bar. We waited for him to come back.

"Who actually taught you to drive, then?" Mike asked me.

"It's a long story," I said. The group all took a long draught, signalling that I could go on. Trev came in, late, and, after effusive greetings, settled down with a Boningtons.

"I started to drive on the Makerere campus. I had a licence for a Lambretta but had not driven a car. A chap, an Oxford chap, a clergyman, I think, called Williams, sold me an NSU Prinz. It was somewhere between a bubble car and a Mini. I was delighted with it." I took a long swig of my Guinness. I could see I had the group's attention. "Yes," I said, wiping the white moustache from my top lip, "it was popular with the group. Trev loved driving it at full pelt towards a swamp and then turning the wheel right round to see how many times it would spin round."

"That's Trev," said Clive. Trev looked alarmed. I wasn't sure what Clive meant and made a mental note to ask him later, when everyone else had left.

"I digress," I continued. "Having acquired the NSU Prinz, the next question was how was I going to drive it? I got in and turned this and that on. Nothing. No go. Solution: I would sit there at the wheel and ask passers-by if they could help me. Everyone was very helpful at Makerere. 'You do this, you do that, they would say, hopping in. I started to get the hang of it and soon could be seen lurching and careering around the campus. People dived for the bushes. It took me quite a while but then, one day, off I went, smiling serenely and waving at passing TEAs. Do you know, Mike, I have this feeling that you were one the many kind 'instructors' who hopped in and showed me the ropes. Is that possible?"

"Not sure, Bob," Mike replied. "It was a long time ago."

"When I come to think about it," I replied, "picking up your story about your dad in Germany, our fathers could be a source of inspiration in life. I have a photo somewhere of a great Italian car my dad drove in Italy during the war. He told me that he had 'found' it under the ground. He explained that as Nazi and Allied armies swept up and down (or down and up) Italy, the locals would bury their cars, the idea being that they would recover them once everything had blown over. Dad had a nose for the places where they would be buried. He told me that he could see where the earth had been disturbed and that he would scratch away with his hands until the roof of the car, just under the surface, would appear. Now, I am pretty sure that he didn't have a licence. He also had a Jeep which he told me he liked to drive up and down steep flights of steps, so he may, I suppose, have had some lessons from the military. I suspect not, though. When I got back from Africa, I bought an old-fashioned Ford Popular, light blue. I liked it. It got me to work, even though I had to push it down the hill and jump in. My wife-to-be was embarrassed by it. It wasn't exactly 'Either it goes or I do' but I got the message. I gave it to my dad. He didn't have a car. He drove it hesitantly around the block. It was a nightmare. There was a lot of traffic in Luton, even then. He came back and handed me back the keys." Niall broke his silence. I had thought, at one stage, that he had fallen asleep.

"I remember you sharing the house, for a while, in Namilyango," he said, in a soft Irish accent. "What was the name of that girl?"

"More drinks, everybody?" I asked, changing the subject. When I got back, I saw that Clive was looking glum. "All right, Clive?" I asked, as I plonked down the drinks.

"I have no motoring stories about my father," he said, "because I was only four when he was shot and killed in Palestine (for which a few years ago I obtained an Elizabeth Cross medal). Somewhere I have photos of him on horseback." He downed half his glass.

"What was he in?" I asked, finding the silence awkward.

"He was in the 16th/5th Royal Lancers, which became the Royal Armoured Corps around the start of WW2. I have no photos of him in an armoured car, unfortunately. I think I told you before that he was buried in Heliopolis Cemetery near Cairo which I visited in 1962 before I knew that he was there."

Trev joined in. "I remember," he said, "careering round in your NSU, Bob. I taught you a few bad driving tricks, like how to change gear without using the clutch. I told you it would come in useful if your clutch cable snapped. The best story," he continued, "was my wife Jean's driving test. We went down to the test centre near the Neeta cinema and, not thinking there would be a problem, I left Jean there in her Fiat 500 and went home. Five minutes later she rolled up at Kibuli. 'What happened?' I asked. She had failed the road signs and he refused to take her out in the yard or on the road for reversing. I was furious, so we drove back down and there he was drinking coffee. I said, very gently for me, 'OK, do you want your kids taught or not? You've failed her. She teaches at Mengo, I teach at Kibuli, so I have to drive her across town through the traffic, often late. Then I drive back through the traffic, arriving late at Kibuli, so no teaching gets done till we get there.' He simply said, 'Get in the car. No reversing. Just drive up Kampala Road'. Then he said 'Park here' - right on the corner of Allidina Visram Street. Jean said, 'But it's no parking. Are you trying to fail me again?' He said, 'Park here. If the police come, tell them you're with me. I'm just going to see my solicitor about my house.' Half an hour later he came out and said, 'Now drive me back to the test centre'. Did that. End of test. PASSED, no problem!!! Jean used that licence when we came back to the UK and drove on the motorway from my parents to Rotherham for a few driving lessons before taking her test there. Passed that one properly!"

Paul came in. "Driving licence stories," I explained.

"I had an English friend," he began, launching straight into it, "called Harry Hunter who visited me once at my parents' home in County Cork, Ireland. He admitted to not having a driving licence and to having failed the test in the UK repeatedly. 'No problem, Harry,' I told him. 'My brother has been driving for years in the UK on his Irish licence and you can get one of those for a pound - no test.' 'You're not serious,' Harry asked. 'I am,' I said.

'We'll get one tomorrow,' I said. I took Harry to the Cork County council office the next day. 'Just go up and ask for one,' I said. I thought I'd better stay close to him in case he didn't understand instructions in the Cork accent. Corkonians speak very rapidly. Harry got to the licence counter.

'Could I have a driving licence, please?' he said. I detected a slightly incredulous tone in his voice.

'OK, fill out that form.' Harry understood and did so.

'There you are,' the clerk said, handing it over. 'Grand. One pound.' Harry paid up.

'Right. There's your licence. Good day now.' Harry's hand stretched out and took hold of the licence with English diffidence. He turned to go, but was suddenly struck by the un-English nature of the whole operation.

'You mean,' he said, 'You've given me a driving licence without knowing if I can drive?' he said. The Corkman looked at him curiously and shot back:

'Sure what would you need a licence for, if you didn't know how to drive?' It could only happen in Ireland. Before, of course, we joined the Common Market."

"Time, gentlemen, please!" called the barman. It was time to go.

John Kakonge

We were sitting on the slow train that goes from St Albans to St Pancras. He had just got back from Bukoba. I was playing with my tablet, like most of the others in the carriage.

"I have always been fascinated by the Congo gold loot scandal," I told him. An article appeared on the screen showing a line of Ugandan soldiers in white uniforms standing smartly in a line. The headline was 'Daudi Ochieng motion and the Congo gold loot'.

The train stopped at Radlett to let more people in. I scrolled down the page. "It says here that Idi Amin led the battle against Moise Tshombe's fighters."

"Mm, didn't know that," my friend said. He seemed to be dozing off. The train stopped at Elstree. I continued to scroll down.

"Oh, it says here that your friend John Kakonge was naïve." My friend woke up with a start. This had clearly stung him.

"Look, Bob," he said, "at the time I was working for Kakonge (a Munyoro and remarkably young to be a key figure) and discussing politics with him more or less daily in some detail. He was far from naïve. He was not enthusiastic for Obote (who had made the huge blunder of replacing him with Grace Ibingira as Secretary General of the UPC at the Gulu party congress, as Obote was afraid of Kakonge's popularity among the youth and saw him as a threat from the left). John was very suspicious of Ibingira, as he believed (probably correctly) that he was working with the CIA. Ibingira more or less admitted this to me some years later, when he was out of prison and I met him in New York." The train stopped at Kentish Town.

"The Tally Ho!" I shouted, uneasy at the way the conversation was going. "That's where the Jazz Club was in the 1960s. Turn left as you go out of the station. Trigg, the road sweeper in 'Only Fools and Horses', lived just round the corner. He was buried in Highgate Cemetery just last week with a full Cockney funeral. We did the Hokey Cokey outside his house to celebrate his life." My friend by now had taken the tablet off me.

"Ah, Daudi Ochieng!" he sighed, seeing his name in the article. "Daudi Ocheng was an interesting figure as he was an Acholi but had become close to Mutesa, the Kabaka, at Buddo. Martin Alliker, my dentist at that time, was Daudi's brother but had been Obote's best man when he married his Muganda wife - a rather political marriage. MPs asked, but did not receive an answer to the question, what had happened to the first Mrs. Obote who was around at Independence.

"In the imbroglio there were many forces at work - the Kabaka Yekka, having worked with the UPC because of their distaste for the Catholic Democratic Party, by 1965 were moving towards separatism. Ibingira, from Ankole, was suspicious of Obote both because he was concerned about possible Nilotic hegemony and because he was more conservative. The summer following the ouster of the Kabaka and the imprisonment of Ibingira, I shared a flat in Nairobi with Matthew Ruikakaire, who became Ibingira's brother-in-law and had been secretary of the UPC youth wing - but fled when the ministers were jailed - so I heard a lot about Ibingira's side of the argument." The train had come to a stop. He paused. The train started again.

"One story characteristic of the time," he said, "in 1966 I took a World Bank delegation out to lunch at the Lake Vic Hotel. Returning to my office before meeting with them to brief them about the Plan and how everything was on the up and up, I found an excited office boy who claimed that half the cabinet had been arrested. I said enough of these rumours I am busy. He told me it was no rumour. He and some other young lads were sitting on the grass outside the planning bureau office when they saw a group of ministers being led away by police in handcuffs, arrested in the PM's office at a cabinet meeting. So I had to meet the Bank to tells them about the events - and about the excellent Plan about to be published!!" My friend was in full flood now.

"Yes," I said, "but what about John's alleged naïvety?" The train was pulling into St Pancras.

"Sadly," my friend said, "John Kakonge was naïve in one respect - staying in Uganda after the Amin coup. He was eventually murdered by a soldier apparently for messing with his woman." We got out of the train. He sped off down the platform.

"Have to rush," he shouted. "Much more about that period. Pretty intense six months of my life. Meeting with the cast of characters throughout. Including Obote." He disappeared into the fast-moving crowd. (BVA)

A Night in Buganda

We met by chance at Schiphol Airport in Holland. My plane had been diverted there because of the the Icelandic volcano eruption. There was too much ash in the air over England. We had both been in Africa at the same time. I had heard that he had become a monk in Holland and was astonished to discover that he was the CEO of one of the world's biggest companies. I asked him if he had any fond memories of East Africa. He replied that he had a recurring dream. I urged him to tell me it. It was one of those moments when one tells all to a comparative stranger or to someone one has not seen for a long time. It is as if one feels safe in that fleeting moment. This is what he told me, word for word:

"I am lying in the bath, enjoying a reverie. You know how you do. Memories come and go about the good times I had in Africa. It is all very pleasant. Something floats up in my mind: a memory of a glistening leg in the half-light of a lecture hall in the School of Education in Africa. I remember the tropical storm that boiled up over Lake Victoria at the same time each afternoon, the rising humidity.

"I remember the lecturer asking us to name a human being's greatest possession. Hands go up. Round the hall she goes, pointing. One by one the answers come: intellect, rationality, empathy, money, knowledge, happiness, religion, health, sex. The list goes on. Why is she leaving me until last? She comes to me. I have always thought of her as pretty, more than that, in fact, and I suspect that that she knows it. My heart is beating. My imagination stirs. I suddenly see the picture of a naked girl in George Bernard Shaw's *A Black Girl in Search of God*, the one over which I had pored, as a child, studying every single detail, in the secret store of dangerous books in the house of the local librarian.

'Imagination, I blurt out, sure that I shall be shouted down by the other students. We are all postgraduates.

'Yes,' she shouts. 'You've got it. That's it. That's what binds things together. That's what makes us human. That's what makes sense of it all.'

"The class falls silent. I can't believe it. I can't believe my luck. It was just a guess. I am not even sure why I said it.

"The door at the back of the room flies open. It is Jones making another of his dramatic entries. He is wearing a waterproof cape that reaches down to the ground. Beard dripping, he sits himself down in the front row. The lecture carries on. There is an enormous clatter as a sub-machine gun slides onto the floor. You can hear a pin drop. He had bought it, he declares, from a soldier the night before, during a raid by the Ugandan army on the New Life Club. I know he is telling the truth because I was there when Obote's soldiers burst in shouting, waving their guns, looking for the Kabaka's supporters. The purge had started. It lies there menacing, absurd, on the highly polished, deep-brown, wood-block floor, black and grey with a shiny barrel and a nozzle with a stubby sight pointing towards her beautiful, jet-black legs. It looks as if it has been used. You can hear rain beating on the roof and loud singing coming from the Pentecostal Church in Kampala Road nearby.

"I get up and pick it up from her feet. I carry it slowly out of the room, go to the dormitory block that we shared with the staff and put it under my bed.

"Later that night, I can't get to sleep. I keep seeing the gun barrel and her legs. The juxtaposition makes me uneasy. I ring her. I ring Mavis, the lecturer. I ring Mavis Ogwang.

'Hello, Mavis,' I say languidly.

'Yes,' she replies sleepily.

'It's me,' I state monosyllabically.

'I know,' she replies fondly. 'Thank you for today. I wanted to thank you personally.'

'My pleasure,' I sigh. 'I wanted to thank you as well, in person, for choosing me.'

'Come on up, quickly, it's getting late,' she laughs gently.

"There is a knock at the door, I hear a voice call, 'How long are you going to be?' It's the cleaning lady."

"That's not what I heard," I interrupted, rather brutally. He seemed to freeze. "I heard that Lawrence did not have a gun at all. He claimed to have bought it together with a a police dog during a raid on the The New Life Club. When asked by friends if they could see them, he suddenly said he could not take them back to his place because he had just remembered that he had some professor's wife in his bed."

"Er, yes, quite," he said, getting up to leave, suddenly remembering who he was now and without further ado he left the restaurant. I think he muttered something about 'Alex's book'. I haven't heard from him since. (CM)

Notes

The Rimbaud texts were awarded a prize (third 'mención de honor') in a competition held in Israel: El Concurso de Poesía Libre de *Artesanías Literarias*: 'El avestruz' -'The Ostrich', 'La casa de Rimbaud''Rimbaud's House', 'La plaza Rimbaud'- 'Rimbaud Square'. 01.07.2007. They were also included in a mixed batch published in Uruguay: 'Infinidad', 'El profeta', 'Intertextos', 'La casa de Rimbaud', 'La Plaza Rimbaud', 'Poesía budista',

Letras Uruguay, nov. de 2008. Go to letras uruguay, Indice de escritores ansd scroll down to Gurney, Robert –Inglaterra.

See also 'La plaza Rimbaud', *Con voz propia*, revista literaria, 3 de marzo de 2011. Edición y dirección: Analía Pascaner. Suscripción y colaboraciones, San Fernando del Valle de Catamarca, Catamarca, Argentina.
http://convozpropiaenlared.blogspot.com/2011/11/robert-gurney.html
'The Snake', first appeared in http://www.tea-a.org, a virtual magazine dedicated to the TEA, Teachers for East Africa overseas aid programme (strong in the 1960s). Type 'Gurney' into Find. TEAA (Teachers for East Africa Alumni) Newsletter No. 30, January 2014. Published and edited by: Ed Schmidt, 7307 Lindbergh Dr., St. Louis, MO 63117, USA, 314-647-1608, eschmidt1@sbcglobal.net.

'The Mercenary' (the Spitfire pilot text) was published as 'El piloto de Spitfire' in *Isla Negra* 2/50, Especial. Casa virtual de poesía y literaturas. Lanusei, Italia. Dirección: Gabriel Impaglione. Octubre 8. 2005. http://es.groups.yahoo.com/group/islanegra/ http://isla_negra.zoomblog.com/; 'The Calf' was first published in Spanish as: 'El becerro', in *Isla Negra* no. 60, January 2006, Sardinia, editor: Gabriel Impaglione. http://es.groups.yahoo.com/group/islanegra/.

'Rebels versus Assassins' was inspired by Niall Herriott's short story 'Close Shave – with a Cut-Throat Razor', in his *Strings and Rindabytes, Tales and poems on life, love and lunacy,* The Carraig Press, Cork, 2009.

'The Dead Man' was published in Spanish as 'El muerto', in *Isla Negra* 2/58, Casa virtual de poesía y literaturas. Lanusei,Italia, diciembre 2005. http://isla_negra.zoomblog.com and in *Veinte Narrativas: Antología de Narrativa Iberoamericana del siglo XXI*, Ediciones Lord Byron, Madrid, 2008, edición a cargo de Leo Zelada. It was first published in English: 'The Dead Man', microfiction, in TEAA (Teachers for East Africa Alumni) Newsletter No. 29, July 2013. Published and edited by: Ed Schmidt, 7307 Lindbergh Dr., St. Louis, MO 63117, USA, 314-647-1608, **http://www.tea-a.org.**

'The Lazy Man' was published in Mexico in Spanish and English in the second volume of the Seven Deadly Sins series: 'The Lazy Man', 'El perezoso', en antología de cuento breve: *Pereza*, serial pecados II, BENMA grupo editorial, México 2013, editoras Elena Arroyo Hidalgo, Ma Guadelupe Arroyo Hidalgo, Susana Arroyo-Furphy, páginas 57-59 y 125-127. 'El perezoso': traducción de las editoras con revisión del autor. Primera edición: mayo de 2013. ISBN: 978-

607-95988-4-6. Benma.editores@gmail.com, grupo editorialbenma.blogspot.com and in El Salvador: *Diario Co Latino, El Salvador,* Más de un siglo de credibilidad, www.diariocolatino.com. NO. 1212 / SÁBADO 17 / AGOSTO / 2013 FUNDADO EL 24 DE MARZO DE 1990 Un cuento español-inglés de Robert Gurney exclusivo para Suplemento 3000; 'El perezoso', 'The Lazy Man'. http://www.diariocolatino.com/attachment/3696/tresm1212.pdf;

The micro-fiction 'A Night in Buganda' was published as 'Una noche en Buganda' in the anthology of short stories *Lujuria (Lust), Antología de cuento breve* a cargo de Susana Furphy, primer volumen del II Serial: *Los siete pecados cardenales (The Seven Deadly Sins)*, Benma, grupo editorial, México DF, 2013; also 'Una noche en Buganda', diariocolatino, suplemento Tres Mil, El Salvador, via:http://www.diariocolatino.com/es/20090220/tresmil/. See also 2013, February, 'Una noche en Buganda', Con Voz Propia, Argentina, dir.A.Pascaner,http://www.convozpropiaenlared.blogspot.com/.

A longer (unpublished) story 'The Cahir', reduced to 600 words, was published as 'The Greedy Academic' and 'El académico insaciable' in the Seven Deadly Sins series produced by Benma, grupo editorial, México DF, 2014.

A micro-fiction, 'Anger in Africa', 'La ira en Africa', borrowing elements from several of the stories in this book, appears in English and Spanish in the *Antología de cuento breve* a cargo de Susana Furphy, primer volumen del II Serial: *Los siete pecados cardenales (The Seven Deadly Sins)*, Benma, grupo editorial, México DF, 2014.

'The Bullet Car' will be reduced and sent for consideration for inclusion in the 'Envy' issue of The Seven Deadly Sins anthology being developed by the Hermanas Arroyo and Benma in Mexico.

CONTRIBUTORS

Robert Gurney

The author of this book was born in Luton, Bedfordshire and attended Luton Grammar School. He lived in Uganda between 1964 and 1967, key years in Uganda's history. Robert has compared the memories of those eventful years to a compressed file. He was selected to join the TEA scheme (Teachers for East Africa, an Anglo-American joint aid programme). After graduating from St Andrews, he arrived in Uganda with high hopes – his decision to go there was part and parcel of the idealism of the sixties - it was difficult for him to know what to think as the country lurched from democracy towards dictatorship. In 1965 he completed the Diploma in Education at Makerere University College, Kampala, Uganda, part of the University of East Africa (now Makerere University). Teaching practice was at secondary schools in Kampala and in Tororo on the Uganda/Kenya border. In 1965 he began a full-time post at Kitante Hill Senior Secondary School, where he taught English and French. He was put in charge of games and launched a variety of activities by badgering the European clubs in Kampala to open up their facilities to the children. The pupils were from poor backgrounds. Clubs opened up their swimming pools, tennis courts, badminton courts, etc. While in Kampala, he concentrated on developing his French, obtaining the Saint Cloud audiovisual method certificate offered by the French Embassy. He lived in a small, mainly French community on Nakasero Hill among French Embassy staff and families from Rwanda and Congo. He created a series of educational French programmes for Uganda TV. He visited Kenya, Tanzania, Rwanda, Burundi and Zaïre (now the Democratic Republic of the Congo). In 1965 he taught French, briefly, and on the same voluntary basis as that of the French for Schools and Colleges TV programmes, at Bombo Sudanese Refugee Camp near Kampala. On his return to the UK from Africa he gained a PhD in Spanish from London University. He lectured at Middlesex University, specialising in Spanish and Latin American poetry. He writes in Spanish and English. His books of poetry and short stories have enjoyed some success in Latin America and Spain. His poems have been awarded prizes in Israel and Argentina. His bilingual book of poetry *The Dragonfly/La libélula* was launched at the Café Comercial in Madrid on The Day of the Book on 23 April 2013, where he was introduced by Ian Gibson and the Peruvian poet, Leo Zelada. His book *The Pawn Shop/La casa de empeño* comes out in Madrid on 23 April 2014. He and his wife Paddy live in St Albans. They have two sons and three grandsons. For more details: verpress.com.

Clive Mann

Born 1942 in Colchester, Clive saw little of his father who was a professional soldier killed in Palestine in 1946. His earliest memories are of V1 (Vengeance 1) rockets ('doodlebugs') coming over and fleeing into the air-raid shelter at the bottom of the garden when the engines cut out. Next door was a bakery where German POWs worked unguarded. Occasionally they would baby-sit him and carve toys from scrap wood. He attended St John's Green Primary School, and then Colchester Royal Grammar School, founded 1206 and granted Royal Charters under Henry VIII and Elizabeth I. Dr Clive Mann first visited

Sub-Saharan Africa in 1962 when he undertook undergraduate ornithological research on the Red Sea Dahlak Islands of Eritrea (then Ethiopia). The results were published in the *Bulletin of the British Ornithologists' Club* and *Ibis*. At that time he was studying Zoology and Anthropology at University College, London, where he was an active member of the Anti-Apartheid Movement. He was particularly influenced at UCL by Peter Medawar (Nobel laureate), John Maynard Smith (evolutionist/geneticist) and Alex Comfort (author of *Joy of Sex*), all members of the Zoology Department. Having completed an MSc on the taxonomy of babblers (a family of birds found chiefly in Africa and Asia), he wrote his PhD thesis on the taxonomy of birds. He was one of the team that produced *Birds of East Africa,* Britton, P. L. *et al.*, 1980, East African Natural History Society, Nairobi. Other publications on African birds include: Cheke, R. A. & Mann, C. F. 2001. *Sunbirds: A Guide to the Sunbirds, Flowerpeckers, Spiderhunters and Sugarbirds of the World*. Christopher Helm, London, refers to the birds of Tanzania, Kenya and Uganda and is an important reference point; Cheke, R. A. & Mann, C. F. 2008. 'Families Nectariniidae and Dicaeidae', in del Hoyo, J., Elliott, A. & Christie, D.A. eds, *Handbook of the Birds of the World,* Vol. 13, Lynx Edicions, Barcelona, 2008 is an update of the previously mentioned *Sunbirds. The Birds of Borneo*, BOU Checklist 23, British Ornithologists' Union/British Ornithologists' Club, Peterborough, 2008. Erritzøe, J., Mann, C.F., Brammer, F.P & Fuller, R.A. *Cuckoos of the World,* Helm, London, 2012. He edited section 'Family Motacillidae' in del Hoyo, J., Elliott, A. and Christie, D.A., eds, *Handbook of the Birds of the World,* Vol. 9, Lynx Edicions, Barcelona, 2004. He has published papers on East African Birds in *Bulletin of the British Ornithologists' Club, Ostrich, Scopus, Journal of East African Natural History Society, Safring, Auk* and *Bulletin of African Bird Club*. Other bird publications have appeared in *Belalong – a tropical rainforest* (Earl of Cranbrook and Edwards, D.S., 1994, RGS and Sun Tree Publishing, Singapore), *Tropical Rainforest Research – current issues* (Edwards, D.S., Booth, W.E. and Choy, S.C., 1996, Kluwer Publishing, Dordrecht), *British Birds, Forktail, BirdingASIA, Oriental Bird Club Bulletin* and *Brunei Museum Journal*. In the academic year 1964-65, Clive completed the Diploma in Education at Makerere University College, specialising in Biology, Chemistry and History. At this time he taught Sudanese refugees on a voluntary basis at Bombo. Between 1965 and 1967 he was Head of Biology at Soroti Senior Secondary School, Uganda and in 1969-1970 Head of Biology and, briefly, Acting Deputy Principal at Kabarnet Boys' High School, Kenya. From 1970 to 1975 he was Head of Biology at Kapsabet Boys' High School, Kenya. He is past Chairman of British Ornithologists' Club, and the present Chairman of the Trust for Avian Systematics (previously Trust for Oriental Ornithology).

He is a Fellow of the Linnean Society and Member of British Ornithologists' Union, amongst other organisations, and a past Member of both American and Australasian Ornithologists' Unions. His ornithological studies have resulted in much travel world-wide. Two books that he has co-authored have been declared 'Bird Book of the Year'. He was Senior Education Officer in Brunei 1981-1991, ornithologist on the Royal Geographical Society's expedition to Brunei 1990-1992. When not abroad, he taught in London and retired in 2002. He now spends his time on bird research, autobiographical writing and traveling.

Brian Van Arkadie

Brian grew up mainly in Kentish Town, near Queen's Crescent Market, in North London. His surname is of Sri Lankan Dutch Burger origin, his father traveling to the UK as an army volunteer in the first World War. He attended Quintin Grammar School in Soho. Today one of its buildings, where the head offices were based, is part of the University of Westminster's Regent's Street campus. In those days it was next to the cinema where the Lumière Brothers showed their first films. He is a Londoner. He did his first degree, in Economics, at the LSE. He gained his PhD at Berkeley: *Investment Behaviour in the US Steel Industry* (Models, Regressions, etc.). He was Fellow of IDS, Sussex 1969-71; Fellow of Queens' College, Cambridge, 1971-75; Director, Cambridge University Centre for Latin American Studies, 1972-75; Professor, ISS, The Hague, 1975-89 (sometime Deputy Rector and Dean). He has published books on Economic Accounting, Palestine, Viet Nam and the Baltic States and a number of studies of economic policy in Tanzania. He was in at the founding of the Movement for Colonial Freedom (Central Hall, Westminster 1954) and organized the Berkeley protest against the Sharpeville massacre (1960). He has always experienced a tension between his being a technocrat and a politico. Between 1963-65, on study leave from Yale University, he was visiting fellow at the EAISR (East African Institute of Social Research which later became the Makerere Institute of Social Research). In 1965 he was economic advisor on Eastern Africa to UK's first Ministry of Overseas Development (Sir Andrew Cohen the PS and Barbara Castle Minister). From 1965 to 1966 he was Chief Planning Economic Officer to the Government of Uganda and editor of the Second Five Year Plan. He was Chairman of Mission on Land Settlement, Kenya, in 1966, and Economic Advisor to the Government of Tanzania (1967-1970). During the 1970s he was a consultant in Tanzania and Kenya engaged on a variety of assignments. In 1981-1982 he worked as an advisor to the Tanzanian government on economic reform. As Consultant to the Ugandan Ministry of Finance, he worked on a number of assignments between 1983-2008. Professor of Economic Development at the University of Dar-es-Salaam, between 1987 and 1991, in 1992 he initiated the Economic and Social Research Foundation, Dar-es-Salaam, in which his role, during the 1990s, was senior advisor. He is currently advisor to REPOA (Research on Poverty Alleviation) in Dar-es-Salaam. Since 1989 he has been heavily involved in economic policy work in Viet Nam for which he was awarded the Campaign Medal by the Vietnamese Ministry of Planning and Investment in 2012. In a recent conversation we had at Brian's house in Cambridge (May 2013), we discussed Viet Nam's transition from arch-communist state to capitalist tiger. He gave me a dedicated copy of his co-authored book *VIET NAM, a Transition Tiger* (Brian Van Arkadie and Raymond Mallon, Asia Pacific Press at The Australian National University, 2003) which describes the process admirably and points to his role in it.

David Smith

After graduating in Economics from the University of Leeds in 1964, David Smith studied at Makerere University College of the University of East Africa, obtaining a Diploma in Education in 1965, specializing in the teaching of Maths and Geography. From 1965-1970 he taught at Kololo Senior Secondary School in Kampala, Uganda, teaching Higher School Certificate Economics and School Certificate Geography. He was also Careers Master and jointly ran the School's rugby team. As well as playing rugby, he became heavily involved in the Theatre Group, appearing regularly at the National Theatre of Uganda where, among other roles, he played The Common Man in Robert Bolt's play *A Man for All Seasons*. He also acted for Theatre Limited and appeared in Uganda Television's version of *Juke Box Jury* and in other programmes. Following his return to the UK in 1971, he lectured at Erith College of Technology/Bexley College, becoming Senior Lecturer in History and Head of Academic Studies. He retired in 2004. Although teaching mainly Economic & Social History, he will probably be best remembered for his always oversubscribed course on the History of Rock Music! He obtained additional qualifications in Educational Management (distinction), Curriculum Design and Development (distinction), and Interdisciplinary Statistics from the Open University, and Further Education Administration from City and Guilds. His academic interest has been the research of British cartographic history. He has written three books, with *Antique Maps of the British Isles* (1982) being an Evening Standard Christmas Book Choice in 1982 and a Readers Union Book Club Choice in 1983. He has also written over 70 articles, book reviews and contributions to other books. All three of his books are recommended in the British Library's *Select Reading List on the History of Cartography* in *Information Sources in Cartography* and in numerous select bibliographies. Writings include entries for the *New Oxford Dictionary of National Biography* (2004); guides for the Royal Historical Society and the Historical Association; and articles and reviews for *Imago Mundi, Cartographic Journal, Modern History Review, Industrial Archaeology Review, Mercator's World, Map Collector, Map Forum, Bulletin of the Society of Cartographers* and the *Journal of the International Map Collectors' Society.* David has lectured for the University of London, the Library Association, the British Cartographic Society, Bexley Adult Education, the International Map Collectors' Society, and local history societies, and at the University of Cambridge and Bexley Book Week. He has been a Fellow of both the Royal Geographical Society and the British Cartographic Society. Consultancies include television programmes on map history, and on the identification of land contamination using early maps for the major London legal firm of Nabarro Nathanson. In between time he has managed to run two London Marathons for charity. He has also travelled very extensively, including Ethiopia, Kenya, Uganda, Tanzania, Ruanda, Zambia, Zimbabwe, Botswana, South Africa, Swaziland, Namibia, Gambia and Senegal in sub-Saharan Africa alone. For some time he ran an antique map export business.

Andrew Carothers

Andrew was born in Kenya. His father was a leading Kenyan Psychologist whose work was quoted by Marshall MacLuhan. His father first went to Kenya as a Medical Officer employed by the colonial government. As such he was posted all over the place to do general medicine - everything from delivering babies to amputating limbs following lion attacks. One of his first postings was to Lokitaung in the remote Northern Frontier District. There were no roads then, and he had to get there by camel train. Later, he was appointed to take charge of Mathari Mental Hospital near Nairobi, and during the war years he doubled as medical officer to East Africa Command. McLuhan's 'big idea' was that peoples' view of life is largely determined by how information reaches them (summed up by his famous aphorism: 'The medium is the message'). This was similar to Andrews's father's view of the fundamental importance of literacy to human psychology. Andrew attended primary school in Kenya. He graduated in Mathematics from the University of Bristol in 1964. In that year he signed up for the Teachers for East Africa (TEA) scheme. His reasons were partly that he couldn't think of anything better to do, and partly that he wanted to return to the place of his birth, where he spent the first seven years of his life. Kampala for him was a delightful place (pre Idi Amin), with a vibrant nightlife, and full of gossip and political intrigue, most of which passed him by. After Makerere, he was assigned for the next two years to teach Maths and Physics at a boys' secondary school, beautifully situated near the town of Nyeri about 100 miles north of Nairobi. For more than a year, he shared with a fellow TEA a house with a veranda that looked out across 40 miles of bush and forest towards Mount Kenya. On clear nights, one could sometimes see the glaciers glinting in the moonlight. Andrew enjoyed mountaineering in Kenya. On one particularly clear day on the summit of Mount Kenya, he saw the snow-capped peak of Kilimanjaro glistening 330 km to the south. There was excellent trout fishing to be had in the nearby forest streams, and he passed many an idle hour there in the company of colobus monkeys, colourful turacos, fish eagles and, on one memorable occasion, a pair of rhinos. In contrast to this idyllic situation, the headmaster was a real pain in the neck – a stuffy old-style colonial, who also happened to be a C of E minister. The teaching experience itself was very rewarding. The boys were highly motivated, seeing education as the key to avoiding a life of unremitting manual labour, and intelligent, having been selected from the top few percent from the primary level. When he looks back at what was expected of them – to study in a foreign language from an early age, with little or nothing in the way of books nor any tradition of education in their family backgrounds – he is astonished at their achievements. From 1967-1968 he did supply teaching in Inner London. From 1968-1969 he studied for an MSc in Biometry/Applied Statistics at Reading University. From 1969 until 1972 he was a Research Assistant, in the Dept. of Statistics, Edinburgh University, conducting research on problems of censusing wildlife populations. From 1972 until 1975 he was a Research Assistant in the Department of Animal Genetics, Edinburgh University. In 1974 he married Jacqueline. They have two children, Anna and Ravi. From 1975 until 2005 he was Head of Statistics, MRC Human Genetics Unit, Edinburgh, with research and teaching in human genetics. In 2005 he became Honorary Reader, School of Public Health, Edinburgh University Medical School. He obtained his PhD in 1981 and his DSc in 2004. Retired now, he enjoys hill walking, travel, photography, natural history and languages: Russian, French, Swahili, German and Chinese.

David Simmonds

David Simmonds attended Ilford Grammar School. He describes himself as "one of those oiks that was, like a winkle from its shell, picked out of a 'jellied eels', 'roll out the barrel', 'East End' kind of world by the 11+ exam. A posh grammar school left me forever after with a foot in each camp. A common experience for many in those days." He graduated from Bristol University with a degree in Pure Mathematics in 1964. This was at the height of the Cold War.

Armed with a Maths degree he explored what the world could offer him. He was faced with interviews at various defence and financial establishments. Revolted by such outfits, he faced the dilemma of what to do with his life. Fortunately, a friend who had been born in Kenya drew his attention to a postgraduate course at Makerere in Uganda. At interview he was declared unsuitable. However, there was a shortage of Mathematics teachers and at the last minute a phone call offered him a place on the Diploma in Education course where he specialised in the teaching of Maths, Physics and Biology. (He eventually managed teach some Biology to junior classes.) In East Africa he did his teaching practice at Kololo School and Kibuli School, Kampala, under an eccentric headmaster, 'a real Wackford Squeers'. His first full-time teaching post, at the Aga Khan High School in Nairobi, found him once again under another eccentric head, an extreme religioso who was scandalised when Dave tried to excuse himself from Grace before the meal of welcome, saying that he wasn't into 'that sort of stuff'. His honesty (his wife calls it his 'bloody-mindedness') got him into further trouble when he revealed that he wasn't motivated by any vocation but by a desire to escape from the world of banks and bomb-making industries. The headmaster tried to have him removed but, fortunately, he found a staunch ally in the Kenyan Minister of Education. East Africa was beginning to move from a missionary-led education system to one staffed by professionals and experts in the subjects taught. [Another, mild-mannered member of this group was anathematised by the headmaster of another rare, Christian sect school for putting up a picture of the Beatles on his bedroom wall.] In 1966 Dave met Frances Kay (TEA 1965 intake) in Mwanza and they married in 1967. They were both posted to a school in Tabora (Tanzania). In 1968, after the arrival of their first son, they returned to the UK where Dave completed an MSc at Leicester University in Mathematical Physics. On completion he tried to enter the field of Computational Quantum Physics as a research student but, in the event, for financial reasons he had to settle, between 1969 and 1973, for a lectureship at Farnborough College of Technology and Frances took up teaching again. In 1973 they moved to Scotland, Frances's home, and until his retirement in 2003 he lectured at Robert Gordon University in Aberdeen. In addition to his lecturing, he was responsible for starting up various new degree courses, supervising PhD students, and so on. Ultimately, while involved in various European-funded initiatives, he became disillusioned with the mercenary attitudes that were creeping into his profession and took early retirement. He now devotes his time to doing the many things he couldn't do when he was working: keeping up with mathematical physics, studying languages, painting, reading, writing. Dave has a unique, almost surreal view of reality and life in Africa and elsewhere that chimes well with the author's own experience. The main contributors to this book were, in the main, from a working class grammar school background. They were thrust into a world that had been, up until that point, an extension of middle-class British life and, in parts, the preserve of aristocratic circles.

Trevor Wilson

Educated at Huddersfield College, Trevor moved on to Bristol University in 1961 to study Chemistry. His most notable achievements there were playing first XV Rugby and meeting Jean (Geography 63-67). Their meeting was achieved through the good relationship with the Union Bar Manager. Using a secret knock on the beer chute door, Jim allowed the Rugby Team to climb up the chute and gate crash the Freshers' Week dances. With no real career idea in mind, Trevor applied and was accepted on the TEA scheme run by the then ODM. They sailed from King George V dock in late Summer 1964 on the Rhodesia Castle with its lavender coloured hull – how tiny compared with modern cruise ships. Friendships developed swiftly. Three Universities were strong supporters of the scheme and several TEAs knew each other, if vaguely, already; Bristol Johnny Morris, Alan Hawley, Dave Marshall, Mike Battison, Trevor himself, Charlie Barton; Oxford Kenny, Hugh, Hugh; St Andrews Bob, Alex, Maurice. Then there were the characters - like Dave Smith ("Smiffy"), Ken Evans, and the girls – he never expected them!! He thoroughly enjoyed the Dip.Ed. course at Makerere despite Prof. Lucas who was clearly incompetent but he gave Trevor a grade 1 on teaching practice at Maseno near Kisumu which made him decide to give teaching a go as a long term career. After being posted to Kibuli, and joined by John Warren, he had the trauma of the anti-American riot, which gave them time to prepare for their new building. Funded by USAID, John and Trevor designed the whole of the laboratory layout and with almost a new staff they were up and running. It was easy to get back to England, if you knew how! Trevor broke his contract by mutual agreement after twelve months, to go to his sister's wedding and to meet up with Jean again. He broke his second contract after ten months to go home to get married. Each time he had paid leave at four days per month and a proportion of the fare back to Uganda. He and his wife's final contracts were an extended 36 months. Rugby, game parks, car crashes and Mombasa beaches are all well documented by others but the lasting memories are of great friendships and super students. Teaching was a pleasure. He and his wife only left to avoid staying forever. He was TEA rugby Skipper in 1965, Captain of Kampala RUFC in 1969 and played for the Uganda team 1965-1970, of which he was Captain in 1969. He played for East Africa from 1966 until 1969. Not wanting to settle in England, Trevor spotted a teaching opportunity in Cyprus with the British Council and arrived there in Sept 1970. Teaching in an Armenian school in Nicosia was a total contrast to Africa. The climate was excellent, they still had the beaches and cheap living. It was idyllic for four years. Rugby continued a while but then changed to golf, on a dry dusty course which actually crossed the "Green Line" boundary between Greek and Turkish Cyprus. Nicosia was a hot bed of spies! Maclean had collected orders from contacts in Trevor's school and they were partly there to balance the powerful Arabic and Russian forces at work. Say no more on that. Their students, after Sixth Form, went mainly to University in Yerevan (Soviet Armenia) and Moscow. Suddenly all the Americans were leaving, and his golfing friends were giving him signals to do the same. Luckily they left and their personal affects were on the last ship out of Famagusta before the Turkish invasion. A superb four years including the arrival of son Steven. Arriving in England with no job, house, or car and another baby on the way, they found a teaching post and made home in Stafford where they have lived ever since. Dedicated to the Comprehensive School philosophy, Trevor quickly progressed to Head of Chemistry, Head of Upper School and Deputy Head, moving between three Staffordshire schools. He was acting Head teacher four times for extended periods but had no aspiration for a permanent post. He became heavily involved in Union (ATL) activities, particularly the fight for fair education funding for the forgotten Shire Counties and the regional funding formula. The Chief Education Officer seconded Trevor to develop a financial model to show the impact of the proposed National Sixth Form Funding Formula on all Staffordshire schools. This proved very useful for their future planning. He was President of ATL Staffordshire. Family life, golf, hill walking, theatre, opera and ballet are all strong interests. He has been Captain of his golf club and a financial director for twenty six years and is still managing a handicap of 9. Since retirement appointment as a Magistrate in Staffordshire has been an amazing experience, with a totally different initial learning curve compared with his science background but with many similarities to the management of people gained in education!

Mike Tribe

Mike Tribe's experience has given him a unique insight into the issues that have exercised Uganda in the past fifty years. While at the University of Sheffield he was Treasurer of the UK United Nations Students Association. On graduating in Economics in 1965 he won a Ministry of Overseas Development scholarship to join the two year African Studies programme at Makerere University College, Uganda, his dissertation for which was on the Ugandan housing market. He became a Lecturer in Economics at what became, in 1969, Makerere University, leaving in December 1971 at the time when many left Uganda owing to the turbulence of the Amin period. While at the University of Glasgow in the mid-1970s he was involved in research on social security systems in developing nations. Then at the University of Strathclyde he worked on the cane sugar industry, collecting data in 1978-79 in five African (including Kenya and Ethiopia – but not, mercifully, Uganda) and five Asian countries. His Strathclyde stint included a two-year secondment to the University of Cape Coast, Ghana. He then spent about 20 years at the University of Bradford, during which time he worked on a case study of small-scale milk production in Bungoma, Western Kenya. With the return of stability to Uganda in the nineteen-nineties he went back to Makerere to lecture on a Masters Programme in the Economics Department, and also contributed to short courses at the Uganda Management Institute.

Colin Townsend

Colin was born in Southend-on-Sea in 1942. He attended Southend High School for Boys but was transferred to the Prince of Wales School, Nairobi, in 1957 when his parents moved to Tororo, Uganda, to supervise the completion and staffing of the technical school now known as Manjasi High School. In 1959 he joined a sailing trip organised by the teacher who ran the school sailing club and who had a 30ft sailing boat. They sailed from Mombasa to Zanzibar, Dar-es-Salaam and back - a fabulous trip. Around the same time he and one of his brothers climbed Kilimanjaro. They went in from the north side where in those days you could drive up to 11,000 ft or so. They got up to the hut that evening and the following day they were up at 3.00 am, went up to the crater summit to see the sunrise, and then all the way back down to the car and back to Nairobi on the same day. Returning to England to study for a degree at London University seemed rather dull after such adventures. Not having a clue what to do with his life he followed the family tradition and went into teaching. His elder brother Norman, now deceased, had been in the TEA scheme two years earlier and it seemed like a great way to get back to East Africa. Colin joined the Rhodesia Castle with the rest of the TEA gang. He was on deck playing table tennis when they collided with a German freighter. They all rushed to the side of the boat and he recalls seeing guys in their underpants running around on the deck of the freighter - being a lot smaller it must have really shaken them up. The boat returned to Southampton but was soon on its way to Mombasa again. At Makerere he was sent to Kisumu for his first teaching practice and then to Tororo for the second. Eventually he was posted to Kianyaga High School - on the slopes of Mount Kenya, a little south of Embu. He did the usual safaris to Serengeti, Lamu, Samburu, etc and, as was the way in those days, stayed with other TEA and Peace Corps people whenever possible. After his stint with the TEA he returned to England, having decided that, much as he had enjoyed teaching, he knew it wasn't something he wanted to do for the rest of his life. He visited a youth hostel at Keld (the highest in England, he believes) on the moors in Yorkshire which was run by the parents of a good friend. It was a miserable wet night and he got talking to the only hosteller who had arrived that day. He worked in computers and it sounded most interesting to Colin. A couple of days later he returned to London and applied for a job. After an interview or two and an aptitude test he was offered a position and spent the next few weeks learning how to programme computers. This led to a job working on the first automation of the holdings of the British Library and also to the automated publication of British Books in Print by Whitakers (of Almanac fame). After seven years his feet started to become itchy again, aided by the endless series of strikes leading to shortages and power failures in the early 70s in Britain. He applied for a job with a consulting company in Canada and was accepted into their Ottawa office, arriving in 1975. After a number of consulting jobs he began to specialise in the document management area and formed a partnership with a colleague to sell and support an Australian product that he had been impressed with, having seen it on a trip to Washington. They were granted the Canadian rights and for ten years they sold, supported and consulted to various levels of government and private industry. Eventually the Australian company was acquired by Hewlett-Packard and they lost their exclusive rights in Canada. He was at retirement age and decided to quit while the going was good. His business partner, ten years younger than he is, still works in the field. Since retiring he has taken a volunteer job at an organisation that refurbishes and recycles equipment for the disabled such as wheelchairs, walkers, bed lifts, electric wheelchairs and scooters, etc. He has learned a lot while having a good time doing this work. Otherwise he fills his time with playing golf and badminton, theatre and concerts, and the occasional trip to the UK to visit his wife's family and to New Zealand to visit his younger brother.

John Warren

John Warren responded to the call of Africa through advertising leaflets distributed in the bar of Swansea University during the latter part of a three year sojourn, where only the Africa section of the Geography course represented genuinely stimulating reading in an otherwise barren environment. The interview by the Ministry of Overseas Development was more impressed by his Grade 1 achievement in "O" Level Woodwork, than a degree in Geography/Biology and resulted in his acceptance on the premise that such practical knowledge was as valuable as academia. Missing the outbound boat trip from Southampton by first flying to Aden to catch up with a services girlfriend - the boat being delayed by a collision in the Bay of Biscay - allowed a further two weeks of experience in Aden before ending up in Mombasa and the trip via the East African railway to the Pearl of Africa and Makerere University. The post graduate Teacher Training year involved teaching experience in Budo, where he learnt how to fend off the demands of local politicians' drivers to obtain six form girls, to clean the baby rhino in the school zoo and to realise that placing written information into the general office for typing was a wasted effort and that learning to type was an essential life skill. Extended teacher training in Kapenguria demanded taking over a Biology department – a singular experience that altered his whole attitude towards nature and nurture. The school farm, an essential commodity, alive with ticks and fleas, honed his organisational skills into marshalling young people into dismantling, DIY whitewashing and animal husbandry. He retains the firm view that teaching science should be a guided practical activity allowing young people to obtain a personal experience of science and its philosophy. Following a year out - a return to Aden - the now married young man returned to East Africa to take up a post in Kibuli Secondary School in Kampala. A school riot and the practical issues of establishing a newly built school convinced him that Geography was a complete waste of time and that Biology, in unbelievable profusion around the school, was worthy of energetic presentation to young people. Leaving Uganda for a post in Cheltenham Grammar School was so retrograde that a further posting to Hong Kong was a necessary stimulus that resulted in a Head of Science position allowing application of the principles of practical science. Tiring of information presentation alone, an association with a local doctor allowed absorption of the principles of anaesthesia and the establishment of a Hong Kong company for the distribution of British made products in such remote areas as Urumqui, Chichihar, Shenyang and Shanghai, with responsibility for distributor support and training throughout South East Asia – an extended application of teaching skills. A return to UK established a consultancy company on medical equipment and latterly, aesthetic technologies, which he continues to service.

Niall Herriott

Part of Niall Herriott's childhood was spent in the Far East and it certainly made a big impression on him because he felt he was back in the real world when he went to another tropical underdeveloped country with Teachers for East Africa in 1964. He spent three years teaching biology at Namilyango College in

Uganda after the Dip. Ed. Course at Makerere University. As with some other T.E.A.-ers, for him the culture shock of re-entry into 'civilisation' was greater than going to East Africa in the first place and so he soon found himself back in Africa – Ghana - for a further two-year contract. Although he had studied Science in University College Dublin, writing was always his first interest. He soon realised, in London, that this was not going to keep that dreaded wolf from the door so he went back to university in Lancashire to do an M.Sc. in Environmental Resources. This has led to a rather chequered career. Much of his life has been spent in coastal areas in the West of Ireland, particularly Connemara where he helped to raise a family. He feels he is now actually in his seventh career devoting most of his time to writing, though this is more of a hobby than commercially driven, as he is now a "pensionista". The other careers were, in this order, journalism, teaching, marine biologist, shellfish farming consultant, businessman (abysmal failure!) and finally ecologist (working on contract for wildlife agencies, forestry and farm improvement schemes and community groups). He still, in retirement, dabbles in ecology in a practical, hands in the soil way. He lives now in the countryside in West Cork and for part of the year in a mountain village in Andalusia in Spain. Most of his writing efforts have been in the scientific and technical field but recently he has published a book of poems – *Beachcombers* – available from lulu.com and a book of short stories – *Strings and Rindabytes* – available from the author and shortly available on Kindle. A couple of the stories are based on events in Uganda that he experienced. He has read his work at numerous venues in Ireland and elsewhere and has been published in several literary journals. He is working on a sort of memoir, which tries to explore the humourous side of various life experiences. He has recently been working on radio plays and is determined to write a novel, despite a number of false starts.

Mike Clarke and Lilian Hayball-Clarke

Mike grew up in the UK at Burnham-on-Crouch, Lilian in Southampton. The travel bug bit earlier than usual, and they met up in Kololo Senior Secondary School, Kampala in the late sixties, working for the Ministry of Overseas Development, the MOD. Mike was Lilian's Science Head of Department and proved indispensible as co-driver to drive all the way from Kampala to see her South African penfriend Anika get married in December 1968 in Johannesburg. That 10 day journey together was the beginning of their lasting, life-long passionate friendship, resilient to change today. Before Lilian arrived in Uganda, Mike found himself living on Makerere University campus in 1966. He made friends with the TEA group and Makerere University lecturers.

Mike regularly played and sometimes coached squash and rugby. The players traveled huge distances by dirt road to play rugby on the weekend, for example to Nairobi, Mombasa, Fort Portal and Mbarara. Being tall for rugby, 6'4" at least, Mike played on the wing and because of his running speed down the line and his beard, he became known as the 'galloping guru'. Lilian came out to teach Biology at Kololo in 1967, and her interest in black and white photography provided the rugby teams with prints to buy. The darkroom was under the stairs at home and there was just time for her to develop and print off pictures of the highlights of the afternoon's game between the finish and the evening social. Rugby was and is Mike's first love, after motorbikes and fast cars, that is. He played rugby for Croydon in the UK, and on the Kampala side in Uganda, and finally in the Uganda team: Idi Amin came as both a player in the opposing team and a spectator to games in Kampala in the early 1970s. Their UK university qualifications, teaching certificates and experience enabled Mike and Lilian to inspire Ugandans taking 'A' levels to reach the dizzy heights of being accepted onto a number of different UK university courses including Oxford and Cambridge. This was job satisfaction of the highest order. One year Lilian took Biology students to study with researchers at Queen Elizabeth National Park, where buffaloes were infected with bovine TB. Accompanying the researchers, Ugandan marksmen on the back of open trucks sighted and brought down infected animals, those that on the run with the herd could not keep up. That was how they were identified. The dead buffalo would be hauled round so that it faced east, the throat cut and bled, until the parts of the flesh free of infection were considered suitable for removal and consumption by religious locals. During their seven year stay working in Uganda, Mike and Lilian were part of the Science Team that wrote Student and Teachers' Guides for East African Secondary Schools. With this experience and with other writing, Lilian was awarded the MIBiol from the London Institute of Biology. Between terms of teaching a full timetable of sciences to 'O' and 'A' level, Mike and Lilian continued to travel around East Africa. The Kenya coast was an annual pilgrimage to the campsite at Malindi where Mike could play squash at the Driftwood Club and where the moon landing was watched on TV at the Malindi Golf Club. Once they went over the borders to Rwanda and Burundi to see the Pygmies and the Wolfram mines, important in the production of tungsten. Lake Rudolph was also quite a drive, and the men who herded cattle there would pause to play *mweso* under a tree, gathering up hard tree beans as counters only to let them down along rows of depressions in a wooden board or in scooped holes spaced in rows along the ground. The aim was to let down and gather up the opponents' beads in a complicated sleight of hand ritual designed eventually to result in one outright winner. A game could last hours if not days, played by men only. In Uganda Mike and Lilian continued to teach the Sciences at Kololo, Mmengo and Kibuli Secondary Schools in Kampala, in one school taking over the timetable and trying to keep everyone happy. "I don't teach after ten o'clock!" was one outburst that was difficult to accommodate. Finally, Idi Amin had a dream in the August of 1972 'To keep Uganda for the Ugandans', the newspaper report read. By the end of 1972 most of the East African Asians had been displaced, to put it mildly. Contracts for Mike and Lilian ended in March 1973; they joined in the crazy leaving parties held by departing expats at the rugby club. Not everyone left Uganda then, or indeed at all, but Mike and Lilian quietly drove their two cars over a remote border one sultry night and stayed with rugby friends in Nairobi, Kenya. After brief trips to South Africa and Ethiopia to stay with more rugby mates, they departed for the UK, only to escape the cold Spring climate and the 3 day week by spending three months in the warmth of the south of Spain. Subsequently, Mike and Lilian learned SCUBA as a buddy pair, and enjoyed diving and Science teaching careers in the UK and in countries round the equator, in Brazil, Papua New Guinea, Australia and the Cayman Islands. They wrote more science texts and teachers' guides in Papua New Guinea in the 80s, had a serendipitous spell of eight years teaching and diving in the Cayman Islands, where they married, and finally retired in 2009. Lilian and Mike are now happily living in Cyprus, and the sun still shines.

Charles Good

Charles Good is Professor Emeritus of Geography at Virginia Tech. He received his B.A. (1961) from The College of New Jersey and his A.M. (1965) and Ph.D. (1970) degrees in Cultural Geography from the University of Chicago. Charles was a secondary school teacher in Uganda from 1961-63 with the intergovernmental Teachers for East Africa (TEA) programme. Part of the induction process involved eating mint peas in Parliament in London! He taught at Lubiri Secondary School, which was and is located inside the grounds of the Kabaka's Palace, the Lubiri, in Kampala. This post gave him special insights into what was, in effect, the heart of Kigandan culture. Charles's general research interests include medical and health geography, international health, community health ecology, ethnomedical systems, and Sub-Saharan Africa. Early in his career he was a Senior Research Associate at Makerere Institute of Social Research in Kampala, Uganda. He was a Research Associate at MISR in 1967-1968, although most of that twelve month period was spent in Ankole district where he did his Ph.D field research. He lived in a rented house of the outskirts of Mbarara in a neighbourhood called Nkokonjeru, where the last two Nkore kings are buried. He was a Senior Research Associate at Makerere from May to August, 1972. Charles was Visiting Professor and Research Associate in the Department of Community Health, Faculty of Medicine, at the University of Nairobi, 1977-79. During this period he conducted intensive fieldwork on traditional medicine/ethnomedical systems in Kenya, sponsored by the National Science Foundation (USA). That study led to the publication of *Ethnomedical Systems in Africa, Patterns of Traditional Medicine in Rural and Urban Kenya* (Guilford, 1987). His publications include *The Community in African Primary Health Care* (Mellon, 1988). His most recent book is *The Steamer Parish: The Rise and Fall of Missionary Medicine on an African Frontier* (University of Chicago Press, 2004). The latter examines the processes and social and health consequences of the introduction of Western-type medicine in Malawi. Charles has lived and worked for over six years in several African countries, with the longest periods spent in Uganda, Kenya, Tanzania, and Malawi. The National Science Foundation (NSF), the National Geographic Society (NGS), USAID, Harvard School of Public Health, and Virginia Tech have supported his research. In 1995 Charles was a member of the Peace Mission of the Presbyterian Church USA to the Republic of Sudan, which included meetings with top government officials and unaccompanied visits to safe houses and internal refugee camps in the Khartoum area. In 1997 Charles developed and conducted a baseline study in northeast Tanzania called "Mobilizing Traditional Healers to Prevent STDs and Combat the Spread of HIV/AIDS," under private contract with USAID. This study was coordinated through the Tanga AIDS Working Group. Charles works (2003-current) with a Presbyterian group in Virginia that helps support a hospital, food security, primary and secondary schools, and scholarships for secondary school and nursing college students in southern Malawi. He is also involved with an international alliance of researchers concerned with the omnipresent problem of witchcraft accusations and their harmful consequences for public health and human rights in Sub-Saharan Africa.

Charles Barton

Charles was born in Bristol, England in 1943 between bombing raids. His family is from Devonshire and South Wales (Port Eynon). He gained a B.Sc. in Physics and Mathematics from Bristol University in 1964, then a Dip.Ed. from Makerere College, Kampala in 1965. He taught Physics and Mathematics at Nakuru High School for one contract from 1965 to 1967, driving back to London via Cape Town. He became a graduate of the Institute of Physics Studies in London, then worked in the Sahara (Libya and Niger) for two years exploring for oil. He returned to Kenya for a second teaching contract - Mathematics and Physics again, at Kangaru School, Embu - then married Nancy Webster from South Africa and drove back to London, via the Congo this time. He moved to Australia and was awarded a Ph.D. in Geophysics (Palaeomagnetism) by the

Australian National University in 1978. Post-doctorate research at Edinburgh University and the Graduate School of Oceanography at the University of Rhode Island involved working on magnetic properties of lake and marine sediments for dating and climate history. He returned to Australia in 1984 to run the national geomagnetic observatory and survey programme at Geoscience Australia. He visited the North Magnetic Pole with Canadian colleague Larry Newitt in 1994, achieving the closest ever recorded approach. He did likewise at the South Magnetic Pole in 2000, becoming the first person to "reach" both magnetic poles (fulfilling James Clark Ross's ambition). He spent his spare time in Africa climbing mountains, a hobby he continues with today. He has two children, Rebecca and David. His wife Nancy died of cancer in 1995. He married Jennifer Lambert in 2004. They live on a toy farm of 230 acres (Oakey Creek, Wee Jasper) near Canberra, Australia, cultivating weeds and wombats. He is still crawling up mountains, assisted whenever possible. He attended a Science meeting (for eGYAfrica) in Nairobi last year and visited Mike and Judy Rainy on their ranch in Kajiado. They are still involved in the safari business, specialising in the Maasai Mara-Serengeti migrations. Andrew Carothers visited him in Australia recently. The fabled International Association of Geomagnetism and Aeronomy elected Charles as their President.

Clive Lovelock

Clive attended Woodhouse co-educational Grammar School in Finchley, London, where he was born. Graduating in History from Bristol University in 1964 he was steered, as were several others, towards the TEA scheme by the careers officer. At Makerere he was instrumental in setting up the Jazz Club. He did his first Makerere teaching practice at Kisumu, Kenya. The school was literally on the Equator. His second teaching practice was at the Aga Khan in Nairobi. He was finally posted to Old Moshi Boys' School in Tanzania. He thanks Don Knies, the American lecturer in charge of Placements, for allocating him to that excellent school. 1968 to 1969 saw him back in London where he saw a lot of Clive Mann, Bob Gurney, Niall Herriott, Dave Marshall, Dave Smith, and others from East Africa. He completed a PGCE in TEFL at the London University Institute of Education just at the time when the ELT profession was taking off. Via International House in Shaftesbury Avenue he found himself teaching EFL in Japan. From 1969 until 1970, Clive was an EFL teacher at the International Language Centre Osaka, Japan and from 1970 until 1971 he was Director of Studies. From 1971 until 1973 he was Director of the ILC Osaka school. In 1974 he was awarded an M.A. in Applied Linguistics at Essex University (in those days a relatively new subject area). From 1974 until 1977 he was Director of Education ILCs Japan (Tokyo, Osaka), and from 1977 until 1978 Director of Studies, ILC Paris, France. 1978 to 1981 saw him working as a freelance EFL teacher in Paris. At the end of 1981 he went back to Japan for the third time to start an in-service English training and translation company for corporate clients, also with a teacher training department, in partnership with a former colleague from ILC Tokyo. Their H.Q. was in Kobe. They subsequently opened branches in Tokyo and Nagoya. By 1990 they had about 60 full-time teachers, plus part-timers. In 1991, stressed out, he resigned as a director of the company. He then started teaching part-time in universities. He obtained a tenured post with a university in Osaka in April 1993. Eventually he was made Professor. Mandatory retirement came in 2010. Since then he has been doing part-time teaching at various universities in Osaka, Nara Prefecture and Kyoto.